A Portrait in Time

BARBARA
DONLON BRADLEY

PRAISE FOR A PORTRAIT IN TIME

"This is a story of mystery, adventure and love that will capture the heart and imagination of all those who read it."

— CHARLOTTE MORGAN OF ROUNDTABLE REVIEWS

". . . a marvelous time-travel featuring a strong, independent, modern-day heroine... a true must-read for any lover of time-travel romances. If you've never taken the plunge, then I heartily suggest this for your first venture into time-travel."

— JUDITH RIPPELMEYER OF ROMANCE REVIEWS TODAY

. . . Barbara Bradley has written a compelling story with A Portrait in Time. This is a fast paced novel full of subplots, twists, and turns that keep the reader turning page after page . . .

— LORETTA PRIDGEN CHESAPEAKE ROMANCE WRITERS
'PEAKE NEWSLETTER OCTOBER 2001

[Barbara Donlon Bradley] expertly weaves subplots into the story, each building upon the other with supporting characters that grow as the stories evolve.

— JAN CROW SIME~GEN REVIEWS

This book is dedicated to my family. Especially my husband, who calmly understands when I growl, "Leave me alone. I'm writing." And my mother-in-law who told me I was joining RWA and the Chesapeake Romance Writers. It was the best thing I could have done.

I also have to thank the Chesapeake Romance Writers; their love and support showed me I had what it took. Without them I couldn't have done this.

CHAPTER 1

*A*lex Thibodaux held the telegram in her trembling hands. Her world crashed in around her when she read the four words on the sheet of paper.

I need you. Grams.

She stood there in shock. Her grandmother was her best friend growing up. Always there when she needed someone to talk to, a shoulder to cry on. Was she ill? She had to go. Turning to her assistant, she asked, "Where is Dr. Martin?"

"Last I heard he was going over the data from last night's telescope readings. You'll probably find him in the tomb."

Alex nodded absently as she forced herself to move. Her footsteps echoed down the hallway as she headed toward the room labeled the tomb.

It got its name because to get to it, you had to travel down three flights, then through several dimly lit corridors. A lot of the newer employees didn't like to venture down that far, but it had never bothered her. Dr. Martin loved the room because he could hide away in there for hours without being disturbed.

The door creaked as she pushed it open. The fluorescent lamp on the massive desk illuminated the doctor's balding head.

She felt the cold metal of the door as she held it open with her palm. "I hate to disturb you."

"Oh Alex, please, come in." Dr. Martin shoved his black glasses back up his nose. "The data here is very interesting. The quasar we've been studying is starting to pick up speed. See?"

He stood and spread out the sheets he had been scrutinizing.

She sat in the old wooden chair in front of the desk. "Doctor, I need to take some time off."

"Off. Well, you need to speak to the... You want time off?" He eased himself back into his old leather chair.

"Yes, sir." Alex gave him a tiny smile. This was the first time she requested leave in the five years she had worked with him. "It's my grandmother."

Dr. Martin pulled his glasses off his nose and chewed on one stem. "And here I had hoped you found some young man."

Their running joke, Alex didn't date. She never let anything inside the tight shield she had erected around herself. Alex didn't look like the stereotypical female scientist. Blonde hair, bright blue eyes with twenty-twenty vision, and a curvy figure. When she first started working here she had probably heard every blonde joke out there. But her no-nonsense way let people know quickly she was there to work, nothing else. Her serious attitude and controlling ways didn't win her any friends, but she didn't need them anyway. Grams was about the only one who could get around her facade. Grams. "Doctor..."

"Sorry. How long do you think you need?"

Alex sighed. "I don't know."

He placed his glasses back on as he stared at her. "You haven't called her?"

She flushed. The thought never entered her mind. The telegram had flustered her, something no one else would believe.

"Use my phone." He pointed to the 1940s-style instrument that graced his desk.

Alex clutched the cold receiver in her hand. Her grip tightened as she dialed in her grandmother's number. The phone on the other end rang seven times before she hung up. "There is no answer."

"Call the airline. I'll clear the time off for you."

~

*a*lex's jeep flew down the shell road that led to her grandmother's house. Why the areas around New Orleans used shells to cover their dirt roads instead of gravel was beyond her. She could hear them crunch and pop as she followed the road.

All she wanted to do was get to her only living relative.

Tires screeching, she stopped the jeep she rented in front of the house. Alex climbed the three stairs it took to reach the porch in one step. The handle on the front door turned with a rattle. It looked like her grandmother never had the knob tightened. Leaning against the door she shoved hard. The door flew open, banging against the wall.

"You didn't have ta put your whole weight into it. It don' stick that bad right now."

Alex breathed a sigh of relief when she heard her grandmother's voice. The door swung backward, stopping as it smacked Alex in the back. "So I noticed."

"You okay, Grams?" She felt the hairs on the back of her neck stand up. Her grandma didn't look sick, so why did she send the telegram?

"I'm fine, Alexandra."

Alex cringed. She hated her given name, but she could never get her grandmother to use anything else. "So why did you call me home?"

"I needed you."

"You had me run all the way from California because of your telegraph." Alex's brow crinkled. "What was so important?"

"You'll find out tomorrow. Now, how 'bout some nice cold lemonade?" Her grandmother turned and headed into her small kitchen.

Alex wanted to smack her head. Her grams was up to something, and since she dragged Alex all the way from California it had to be big. What? was the question. And why tomorrow instead of now? A small sigh escaped her lips as she followed her grandmother.

~

*A*lex didn't see the low-hanging beam until it was too late.
Bam.

"Oh man," she mumbled as she rubbed her head, glaring at the offending beam. Staring around the musty old attic, she sighed. Boxes were stacked everywhere. Why did she agree to climb into the proverbial black hole? The photo album her grams wanted was probably lost forever.

Her grandmother's voice floated up to her from the first floor. "Alexandra, you okay up there?"

"Yes, Grams." She looked around once again, grateful the evening air had started to cool off the stifling heat of the attic. "Grams? When was the last time you cleaned up here?"

"Don't know, maybe thirty years? Before yer gran'pa passed away."

Alex shook her head. Three hundred years sounded more like it. Cobwebs hung everywhere. The single bulb above her head cast more shadows than dispelled them. Tucking a stray honey-blonde hair behind her right ear she asked, "Which box should I look for the album in?"

She could hear her grandmother's cane tap against the wood on the floor below as the woman thought. "Let's see. Las' time I had it out was the day you were born. Go in about ten paces and turn left. It should be in the top box."

Alex's brow shot up, but she did as her grandmother instructed. Pushing several cobwebs out of her way, she hoped she found it soon. The attic hadn't cooled down enough for her tastes. She stopped in front of a pile of boxes. Pulling the lid off the top one, she found a leather-bound book embossed with an intricately engraved oak tree in gold leaf. Inside, on the first page, the face of her grandmother as a child stared back at her. They both shared the same aristocratic nose. The bright eyes and rosy cheeks in the picture made Alex smile. Although her gram's chestnut-brown hair had turned to a feathery white texture, a youthful light still glowed in her grandmother's eyes.

She grinned. Her grandmother could still surprise Alex with her sharp memory. "I found it."

"Good. Meet ya in the den." The tapping of her cane faded as Betsy

Thibodaux moved away.

Alex climbed down from the attic and headed for the den. She seated herself on an overstuffed blue couch before her grandma walked in the room. Her grandmother didn't move as fast as she used to.

Although her grandmother had turned ninety-three four months ago, knowing where to find the book proved she was still sharp as ever. After she settled down in her favorite chair, Alex handed her grandmother the family album.

"Now, sweetie, I want to tell you the story of..." Grams' voice dropped off as she hunched over the album, flipping the pages in search of a specific picture. "Ah, here we are. Trey..."

"Trey?" There weren't too many men with the name of Trey outside of the Crescent City. "A true boy from New Orleans, eh?" Alex took the album her grandmother thrust at her.

"Now, don' fool wi' me." Her grandmother patted her hand. "His full name was Montgomery Brice Dalton. They called him Trey because he was the third."

Alex rolled her eyes. When the letters started dropping from the ends of her grams's words the stories got wild. "Yes, Grams."

Betsy's cane pounded against the floor. "Don' you 'yes Grams' me. Dis is true life."

The smile Alex tried to hide faded as her gaze fell on the picture. Like all the pictures taken in the late eighteenth century, Trey looked stiff. He didn't smile, but humor shone through in his eyes. She wondered what went on in the background to cause that look. His attractive, chiseled features affected her. His eyes held hers, as though he actually stared at her instead of at the camera.

"My papa tol' me about him when I was a chile. His daddy made him go to France during the war. Wanted him to become a ship's captain. Just as the war ended, he heard about his parents' deaths and returned home. When he came back, he rebuilt the family plantation. Made a name for heself."

One of Alex's blonde brows shot up. "And you remember the stories, Grams?"

Betsy Thibodaux straightened her spine. "Of course!" She tapped the side of her head. "Still sharp as a tack. Where do you think you got that scientific mind from? Anyway, he was friends wi' my grandpa. Nice looking man that Trey. One that could turn a lady's hade.'"

She knew her grandmother could spin more yarns than anyone she ever met. Laughter bubbled up inside her.

"He fell in love wi' a woman from our family."

Alex's gaze slid to her hands when her grandmother looked her in the eye.

"In fac', she had the same name as you. They had what you call a whirlwind affair. Papa tol' me about their life, but I guess I jus' don' remember ever'thing."

Alex coughed. An elephant would have an easier time of forgetting. "Go on, Grams."

"Papa say she was real pretty. Very sophisticated. Trey fell for her like a ton o' bricks. They were very happy, for a while. But somethin' happen, an' she had to go away. Papa say Trey pined and pined for her. He didn't wan' to live without her."

"Talk about your Romeo and Juliet," murmured Alex. "Did she ever come back?"

"Not sure. Would you like to see a picture of her? I have one in here somewhere." Alex's grandmother flipped through the family album. After a fruitless search, she yawned. "Well, I'll find it in the mornin'. Why don' you go on to bed? Tomorrow I plan on making my famous praline pancakes."

Alex gave Betsy a quick peck on the cheek. Sleep sounded great. She stretched her back as she walked toward her room. "I'm looking forward to it, Grams. Good night."

Once Alex had closed her door and turned out the light. Betsy reopened the album. Gently, she traced the picture of the woman Trey loved, a woman who was the spitting image of her granddaughter.

"Tomorrow is a whole new day, Alexandra."

*A*lex woke early the next morning. Her nightshirt stuck to her body. Her grandmother didn't believe in air-conditioning, and the room had started to heat up already. She pushed aside the delicate lace curtains and slipped her hands under the weather-beaten wood of her bedroom window. Her muscles flexed as she pulled up, forcing the window to rise upward with a loud groan.

The air in her room filled with the fragrant aroma of magnolias. This one smell let her know she was back home.

After dressing, she tiptoed down the golden oak stairs, hoping she wouldn't wake Betsy, if that was possible. Grams always woke before anyone else, no matter how early they rose.

Peering into the pale yellow kitchen, Alex sniffed the heady aroma of freshly perked coffee, but found no sign of her grandma. Pouring herself a cup she sat and inhaled. One cup and she'd start in the living room. She knew her grandmother too well. She was probably napping somewhere in the house.

About fifteen minutes later she found her grandmother sleeping in her favorite chair in the den, where they had been the night before, the photo album still clutched in her gnarled hand. Just as Alex turned to let her grandma nap a little while longer, the book slipped from Betsy's grasp and dropped to the rag carpet.

An embossed card fell out.

Bending down, Alex picked up the card.

"I see you found the invitation."

"Good morning, Grams," Alex said. "Is this why you wanted me here? For the reopening of the Dalton plantation?"

"Now, would I call you home for something silly like that?" Betsy banged her cane against the floor several times before she could get up out of the chair. "These old bones get more stubborn with each passing day."

Alex shook her head as her grandmother headed for the kitchen. "Can I help?"

"Everything is under control, dear." Betsy shooed her away. "Go sit down, it will be ready in no time."

Within an hour, Betsy's praline pancakes sat on the gray Formica-topped metal table, filling the kitchen with the aroma of roasted pecans, vanilla, and melted butter. Grabbing the butter and the syrup Alex made short work of the stack on her plate.

"I had forgotten about the Dalton plantation until you found the card. Why don't we go?"

Alex placed her utensils on the edge of her plate. So it was the plantation she wanted Alex to see. Why? "If it's okay with you I'd rather stay here."

"I thought it would be fun." Betsy got up and placed a few more pancakes on Alex's plate. "They also have a portrait of that woman that Trey loved in the sitting room. You should see it."

Alex pursed her lips. She wanted her to see some painting? Really? "So?"

Betsy watched her for a few minutes.

Alex felt heat climb up her neck and face under her grandmother's scrutiny. When her grams wanted something she always got her way. "I don't really want to go. I need to get back to work in California, Grams."

"Pish posh. You will go with me. It ain't gonna hurt you none." Betsy stood up from her chair. "When was the last time you took any vacation time. A day or two ain't going to do any harm. Then you can get back to your job."

Alex knew she could argue with her grandmother, but she would end up giving in anyway so why fight her? She sighed. "Give me an hour. Then we'll go."

Alex's grams smiled.

"Are you sure you're up to this?" Alex asked, hoping to talk her grandmother out of going.

"Yes, honey," she replied, giving Alex a look as tender as it was mysterious. "I've been waiting for this most of my life."

～

*A*lex's hair whipped in the wind. She shifted into fourth gear before sparing a glance at her grandmother. She would have put the roof on, but her grams said a little wind wouldn't hurt her. Watching gray hair pull itself free from her grandmother's bun made Alex wonder.

"What you call this thing?" Her grams shouted to be heard.

"Jeep Renegade."

Her grandma watched the rice fields go by as she looked out the passenger window. "Damned box."

Alex fought a grin. Her grams would call a stretch limo a box; she didn't care for 'the contraptions,' her word for cars. "We didn't have to come, you know."

"Yes, we do." Her cane banged the floorboard. "You need to see that painting."

"Yes, ma'am." Following the signs, they pulled onto the shell road that led to the plantation. Alex didn't look forward to this. Whatever her grandmother was up to she knew she wouldn't like.

Her brown boots hit the white shells with a pronounced rattle. She quickly made her way around the green jeep to help her grandmother out.

Her grams straightened the hem of her flower-print dress, ground her cane into the shells, and moved toward the plantation, mingling with the flow of arriving tourists.

The sounds of people laughing and talking as they headed in the same direction did nothing to calm her nerves. The large white two-story box-type home towered over her, blocking the rays of the sun. Her throat went dry. She straightened her shoulders. Alex knew she was being silly, but she just couldn't shake the ominous feeling that was starting to fill her.

This area, like all the land near New Orleans, was flat. The city was below sea level, making it a perfect place to grow rice, which the land surrounding the plantation still did.

A child's cry caught her attention. Alex wanted to cry too. She didn't want to be here.

~

*A*lex hung back behind the crowd as the guide led them from room to room. Her dread grew with each room the tour entered. By the time they entered the sitting room with the rest of the tourists, she wanted out. She rubbed her arms. Her white long-sleeved poet's blouse didn't help to keep away the sudden chill.

Her grandmother begged the guide for a few minutes of rest before moving on, giving them both a few minutes alone in the room without the other tourists or guides. "See, Alexandra, there's the painting I tol' you about."

Alex stared at the painting. The picture was an exact likeness of her, but in period clothing. Instinct said she looked at herself, but Alex knew she never posed for a picture like that. The young woman sat serenely on a chair, her deep green skirt draped around her. "Grams, she looks just like me."

"Interesting, no?" Her grandmother nodded. "No one knows where the picture came from, or who painted it. Look at the spot on the right side, just behind the chair. The brush strokes are different, as if something's been removed. I think someone used this picture to taunt Trey. Whoever sent it put something or someone in the background to anger him and he had whatever had been in the painting removed."

"Grams," Alex admonished.

"It's true. Go up and look and you'll see the same thing."

"Are you kidding?" Alex stared at her grandmother. "What if someone sees?"

"Who's going to see?"

Alex glanced around to see if anyone watched. Ignoring the velvet ropes, she slipped one side off the pole, so she could walk up to the painting to study it closer. Her brow creased. Alex knew a little about art and the strokes made by a brush. Betsy was right. This painting had been altered. She reached out to touch the brush strokes on the woman's face. A strong tingling sensation assaulted her. It shot up her arm and spread through the rest of her body.

Too late, she tried to pull her hand back. The sensation continued, overpowering her. She felt like Cinderella when the fairy godmother cast her spell. She saw the outline of the woman's face turn a golden color, like a thousand fireflies had taken alight. The face turned toward her, as if to say, 'It's about time.'

The light circled around her body, covering her and squeezing away her breath. Slowly, she crumpled to the floor.

~

*H*er mind registered the movement of air on her face when she started to regain consciousness. The polished wooden floor felt cool against her cheek.

"Do you think she's all right?" Alex heard a feminine voice ask.

"Yes. Her color's returning. She should be fine." This one sounded closer, also female.

"Where do you think she came from?" asked the first voice.

"How would I know?" A cane thumped the floor. "We found her at the same time, Fleurette."

There was a short pause before she heard one of the voices ask timidly, "What sort of clothes are those, Miss Rose?"

"Nothing a lady would wear."

Alex took a chance and opened one eye. Although she didn't recognize the voices, the thumping cane could only be her grams. Two sets of eyes stared back at her. One set belonged to an older woman dressed in a long gray dress. The other belonged to a young black woman, who wore a simple brown dress with a white collar and white cuffs. The style of their long dresses was from the late nineteenth century.

One quick glance around revealed that her grandmother was nowhere to be seen. What was going on?

"She's awake," the young black woman said.

The cane thumped again. "I can see that, Fleurette."

The two women in late nineteenth-century costumes must have been looking for stragglers before the next tour. Rubbing her head absently, she sat up. "I'm sorry. I didn't mean to faint. Let me get out of your way."

"You all right?"

She nodded. "Fine. Um, let me find my grandma and we'll—" She stopped talking when she glanced at the wall. The painting was gone. So were the velvet ropes that had surrounded it. Color drained out of her face.

"Oh dear, she gonna faint again." Fleurette started to fan Alex in earnest once more.

She put her hand out, touching the black woman's thin wrist. "Please, stop. I'm fine, really, it's just—" Looking around stopped Alex again. She noticed the furniture wasn't crowded into areas to allow room for tourists to walk through. The room suddenly looked lived in.

She stood up. "I've got to get out of here." Her boots pounded against the oak floor. Once she hit the porch, she stopped again. Her heart started to beat faster. The vending machines were gone, along with the sidewalk and the shell road. There were no cars, or families with children yelling for attention. All she heard was a dog barking in the distance, and the pounding of horse's hooves.

She started to hum the theme to the *Twilight Zone* as she looked around. Alex expected to find Rod Serling standing nearby doing his prologue.

She looked down at her boots. "Okay," she said out loud. "This is only a dream. I must have hit my head when I fainted. That's all. In a few minutes, I'll wake up and Grams will be standing there laughing at me for being so silly."

The pounding hooves she had heard before stopped in front of the stairs where she stood, forcing her to look up. Her eyes widened. "Oh God."

Trey Dalton, still astride his horse, towered over her. His picture didn't do him justice. No humor shone in his eyes now, only anger. Jet-black hair clung to his cheeks. His breakneck ride to the house had mussed the shimmering mass. Alex felt an urge to brush his hair back from his face.

A muscle throbbed in his jaw. Trey didn't believe Jessie when he ran out to the fields to tell him that a woman had just appeared in the sitting room, but here she stood. "Madame, what right do you have to invade my home?"

Alex looked at him, and then back at the doorway she had come through, now crowded with the curious. Turning back to him, she gestured helplessly toward the door. "I…" Her eyes rolled to the back of her head as she crumpled into another faint.

CHAPTER 2

*A*s Alex floated slowly up toward consciousness, the voices around her became more distinct. The smell of pipe tobacco mixed with magnolias assailed her nose. Home. They reminded her of home.

She opened her eyes, and sat up, praying she'd find herself back at her grandmother's. Nope. Her shoulders slumped. She found herself in the sitting room of the Dalton plantation on a soft yellow chaise. Still wearing nineteenth-century clothing, and leaning on a cane, stood Rose. A fan hung from her wrist.

"Well, Trey, who is she?" asked Rose.

Trey Dalton stood near the head of the chaise. "I don't know, Aunt Rose. Do you?"

She thumped her cane. "She has shown up at your house, unescorted."

His eyes slid over to Alex.

Alex stared deep into his emerald-green eyes and swallowed hard. This had to be a dream. He was too good-looking for it to be reality. His picture didn't do him justice, but then, photography was in its infancy back then. He had a bit of a pirate look, with shoulder-length black hair, broad shoulders, a lean waist, and a face that would make many a woman's heart beat faster.

"You gonna speak, chile?" Rose asked.

Alex turned toward the woman standing nearby. If this was a dream she had a very good imagination. The detail of the room was perfect. She could even hear the ticking of the grandfather clock that graced one wall. In fact, it was a little too perfect.

Rose looked just like her grandmother's best friend, Mary. As she studied the woman she realized there were subtle differences, but the resemblance was uncanny.

"Look at the way she's dressed. It's scandalous," Rose said.

Alex looked down at her poet blouse and jeans. "What's wrong with the way I'm dressed?" The way they both stared at her when she spoke made her frown.

Rose's fan snapped open. "Why, the fact you're wearing trousers."

Alex arched one brow. "You mean you've never seen a woman in pants before?"

"Well." Rose fanned herself. Gray hair stirred in the soft breeze. "Out west, but she wasn't a lady."

Alex examined Rose's style of dress. A high-necked, ruffled bodice complemented by pleating at the wrists of the long sleeves. The skirt hugged closely in the front, but the back of the dress stood out behind her. Curiosity got the best of Alex. "Is that a bustle?"

Rose laid her hand on her chest and blinked. "Of course."

Alex stepped toward her. She wanted a closer look at the aunt's clothing. Rose stepped back, gripping her fan like a weapon.

She blinked. Why was Rose afraid of her? "I'm sorry. Did I do or say something wrong?"

A soft blush filled Rose's cheeks. Her fan slid up to hide most of her face from Trey. "We're in mixed company."

"Oh." Alex looked up at Trey, wondering why her heart started to flutter every time she looked at him. This couldn't be good. "I'm sorry—"

"Aunt Rose." Trey cleared his throat.

"Yes, Trey?" Her eyelashes fluttered as Rose looked up at her nephew.

"You're going to be late," he reminded her.

Alex felt his deep rich voice vibrate through her body. With a voice like that she could listen to him all day. Oh, this was not good at all.

Rose sat down in a nearby chair. Grey tendrils of hair floated in the breeze she made with her fan. "Trey, dahlin', I just don' feel up to it, right now. Why don' you be a good boy and send an apology to Mrs. Woods for me."

A frown flickered across his face for a second. Then he sighed and stepped out into the hallway.

Alex didn't know what to make of this. This was too bizarre to be real, at least she hoped so. Maybe she bumped her head, like Dorothy in *The Wizard of Oz*.

It couldn't be some elaborate ruse. She didn't know anyone who could pull this off, and her imagination was never this good before. All it would take is a munchkin pointing her toward the yellow brick road to make her think she had lost her mind.

Cold fingers of dread snaked up her spine. What if all this was true? But, how? Alex took a deep breath. She had to keep a level head if she wanted to make sense of this.

Rose wore a cat-like smile as she watched her nephew leave. Her ivory fan moved slowly in her hand. His aunt had just pulled one of her gram's stunts. Her accent thickened as she manipulated her nephew and he couldn't tell her no. This was getting more bizarre by the minute.

Alex stood up and walked over to the fireplace. The marble mantel was cold to the touch. Okay, so all her senses were working. This was definitely not a dream. She turned to find Rose watching her intently.

"Are you all right?"

"What? Oh yes, I'm fine." Could they be ghosts? Anything seemed possible at this point. "Um, do you live here?"

"Why do you ask?" Rose adjusted her dress, so she could stand up.

"Trying to make conversation?" Alex found Rose's dress fascinating.

She reached out to touch the gown. It surprised her to actually feel the material. So, they were definitely not ghosts. "Wow, is that silk?"

"What would you expect?" A frown creased Rose's brow.

Alex wondered that herself. Everything seemed real. Her mind told her she wasn't dreaming, so how did this happen? Time travel was impossible, wasn't it? What exactly had happened to her? Glancing at Rose's face she realized an answer was expected. "I don't know. Silk is so expensive now."

Rose nodded. "The war drained a lot of pockets. So, what is your name, chile?"

"Alex Thibodaux." She glanced around at the sitting room. The pale yellow walls had new wallpaper on them. The white molding had a fresh coat of white paint, and the white marble fireplace looked new. A beautiful Hessian rug covered the hardwood floor.

Rose cleared her throat. "So, Miss Thibodaux, what are you doing in my nephew's house?"

Alex turned toward the door to see Trey Dalton standing in the doorway. Again, she was awed by what she saw. His shoulders filled the entrance. A chiseled chin with a slight dimple in the center made her think of the classic hero. His deep emerald-green eyes held her spellbound. So green she'd swear he wore—

"Contacts?" she blurted out.

His eyes narrowed. "Why do you want to know whom I am affiliated with?"

Aunt Rose's fan snapped shut.

"No, I mean contact lenses." She didn't like the strange look she received from him. "Your eyes, is that their natural color?"

"What kind of question is that?" He stepped closer. A faint hint of hay and horse filled the air. "I should be asking the questions here, like where did you come from? How did you get into my house? Who are you?"

"Okay, okay. As I said, my name is Alex Thibodaux. I was visiting my grandmother near New Orleans when she wanted to come out to the old Dalton plantation…"

"Old?" He gestured around the room. "I built this place only seven years ago."

"Seven!" Her eyes widened. He must be joking. "What year is this?"

He crossed his arms over his wide chest. "The year? Eighteen seventy-eight, March eighth."

Color drained from Alex's face, as she plopped back down on the chaise. It couldn't be eighteen seventy-eight, could it? "Yeah, right, and I have a bridge to sell you..."

"You're not going to faint again, are you?" he asked impatiently.

"Trey," admonished Aunt Rose. "Perhaps she has been ill."

"No." Alex sat up straighter. Time travel was only a theory. As a scientist she knew that, but what else would explain what had happened? Her eyes widened. Did she actually travel back in time? The clothes, the room, the lack of modern conveniences said yes. What was she going to do? Alex had to think fast.

Time travel did explain their clothes. Dalton wore a classic period costume, or at least it passed as one to her. Alex didn't know all the nuances of fashion to be able to date his outfit correctly. His style of dress looked very elegant next to her jeans.

"So how did you get in my house?" asked Trey.

"With a ticket," she answered absently as she stood up. Trey's presence was a little too overpowering to take sitting down. She ran her hand over the chaise she had been lying on. The thickness and color of soft gray velvet material was new, the white wood had a fresh finish. The one her grandmother owned showed heavy wear and tear.

"A ticket?" His brow furrowed as he followed her movements. "Are you mad, woman?"

That got her attention. How could she explain what she thought happened? But she knew she had to come up with something. No one needed to know a lot about history to know about the insane asylums from this era. "Let me start over."

She brushed the ball of her thumb across her bottom lip. Lying didn't work for her. Alex always got caught. "Like I said, I came to New Orleans to visit my grandmother, who wanted to visit the...your plantation. We traveled together. Things get a little fuzzy at that point. I don't know what happened to her, how I got into your home, or how to get back to mine."

"You've lost your memory, then."

"Yes!" She grasped at that suggestion quickly. Alex edged toward the door. "So, if you don't mind, I'll just be on my merry way."

Trey blocked her way with his well-muscled body. "I have a few more questions first. What manner of clothing is that?"

"Um, traveling clothes. Newest fashion when riding long distances." Alex rubbed her hands on her jeans. She had no clue when Levis had been created, or when women started to wear pants. According to Rose's reaction it hadn't happened yet, or at least it was not commonplace.

"Then you ride?"

"Of course." Her eyes slid to the floor. She had never sat on a horse in her life.

"Show me," he said.

Alex bit her bottom lip as she studied her boots. He knew. Somehow, he knew she lied to him. She looked back into those mesmerizing green eyes. "Now?"

He nodded slowly.

"I'd rather not." She took a few more steps toward the door. Just as she got near it, she found her hand in a steel grip.

"Then explain yourself." His face was a mask, but she could feel the anger rolling off him. Alex realized she didn't want his anger directed at her.

"You'd never believe me," she said. Alex slid her free hand into her back pocket. The fingers of her hand rubbed against something hard. A credit card? No! Her driver's license. She also had some bills and change in the front pocket. But did she want to reveal the truth about where she really came from? Would anyone here believe her or just lock her away?

A timid knock sounded against the door before it opened.

Dalton turned toward the door and said, "What?" a little too harshly.

"Sir?" The younger woman Alex had seen earlier stood in the doorway. "I thought the lady would like something to eat."

"Of course. Please, Fleurette, bring it in," Rose said from where she sat.

Dalton stepped back from Alex. His frustration visible in his stiff back and clenched jaw.

Alex smiled, grateful for whatever respite she could get. She still didn't know how she would explain her predicament to Trey Dalton or his aunt, and she knew, sooner or later she'd have to.

Dalton sat in a nearby chair and watched her eat. Who was she? She spoke with a slight New Orleans accent, but there was a hint of something else. He had watched as a myriad of emotions had danced across her face, anger, frustration, confusion, shock, fear, yet through it all she maintained control. He had never met a woman who could suppress such passion.

Where did she come from? Did one of his friends set up some elaborate prank to fool him? Several did complain he grew up on them. Perhaps one of them hired her. If so, she was very good. Her clothing, hair, mannerisms, even her speech was different. He understood her words, but not the meanings. This woman kept using them in the wrong context. What was "fuzzy" supposed to mean anyway?

Her clothing bothered him the most. The britches she wore were far too snug to be decent, but he had to admit she did look good in them. Damn good. It had been a long time since he had been with a woman. Probably why her style of dress aroused rather than appalled him.

He continued to stare. She had a pretty face, small, with an aristocratic look. Her high cheekbones, and her bow-shaped lips, had a pink tinge to them. He wondered what her lips, moistened by the tea she sipped, would taste like.

Thankfully, Fleurette interrupted his thoughts as she asked Rose, "Ma'am? Should I fetch her proper clothing?"

Rose looked at Trey before she nodded her approval.

Trey agreed. Perhaps if she were properly dressed, he wouldn't have these wayward thoughts. His aunt shooed him out of the room when Fleurette returned with appropriate attire.

~

*A*lex looked at Fleurette and Rose. "Ladies?"

Rose thumped her cane. "Why are you here, Miss Alex Thibodaux?"

"I don't know." She broke eye contact by glancing down toward the floor. "Look, I know I'm an inconvenience. Why don't I just leave? All I need is a taxi."

Rose's brow crinkled. "Taxi?"

Her mind groped for another word as she looked up at Rose again. "Hack?"

"Out here?" The cane thumped again. This young woman didn't behave like any of the young ladies Rose knew. Yet it could be all a show. There was only one way to test her, with the clothes that came from Trey's mother's trunk. "Besides, you're not dressed properly."

Fleurette silently laid out the undergarments Alex had to wear.

Alex looked at the pantaloons and corset and started to laugh. "You can't be serious."

"Fleurette is the only one about your size."

That sobered her up. "I didn't mean…" Alex looked at Fleurette. "It's just I've never…"

That cane thumped the floor again. Rose didn't know one white woman who would wear an ex-slave's clothing, yet Alex seemed upset that she'd hurt Fleurette's feelings. She decided to keep the truth of where the clothing came from a secret a little longer.

"Are you friends of my grandma?" Alex mumbled, thinking of her grandmother's thumping cane. That thing thumped every time she wanted someone to see things her way. "Do I have to wear those things?"

"How do you expect to fit in the dress without them?" Rose's fan snapped open.

"Okay. Stupid question." Alex eyed the garments again. How bad could it be? "Then let's get this over with."

Rose hid her grin behind the fan. This young woman had a lot of fire. She reminded Rose of herself at a younger age.

~

F ifteen minutes later, after hearing her voice rise a couple times in protest, Trey watched Miss Thibodaux emerge in what was considered proper attire. At least it would have been fifteen years ago. He walked a close circle around her as he examined the dress.

The hoop skirt brushed the ground, covering her legs properly. He found trouble as he raised his gaze up to inspect the rest of the dress. The bodice was too small, or was such a daring cleavage the way women wore them when this style was in fashion? Alex Thibodaux practically fell out of the dress.

He turned beseeching eyes toward Fleurette. The soft scent from Alex's skin tickled his nose. She smelled like she had been rolling in magnolias, his favorite flower.

"I'm sorry, sir. That was the only one I could find in your mama's trunk that I thought would fit her."

Alex turned a questioning look at Rose.

Rose smiled sweetly before asking Trey, "Didn't you save all of Winifred's dresses?"

"Yes," he answered. He didn't have the heart to throw his parents' clothes out when they died. As he glanced down at Alex, he wished he hadn't. The view he had made his body react in a way it hadn't done in a long time.

Although his mother was thin in the beginning, the dress Alex wore attested to that, Winifred Dalton was a large woman in her later years. There should be plenty of material in the larger ones to make a couple of dresses for the slender Miss Alex.

"Could you alter some to fit our guest? And maybe one or two for yourself?" Rose asked Fleurette.

Although he hated his aunt taking over every situation, which was her nature, she made a wonderful suggestion. He didn't know Fleurette could smile so hard.

"Oh yes, ma'am. I sure can." A hesitant look entered Fleurette's eyes. "Then, the lady is staying?"

"No," Trey stated.

"For now," countermanded Rose.

A muscle in Trey's jaw twitched. "Aunt Rose."

"You jus' gonna send her out there unprotected?" She snapped open her fan again. Rose's accent grew thick again.

Fleurette picked up Alex's twentieth-century clothing and headed out the door.

"What will the neighbors think?" he retorted.

"I'll act as chaperone."

"You're leaving in two days." A wary look entered his eyes.

"I've decided to extend my stay." Rose fanned herself.

Trey sighed. He didn't need this, but he couldn't say no to Aunt Rose. "For how long?"

She shrugged. Her fan moved slowly back and forth.

Trey stared down at Alex. His murderous eyes pinned her to the spot.

She hadn't done a thing, yet he looked like he could kill her.

They stood toe to toe for a few seconds, sparks flying between them. Alex could have sworn he fought the urge to throttle her. Then he stalked out of the room.

Once Trey left, she found herself being watched again by Rose Dalton. "That was very nice of you."

"What?" The fan slowed.

"Offering gowns to Fleurette as payment for making me some. Not many folks would think of such a thing." She knew that people weren't known for giving their clothing to their servants. Rose amazed her by making the offer she did.

"Well, they're just going to rot in the trunk they're in, anyway," came her gruff reply. That fan of hers picked up speed.

"Perhaps it would be better if I stayed in town. Mr. Dalton doesn't seem too happy to have me here."

Rose thumped her cane. "My nephew will do as I say."

So that was the problem. "And I bet he doesn't like it one bit, does he?"

Rose's deep gray eyes pinned her to the spot. "Why do you speak so strangely?"

Alex watched her hands as they smoothed down the front of her russet gown's skirt. "Where I come from, everyone speaks this way."

"And where is that?"

"California."

Rose grunted.

Alex wondered how much Rose knew about California. "Have you ever been there?"

"No. Only been as far west as Nebraska."

"Ah." She thought about sitting down, but knew she'd have trouble with the hoop skirt. Instead she wandered around the room, noticing a faint rose pattern on the yellow wallpaper. It dawned on her that Fleurette had taken her clothes, and along with it any proof that she came from the future.

"What happened to your hair?" Rose asked.

Alex turned toward her. Unconsciously, she ran her hand over her collar-length hair. "Is there something wrong with it?"

"Well, it's been cut."

She smiled. Good thing she didn't have a buzz cut. "It's the newest rage where I come from. No one cuts their hair here?"

"Not unless they're ill or... Well, no matter. I'm sure we can fix this problem. Fleurette is a wonderful coiffeuse."

Alex started to move about the room again, gazing at the whitewashed secretary against the left wall. Why would they want to hide the length of her hair? Good thing no one could see her driver's license. Her hair was a lot shorter then. Her driver's license, oh no, her pepper spray. She whirled on Rose. The hoop skirt swung with her sudden movement. "Where did Fleurette take my clothing?"

"To the laundry. Why?" she questioned.

"My clothes, she doesn't have to wash them. I'll do it myself." She walked out the door before hesitating. Finally, she turned back to look at Rose. "Um, which direction is the laundry?"

Fleurette's high-pitched scream filled the hallway.

Alex glanced back at Rose. "Never mind. I believe I can find it myself."

She started down the hall, praying her feet wouldn't get caught in the ridiculous hoop. She hadn't gotten more than two steps when Trey stepped in her path. His hand grabbed her arm in a steel grip.

"Where are you going?" asked Trey.

"To retrieve my things." She tried to shake him off. "A few items in the pockets of my jeans could startle Fleurette, and I believe she found one of them."

Alex didn't wait for any comment. Pulling her arm free, she stomped down the rest of the hall to the laundry room. The doorway to that room was narrower than other doorways that Alex had gone through.

She charged through to find that her skirt wouldn't fit. It got stuck in the doorframe, with the back end tipping up a little too high. The only reason she knew this was because of the sudden draft, followed by someone shoving the dress back down, propelling her through the door. She skidded to a halt, her skirt bobbing around her ankles. Turning, she found Trey directly behind her.

"Keep her away from me. She's a witch," Fleurette screamed. She knelt beside an older black man sitting on an upside-down washtub. He held his eyes while he whimpered.

Alex rolled her eyes. Perfect, what else could go wrong? "I am not a witch. Fleurette—"

"Don't use my name, witch," Fleurette screamed, throwing Alex's keys, pepper spray, ID, and money at her.

She caught the keys and spray in midair. The coins clattered against the hardwood floor. Her bills fluttered in the air as they slowly danced their way down.

The ID landed right in Trey Dalton's hand. His curiosity piqued, he headed to a window to examine the small object in his hand.

"Did you push this button?" Alex asked. Praying they didn't. She knelt down in front of the man, prying his hands away from his eyes. Sitting back on her heals, she sighed. The tears streaming down his face told her someone did push the button and this poor man got a face full of pepper spray.

Fleurette crossed herself. "That evil thing hurt Jessie."

Alex stood and grabbed Fleurette by the shoulders. "I need water. Lots of water."

Trey looked up from the article he examined. "Why, so you can drown the poor man too?"

Spinning to face Trey, she jammed her hands on her hips. "No. He's been sprayed with pepper. It was designed to ward off attackers. Water will help rinse his eyes. Remove the burning sensation."

Alex saw a bucket of water on the floor. The ladle sticking out told her it was drinking water. She knelt down. "Jesse, you need to stick your face in the bucket, and open your eyes in the water. The stuff burns, right? Water will take away the burning."

In the beginning, Jesse refused her request. After the burning persisted, he did as she asked. It took several good dunks before the burning started to ease.

Once sure he was all right, Alex turned to face Fleurette. "I never meant to harm Jesse."

"Then you are a witch."

"No." She bit her bottom lip. How could she explain this piece of modern technology? "Traveling alone is dangerous where I come from. My father wanted to be sure I was protected."

She held up the canister, not sure how to explain the pepper spray. "This is nothing but liquid pepper. When sprayed in the eyes of someone it stops them from hurting me. Gives me a chance to get away."

Fleurette stared at the sleek black canister.

"My father's friend created this for me. He's an inventor. It's not magical." She held it out to the young woman. "Here, hold it yourself. It doesn't do any tricks."

Fleurette continued to stare at the container, making no move to touch it. "Tricks?"

She did it again. When would she learn to keep her mouth shut? "Maybe I'd better leave."

Turning, she found Trey Dalton blocking her way. She moved around him and stepped into the hall.

The floor glistened. Her money. Alex crouched down, gathering the bills and coins that had bounced off her dress and onto the floor. She fought back the tears that threatened to spill. This was turning into a nightmare.

Alex knew Fleurette would give her a wide berth from this point on.

She shook her head slightly, as if she'd be here longer than a few more minutes. She knew this would get her thrown out on her ear.

Once again, she felt the viselike grip of Trey Dalton as he dragged her to her feet.

"Come with me," he said, dragging her to his study.

A dull throb emanated from where he held her arm. She stumbled behind him in order to keep up with his long strides. "You're hurting me."

He ignored her as he pulled her into the room.

The study oozed with masculinity. Large leather chairs, dark velvet drapes, the scent of tobacco. A huge globe sitting next to the massive mahogany desk caught her attention. Something she dreamed of having, yet never bought. His grip on her hand didn't allow her the pleasure of going near it.

He spun on her, keeping her body close to his. Waving her driver's license in front of her face, he demanded. "What sort of witchcraft is this, Alexandra?"

CHAPTER 3

*A*lex closed her eyes. Of all the things he could have reacted to, it had to be her full name. Why? He must have read her driver's license and found it.

Wrenching her hand free, she snapped, "I am not a witch! You've seen photographs before, haven't you?"

"Not with color like this," he shot back. Could it be a hand-painted miniature portrait? He looked at the picture again. The picture didn't do her justice. Her vivid blue eyes glistened, and her soft flesh looked real enough to touch. "Where did you get this?"

She placed her hands on her hips. Mad enough to tell the truth, she didn't care what he thought. "Why, the DMV."

"DMV?" he questioned. Trey went to the window and sat on the sill to study her driver's license again. It amazed him. The slick paper was hard like a rock and as thick as vellum. He banged it against the window to test its strength. Angling it in front of the window he saw an image jump out at him. "What was that?"

Alex shrugged. "You probably saw the hologram."

He looked at her, noticing how the light danced in her eyes when she was frustrated. "Hologram?"

She tapped her foot. He was taking this far too calmly. Why wasn't he threatening to have her locked up? "A three-dimensional image. They use it to stop forgeries."

"Fascinating." He looked back at her color photo. His face paled when he noticed the date.

She tried to get her ID, but Trey kept it just out of reach. "I'd like that back."

"I know, Alexandra, but I'll keep it for now." He slipped it into his shirt pocket and smiled. "How was it made?"

"With a camera." She frowned at him. "Why can't I have it back? It belongs to me."

"I'd like to study it a little more." He looked down at the card. "A color camera."

"Yes." Her foot tapped harder.

"There is no such thing." His smile widened as he crossed his arms across his chest.

"Maybe not now." Alex closed her eyes, pinching the bridge of her nose. She needed to maintain control. "So, what are you going to do? Burn me at the stake?"

Looking up at her, he asked. "For what?"

"Witchcraft. That is what you accused me of."

"True." Trey patted his pocket. He believed the picture a hoax and she a very good actress. All he had to do was watch her. Something he found he enjoyed. Sooner or later she'd reveal her real identity and he had the patience to wait her out. "My aunt is right. As a gentleman I can't force you out the door with no place to go. So, you are welcomed in my home, for now. Aunt Rose will be your chaperone."

"You're letting me stay?" she blurted out, amazed.

"Do you know how to go home, Alexandra?" he asked, expecting her to stumble on her lies.

"No." Alex couldn't look him in the eyes. "Not right now anyway. And please, call me Alex."

"Then where would you go if I forced you to leave, Alexandra?" He noticed a hard edge enter her gaze.

"I don't know," she said. "I'd rather you didn't use my full name."

"No woman who stays here will be called by a man's name. As long as you stay, you will be Alexandra," he replied, wondering why he pushed. Maybe it was the way her eyes brightened when he ignored her request.

She nodded silently. Her body rigid. How could she argue when he offered her a place to stay? He also raised a scary question. What if she couldn't get home?

~

*A*lex rubbed the table one last time before inspecting her work. She smiled at her reflection. The golden oak table glowed from her polishing. Straightening up, she massaged the small of her back. When she asked Trey if she could help with the chores two days ago, his reaction was comical. She swore his jaw hit the ground.

Rap, rap, rap.

She turned toward the window. Rose sat out on the porch banging her cane against the doorsill. Something the woman did about every fifteen minutes. Wiping her hands, Alex stepped out unto the porch. "Yes, ma'am?"

Rose rocked in a rocking chair. "Tea, please, with a sprig of mint."

"Of course," Alex replied. "Anything else?"

"No."

She nodded as she went back inside. She got a drink and a tray from Fleurette and headed out the door.

Rose's eyes lit up when Alex returned so quickly. "Oh, could you get my fan? It's up in my room."

"Of course." Alex set the cup down on a small table beside the rocker where Rose sat.

She searched the room a few minutes before locating Rose's fan. She stepped out onto the porch. "Is this the fan you wanted?"

Rose blushed as she closed the small black fan in her hand. "I forgot I had this one out here. My favorite is the ivory-handled one."

Alex looked down at the jade fan in her hand. Flashing Rose a tight smile, she went inside and searched for Rose's favorite fan. She came back out fifteen minutes later. "Here you go."

"My fan," Rose exclaimed. "Thank you. I didn't mean for you to get it."

Alex knew what Rose wanted. Her grandmother pulled tricks like this all the time. Like her grandma, Rose didn't want to ask anyone to just stop what he or she was doing to pay attention to her, so she used other tactics. Her grams was the queen of them all.

Fleurette came out on the porch carrying a large tray. "Jessie just told me we're about to have company, Miss Rose."

Rose peered down the road. "I wondered when Miss Lulabelle would come visit."

Alex wiped a bead of sweat from her throat.

"Lulabelle?" What a name.

"Yes." Rose picked up her tea. "She's a dear friend. I was supposed to visit her the day you arrived."

Fleurette handed a cup to Alex, then set out a tea for the impending Miss Lulabelle, and a plate full of her pralines before going back inside.

Alex followed behind her. The fewer people she met the safer she felt. She didn't fit in here and knew it wouldn't take very long for anyone to realize that. But she did stay close enough to overhear the two women's conversation.

"Rose! Thank God, you're all right! I hear a rumor that Trey brought some strange woman here and she hurt someone with some strange box. Then I get a message you didn't feel well. Well, I thought the worst!" Lulabelle collapsed into the rocker next to Rose, fanning herself furiously. Squinting against the sun she asked, "Why do you sit in the sunlight? The breeze on the southern porch is so nice about now."

"If I sit on the southern porch, I wouldn't know when you're coming to visit, would I?" Rose questioned. "Now, what are they saying about my nephew and his new guest?"

Alex didn't really want to eavesdrop on Rose and Lulabelle, but the moment she knew that she was the main topic she couldn't move. Their voices floated into the window.

"Well, you know that Trey never has a woman here," Lulabelle said.

"And what am I?"

Alex heard Lulabelle's soft twitter of a laugh.

"My dear, you are his family. In fact, the only time Trey has guests is when you are here trying to get him involved with his neighbors or trying to play matchmaker."

"And who said I didn't invite her?"

"Well, she didn't come with you. Everyone knows that. And she's, well, she's not the type of women you normally bring here."

Alex could hear their rockers squeak as the conversation paused.

"And what would happen if everyone learned that I brought Miss Alexandra here?"

Alex thought she heard a gasp before she heard Lulabelle ask, "Did you?"

Rose's cane thumped against the porch floor. "Lulabelle, you know I hate to find out that people here are gossiping about my family."

"Rose. That was a long time ago."

"Was it? No one has forgotten that Trey went overseas when that stupid war began. And no one has forgiven him for coming home in one piece, and with money in his pocket. So, they make up wild tales about why he went and how he got his money. And any time he can take three steps forward, they shove him back five."

Alex brushed off the chairs around the table as she continued to listen. They must be talking about the Civil War. Their conversation made her wonder what people had said about Trey.

"Well, you can tell all your friends that I asked Alex to come out here."

"You did?"

Alex thought she heard Lulabelle's voice squeak when she asked that last question.

"Yes. She is his fiancée."

Alex bumped into the table she had been polishing for the fourth time at that announcement, upsetting the vase in the center. Water sloshed all over the beautiful oak table. "Oh no."

She quickly grabbed a rag and sopped up the water as quickly as she could. What was Rose doing?

"Fiancée! When did he get engaged?"

"They've been engaged for a while. They met in Paris, when her family was visiting."

"In Paris, really?"

"Oh yes. They were quite taken with each other."

Alex rolled her eyes. She had been wrong all these years. Rose was much better than her grandmother at spinning a yarn. This story was living proof. Paris?

"She is a lovely girl. You really must meet her."

Alex jumped when Rose's cane thumped against the wall. Her hand went to her throat. "Oh please, tell me she doesn't want to see me."

"Alexandra," Rose called.

"Oh no. She does want to see me." Alex wanted to hang her head. Instead, she straightened her shoulders, took a deep breath, and walked out on the porch.

~

*T*rey didn't see Mrs. Lulabelle Woods arrive in her carriage. One of the male servants came out to get him.

"Aunt Rose sent for me? Is she mad?" He had too much to do and she knew it.

"No, sir. She jus' tol' me to come get you."

Trey closed his eyes in frustration. His aunt should have left two days ago, but because of that woman he couldn't stop thinking of, she'd decided to stay indefinitely. He loved his aunt, but her overbearing behavior drove him crazy. In the last two months she'd been there, she introduced him to five different women. All five bored him. Plus, three prospective business partners who wanted only his money, and their new priest, despite the fact Trey hadn't been to church in years. He breathed deep, hoping to clear out some of the tension building in him. She was his father's sister, and the only family he had left. Even with her high-handed ways, he'd always had a soft spot for her. "All right. Let's get back."

He was amazed to see Alexandra acting as the perfect hostess, offering to pour more tea, just as he walked up.

Her head snapped up at the sound of his boots on the porch. "Trey, I didn't expect you."

Rose patted her hand. "I sent for him."

Trey frowned. Did Alexandra just turn as white as a sheet?

He leaned down to kiss his aunt's cheek. He looked at the woman seated next to her. "Why, Miss Lulabelle, what a pleasant surprise."

She flushed. "Oh Trey, you tease me."

He smiled as he rested his hand on his aunt's shoulder.

Rose placed her hand on his as she looked up at him. "Belle has invited us to her party in three weeks."

"Three weeks?" He planned on figuring out the truth about Alexandra before then. "But, Aunt Rose, I thought you needed to get back home."

"Oh no, she can't leave before the wedding," remarked Lulabelle.

His eyes narrowed a little. "What wedding?"

Lulabelle looked right at him. "Why, yours."

CHAPTER 4

"*M*ine," he repeated. It took a few minutes for the words to sink in. He gawked at Rose. What had his aunt done now? "Mine! Aunt Rose?"

Rose tilted her head up, so she could look Trey in the eyes. "I know you wanted to keep it a secret, dear, but Lulabelle told me how everyone has been talking about Miss Alexandra's arrival." She squeezed his hand. "You know how gossip travels. What would you have me do, keep your secret and let everyone think the wrong things?"

His grin was forced. Aunt Rose had painted him into a corner. If he contradicted her in front of Lulabelle, the town gossip, everyone would think the paragon of the Dalton family was a liar.

Trey didn't care about himself. He could just ignore the old biddies who had nothing better to do, but his aunt Rose couldn't. These women were her friends. Without that friendship she would be very lonely, and Trey knew all about loneliness.

It had been his best friend since he came back from France seven years ago. No one had forgiven him for leaving the states just before the war started.

He took a deep breath. Forcing it out, he knew he couldn't contradict his aunt. "Of course not."

Trey smiled at Alexandra, but anger blazed in his eyes. He looked down at her face and watched as her eyes widened in disbelief. Gripping her arm, he pulled her to his side. Her teeth clacked together with the force of his tug. He smiled at Lulabelle as she continued to speak, wondering what the little minx was thinking at the moment.

The tattoo of Alex's heart beat rapidly against her rib cage, as she watched Rose and Lulabelle speak, but didn't hear the words. Trey's hand rested lightly against her side, but every time she shifted, she could feel the strength in his muscles as he exerted just enough pressure to keep her right where he wanted her.

He wasn't going to let her get away from him. She glanced up at him, knowing he must be thinking the worst.

"I am so glad to see you finally settle down, Trey," said Lulabelle. "You've been alone in this house too long now."

Trey nodded as he looked down into Alex's pale, frightened face. "That's what Aunt Rose kept saying."

Rose placed a hand on Lulabelle's arm, forcing her friend to look at her. "Yes, that's why I sent for Alexandra. It's past time for them to get married."

Alexandra tried to discreetly pull out of his grasp. A soft blush filled her cheeks when he tightened his grip. Angry sparks filled the eyes that glanced up at him.

Even in his anger, Trey's heart skipped a beat. Her eyes held a sparkle that captivated him. If she looked this good when angered, he wondered what she looked like when in the throes of passion. He mentally shook himself. Where did that thought come from? Miss Alexandra Thibodaux was the last thing he needed.

Lulabelle leaned toward Rose. "You sure they're in love? They act like they can't stand each other."

Trey pretended he didn't hear Lulabelle's comment, even though she'd said it loud enough for the whole plantation to hear.

There was only one thing to do.

To make this fake engagement real, at least to Lulabelle, he had to kiss Alexandria. Still pretending he didn't hear Lulabelle's comment, he cupped Alex's chin and tilted it up. His thumb rubbed across her soft lips.

Alex gasped at the intimate contact.

It was supposed to be a sweet, chaste kiss, but her hesitant response ignited something deep inside him and in an instant, he deepened the kiss. His body trembled with desire.

The softness of her lips beneath his felt so right. He slanted his across hers, increasing the pressure with every second. The sweet headiness of their kiss filled his senses.

Trey didn't remember wrapping his arms around her, but he found her pressed up against him, making him totally aware of the curves and swells of her lithe frame. She fit perfectly into his embrace.

A soft moan escaped her lips.

He knew they were getting in too deep, but he didn't want to stop. Blood roared in his ears. Desire controlled him. He wanted to bury himself inside her warmth, to feel her body close tightly around his.

Someone clearing their throat caught his ears, but he paid it no mind. A soft whack of a fan against his pant leg brought him back to reality. Reluctantly he broke the kiss. Staring down into Alexandra's eyes, he spoke. "I forgot we have company."

Alex just stared at him for a few moments. No one had ever made her feel what he did with one kiss. She turned her head away from the two ladies, so that they wouldn't see her flushed cheeks and swollen lips.

"I need to get back to work." Trey still held her close. "I'll see you at dinner, sweetheart."

Alex could only nod. She was too flustered by the kiss to be able to answer him properly. Once he walked off the porch she made a flimsy excuse and fled to the backyard, hoping to cool the desire he evoked in her so easily.

∾

A dust cloud danced around Alex as she swept the front porch. She was grateful that Fleurette had tied a kerchief around her hair to hold it up off her neck. At least part of her could keep cool. She had to stop every so often to flap her skirt, so she wouldn't sweat to death. These people had no air-conditioning and wore ten layers of clothing. No wonder so many women swooned. It was from lack of air from the corsets and heat exhaustion. She stood there flapping her dress when their invitation arrived. Alex blushed as the young boy reined his horse in. How much had he seen before she spotted him?

Silently, he handed her a thick envelope before turning and riding off.

She leaned the broom against the side of the house. Wiping a strand of blond hair away from her face, she pulled the invitation out of the vellum paper envelope. The paper's smoothness amazed her. The thickness of the velvet-smooth paper couldn't compare with what she was familiar with. She had never seen quality like this. A gust of hot, humid air pulled at the card, making it flutter in her hand. A ray of late afternoon sunlight played across the black ink of the beautifully handwritten note as it moved.

"And I'm supposed to fit in with these people," she mumbled as she carried the invitation into the house. Just before Alex entered the sitting room she heard Rose's cane thumping methodically against the wood edging of her straight-backed upholstered chair.

Alex stood just outside, in the cooler, dark hallway, staring at the invitation. She tapped it against her palm while she debated. If she gave it to Rose, the woman just might fill it out herself and return it without consulting anyone. If she waited, Trey would probably accuse her of trying to hide it. Alex sighed, a losing situation either way. Taking a deep breath, she swept into the room.

She headed straight toward the fireplace that dominated the room. Without glancing at Rose, Alex leaned the invitation against a candlestick on the white marble mantle. A place Trey would obviously see.

"What you got there, chile?"

Alex felt silly, but she really didn't want Rose to see the invitation first. For one insane moment she thought about hiding it behind her back. She straightened her shoulders and turned toward Rose. "The invitation to the Woods's ball."

"Oh good. I've been expecting that." Rose's cane dug into the carpet as she stepped toward the fireplace. She picked up the invitation from the mantle and placed it into her pocket before walking to a small white Victorian desk near the door.

In one fluid movement, she pulled out the invitation and the RSVP card. Retrieving the pen from its inkwell, she signed it with a flourish.

Alex wondered just how much Rose needed that cane after watching her.

Without looking up she said, "We are going."

"Don't I get a say in this?" Alex mumbled, already knowing the answer.

Rose raised her head and smiled. "You're just going to love this party." She motioned to Fleurette, who had just entered the room. "Have Joseph take this to Miss Lulabelle."

Fleurette inclined her head, before taking the note with her.

Rose leaned on her cane as she stood, then made her way out into the hall and turned left, heading to the back porch.

Heavy footfalls told Alex that Trey had entered the room. Quickly, she spun around and watched one of Trey's finely arched eyebrows rise as he studied her face.

"The invitation came today." A blush rose up her cheeks.

"So, you're talking to me again," he said, moving toward the mantle.

Her blush deepened. She had avoided him since he kissed her. She didn't want to face him after that. The attraction she felt for him confused her. No man had ever affected her the way he did. Talking to him made her feel flustered, like a schoolgirl, not a grown woman with a doctorate. "Your aunt just answered it."

Trey looked out the door in time to see the dust cloud from horses' hooves. "Well, it's too late now."

Fleurette quietly reentered the room to start her dusting.

"Is that all you have to say?" Alex gritted her teeth. "Aren't you going to try to stop this?"

He crossed his arms over his chest. Normally, when his aunt overstepped her boundaries he reacted angrily, but not today. He enjoyed Alexandra's frustration too much. "What would you have me do?"

"Stop her from interfering!" she snapped.

He gave her a disarming smile.

Nothing seemed to bother this man. Furious, Alex stomped her foot. "Oh, come on! Are you some kind of idiot?"

A loud crash vibrated through the room. Alex hung her head. Every time she opened her mouth she said or did something wrong. She knew without looking that Fleurette overheard her and dropped whatever she had been dusting. A quick glance told her it had been a vase. With a swish of her skirt Alex headed out of the house. She got as far as the gravel walk in front before Trey caught up with her. The pressure of his hand on her arm stopped her.

"Where do you think you're going?"

"Away from here." Alex pointedly looked at the grip he had on her arm. She started to walk the moment he let go.

He crossed his arms over his chest again. "Is the game too much for you, then?"

"What game?" she asked as she followed the gravel path.

"The one my friends put you up to," he said to her retreating back.

That stopped her. She turned to face him. "What are you talking about?"

"I figured it out almost from the beginning. Who was it? Manning? Boudreaux?"

Her brow furrowed for a second, then arched in understanding. "Ah, you think I'm some kind of actress, and someone paid me to come here."

"Yes." He suddenly felt uneasy at the spark of anger that entered her eyes. "Of course, you're one of the best. Your clothing, mannerisms, and speech are very good. It seems so real."

"Real. Oh sure, and this is a nightmare." She turned her back to him and resumed a steady pace. "And your aunt?"

"Why, she's in on this game of yours," he said as he started to follow her.

"Of course," she said over her shoulder as she walked away.

He caught up with her. "Are you upset because I found you out?"

"You just don't get it, do you?" She whirled on him. "Look at my driver's license. Do you know anyone who could do something like that? And the money, have you ever seen anything like it?"

As she raised a fist at him, a glint of light caught her attention. Thrusting her sleeve up, she showed him her watch. "Ever see anything like this?"

He grabbed her wrist. The gold watch he looked at had a black face, with several smaller clocks inside. Each of the smaller clocks moved at a different beat from the big one. "What a beautiful timepiece."

"You still think this is a prank, don't you?" She yanked her arm out of his grasp and pulled her sleeve back over her Seiko flight computer watch. "Fine. The game is over. You got me, what a fun joke. Ha, ha, ha." Her hand closed around her skirt and lifted it slightly. "I'll be going now. Goodbye, Mr. Dalton."

Trey watched as she stomped away. "Wait. You forgot your costume."

"Keep it. I won't need it anymore, anyway." She continued her quick pace. Too bad this wasn't a dream. This would be a good time to wake up.

Unfortunately, she knew she was already awake. Time passed normally here. She felt the aches and pains from working, fear of what would happen next, heartache because no one would believe her fantastic story.

Somehow, she had slipped back in time. She shook her head. Steven Hawkins would have a fit. He said time travel was impossible, yet here she was. But how? Wormhole? Tachyon particle? It was starting to sound a bit *Star Trek*ish, and her head hurt because of it. She rubbed her temples. Science dictated that it would take a time machine, not a picture hanging in some old plantation.

～

*A*lex walked several miles before she stopped and looked around. She didn't even know where she should go. Nothing she knew would exist yet. Sitting in some grass just off the dirt road, she removed her shoes and rubbed her feet.

"Okay, idiot. Pride made you walk away. Now what?" She dropped her head in her hands. "If only I hadn't touched that damned picture.

"Time to look at the situation logically." She stretched her feet out in front of her and wiggled her toes before putting her shoes back on. "There has to be an explanation on how I got here.

"Really." She tried to convince herself. Slippers on, she stood back up and proceeded to walk again.

The ground started to vibrate with the pounding of hooves. She turned to see a horse and rider charging toward her. There could only be one person on that horse, and that made her spin and run in the opposite direction. Thankfully, she didn't wear the corset Fleurette tried to force on her earlier. The dress was a little big on her and she could go without and not expose herself. If she had she wouldn't be able to flee.

She ran fast and hard but didn't get very far before a well-muscled arm caught her by the waist and swept her off the ground. The force of landing on the saddle knocked the wind out of her, or she would have complained about being manhandled.

His angry voice sounded in her ear. "We're going to prove who is right, once and for all."

She stiffened.

"How," she shot back. "By visiting your friends?" Silence told her she guessed right. "You won't believe them when they deny knowing me."

Trey said nothing, just pushed his horse harder.

Alex wondered if she had hit a nerve.

It didn't take long before the horse pulled to a stop in front of the male boarding house in the center of town. The two-story brown building stood between the mercantile and the livery.

Alex held her breath as Trey leaned into her to dismount the horse. She felt his warmth just before her back made contact with his muscled chest. His lean body pressed into hers just long enough to send her thoughts flying before he dismounted.

Standing on the dirt road, he lifted his hands in offer.

She glanced at his hands. There was no way she could let him touch her again. Her thoughts kept leaving her when he did. Quickly, she slid down the side of the horse and landed hard.

Trey's eyes narrowed before he grabbed her wrist in a steel grip. "There is no escaping, Miss Thibodaux." He jerked her alongside him.

She made a note to herself. Don't make Trey Dalton mad.

Entering the house, he dragged her along as they walked up the stairs and down the hall to the second to last door.

The proprietor's wife tried to stop them from her spot on the first floor. "Mr. Dalton, you know that ladies are not allowed in here!"

"The lady is perfectly safe. She's my fiancée." Trey ignored the glaring look Alexandra shot him, as he leaned over the banister to respond to the owner's wife. "Nothing will happen, I promise you."

"But, sir!" The woman moved to the bottom of the stairs.

"We will be here for just a few minutes," said Trey. "You can stand there and watch if you like."

The woman did stand at the bottom, ringing her hands as she watched them head toward Mr. Manning's room. Alex bet she was worried that her husband wouldn't be very happy about this. Trey was putting their reputation on the line by dragging her into their establishment.

Once they reached their destination, he placed Alexandra in front of the smooth maple door so when his friend opened the door the only thing he'd see would be her.

After his brisk knock on the door, Alex heard someone shuffling about inside. The door opened slowly.

A handsome young man leaned against the doorjamb, looking her over from head to foot. "My, my, aren't you a lovely thing. Are you another of Miss Russell's doxies? You must cost a pretty penny."

A growl came from Trey's throat before he moved into his friend's line of vision. "So, you don't know the girl?"

"Believe me, I'd remember if I had ever met her before." Beauregard Manning grinned at his friend. "Is she a gift?"

"No," he said a little too sharply. "Where's Boudreaux?"

"Haven't you heard? He sailed to France three weeks ago. His father has taken ill."

Alex crossed her arms. Now she had the upper hand. One delicate brow arched. "So, now do you believe me?"

"I don't know what to believe," he snapped. He turned back to Manning, who still lounged against the doorframe, watching them intently. "So, you're saying that neither you nor Boudreaux sent this young woman to me as a ruse?"

Manning looked at Alex. "Are you an actress?"

"No."

He looked back at his friend. "Well, I don't know about Jacques, but I never hired her. If I had, it wouldn't have been for you."

Alex's cheeks colored at his comment.

"Who is she anyway?"

"My fiancée." Trey grabbed Alex's hand and hauled her back down the stairs. Once outside, he spun her toward him. "Now we know that Manning didn't hire you, but Boudreaux could have."

"But he sailed to France, he might not be back for months," she exclaimed.

"True. Until then you will remain my guest. Once Boudreaux admits he hired you, you can leave."

She stamped her foot in the dirt road. "Look. I'm not some insipid little female. I will not stay in your house if you won't believe me."

"Sorry. To this small town you're my fiancée." Grabbing her hand, he forced her back toward his horse. "What would they think if you ran away? I would be the laughingstock."

"You won't humiliate me either." She stopped in the middle of the street and jerked her arm up, trying to pull free of his hold. "Come and get me when your friend returns from Europe."

"You're not staying here in town."

"Like hell."

In one quick fluid motion, Trey scooped her up and slung her over his shoulder. "You're coming back with me. You will learn to curb that language of yours, and you're going to start wearing a corset. I will not have this town gossiping about you."

She pummeled his back and struggled to get loose. "Put me down!"

"No." He slung her over the horse. His hand held her in place as he swung himself up into the saddle. Urging it with his knees, the horse galloped toward his plantation.

CHAPTER 5

*A*lex realized that she would be going to this party of Mrs. Woods even if Trey had to bind and gag her to get her there. Now that the word was out about their engagement he insisted they acted accordingly, despite most of the town knowing about their visit to Beau Manning's room.

Since their charming ride into town and back three days ago Alex had not said one word to him, but that didn't faze Trey or Aunt Rose, who talked about the party constantly.

Alex ducked into a small alcove, so she could tug at the corset she wore. This new one fit better than Trey's mother's had, but it still was extremely uncomfortable. Trey had followed through on his threat. She hated the torture device, but she had to wear it or be trapped in her room all day long. If it were up to her she'd burn the horrible thing.

Although Trey remained quiet about the party overall, he made the final decisions on her clothes and smiled and nodded at his aunt when she spoke about the party during the meals.

Seamstresses had traveled out to the plantation several times that week to fit Alex for dresses. Dresses she would have to wear her new corset with if she wanted to fit in them. As much as Alex hated it, she knew she had to wear it if she wanted her dresses to drape right.

She took a deep breath before realizing her mistake. It would be easy to bruise a rib if she wasn't careful. After a few shallow breaths she felt the pain subside. How was she going to do this? She didn't have a clue about the etiquette of the 1880s. She paused for just a moment before walking into the sitting room.

She noted several of the servants in the room also. "Miss Rose? Can I talk to you?"

"Of course, my dear."

"Outside?"

Rose nodded before following her.

Alex bit her bottom lip as they walked through the small garden behind the house. She touched Rose's arm as she spoke. "Perhaps it would be better if I didn't go to this party."

Rose's cane thumped against the gravel walk. "Nonsense."

"Miss Rose, you really don't want me there. I'll just embarrass everyone."

Rose stopped walking. "Then you are an actress like my nephew accused."

Alex made an unladylike sound as she turned toward her. "If I were an actress, I wouldn't worry about embarrassing your family."

She could feel the heat of Rose's stare, making her want to explain. "My father was a scientist." Like father, like daughter. "We never went to big social functions, he was always too busy with his experiments."

Rose made an unladylike sound of her own. "You'll do fine."

Alex rubbed her forehead. "Are you always this stubborn?"

Rose paused, studying Alex. "No one has ever dared to talk to me like that."

Alex placed her hand on her collarbone. She really stepped into it this time. Then she heard the oddest thing, Rose's laugh. She just stared at Trey's aunt.

Rose leaned heavily against her cane. "I'll teach you everything you'll need to know. I can't have my nephew's fiancée unprepared, can I?"

Alex rolled her eyes. What had she gotten into now?

"We'll start tonight. I know Fleurette will help."

~

Once Alex heard the house grow silent, she snuck out of her room and met Fleurette and Rose in the kitchen. All three crept to the ballroom. They worked together for the next four evenings. Several things began to happen during this time. Alex learned about the rich Southern culture, something she never paid attention to before, and Fleurette and Rose found a friend.

Rose watched Alexandra with admiration. She felt drawn to her. This young woman had a way about her. Alexandra treated everyone equally. A breath of fresh air to Rose. Her decision to befriend this young woman was proven right night after night.

They were working on dance lessons on the fifth night, when Trey heard Alex's rich, bubbly laughter float up the stairs. Curiosity dragged him out of bed. What made her laugh like that? Why couldn't he make her laugh like that? Trey opened his bedroom door. His hand tightly gripped the door handle while he listened. What could she be doing at this hour?

Quietly, he descended the stairs. Tilting his head, he strained to hear her location. He shook his head in disbelief. She was in the ballroom.

"One-two-three, and one-two-three," Rose said, her cane thumping out a rhythm on the oak floor. "Come on, Alexandra, you're missing a beat."

Alex collapsed into the floor, her dress billowing up around her. "I'll never get this right."

"Yes, you will," Rose said. "You have a sharp wit and mind."

Alex smiled at her. "You got all that from dancing lessons?"

Rose thumped her cane. "You have picked this up quickly and have done little damage to Fleurette's feet."

Alex looked up at the feet in question, then Rose. "They are still intact, aren't they?"

Fleurette giggled.

"See?" said Rose.

"Mr. Trey will be so proud."

"Don't bank on that." Alex laughed. "He thinks his friends sent me here as a practical joke."

"A what?" Fleurette asked.

"A joke, a trick, um." Alex bit her lip. "A ruse, I think."

"Ah, then we'll just have to prove him wrong, won't we?" said Rose.

"You're right." Alex smiled. "I would like to see him eat his words."

Rose wrinkled her forehead. "What?"

"Never mind. It's just a figure of speech."

Fleurette stood up. "You speak very strangely."

Alex pushed herself up off the floor. "Don't remind me."

"Once more around the floor. Then we'll start again tomorrow night," Rose said.

Alex nodded. Taking cues from Rose's cane, she and Fleurette whirled across the floor effortlessly, not knowing Trey watched.

Trey quietly headed back up the stairs to his room. There was so much to Miss Alexandra Thibodaux. Most of it confused him. A week ago, he would have sworn that she was an excellent actress, but a good actress would already know how to dance, wouldn't she? And even after he confronted her, she still continued to talk in her strange dialect, as if that were normal for her. He had spied on her yesterday while she pulled weeds from the garden and had heard her talking oddly to herself. She should have dropped the strange accent when she was alone, but she didn't.

Later that afternoon, she became angry because she didn't understand his curt words when she showed her ankles out in the field. Alex had called him a what? Oh yes, a male chauvinist pig, whatever that was. He could swear he'd been insulted, but not knowing the meaning of her words made him wonder if she ready did swear at him or if he imagined it.

The party was two days away. How would he explain her odd ways? Perhaps he should back out now while there was still time. It might be the smartest thing he could do. Trey wondered how he could go about doing it.

*T*he next evening, after dinner had been served, Trey sat in his office, trying to figure out a way to decline the invitation his aunt had accepted. He held the pen poised above the page while his other hand raked through his hair in frustration. How was he going to do this?

A soft sound of a skirt swishing followed by a thumping cane caught his attention. When he looked up, he saw his aunt walk past. He crossed to the doorway to catch her before she rounded the corner.

"Aunt Rose?"

She turned around to look at him and smiled. "Yes, dear?"

"How are you faring with Miss Thibodaux?" He stepped into the hall and leaned against the doorframe to his office.

"She's a dream. Such good company. I haven't felt this young in years." Her smile softened, and a dreamy look entered Rose's eyes.

"Is she feeling well?" Trey crossed his hands behind his back to rest on the doorframe. "No more fainting spells?"

"No, Trey." Rose's brow furrowed. "Why?"

"Oh good. I just wondered if she feels up to the party at Mrs. Woods's house."

"I'd say." Rose's deep laughter filled the hallway. "She'll be the belle of the ball."

"If you have your way," he teased.

"Why? Afraid I might embarrass you?" came Alex's voice from the other end of the hallway.

Whirling, he faced her. "Are you planning something outrageous?"

A brief flash of evening sunlight from a doorway surrounded her as she advanced on him. "That depends on you."

She was breathtaking, but until he knew the truth, he couldn't trust her. His eyes narrowed. "Meaning?"

"I will behave myself, if you behave yourself." Shadows enveloped her as she stepped past the doorway. She brushed a few stray strands of hair from her face.

"I am a gentleman." He swallowed hard. Flashing eyes and a sultry voice had his desire rising. No other woman could get him to react like this.

"Then we'll have no problem, will we?" She gave him a cocky grin.

Trey stared as she walked away. Tomorrow was going to be one hell of a day. He shook his head. Now that woman had him swearing.

CHAPTER 6

Set up on the Woods's front lawn, the party was already in full swing when they arrived at three P.M.

Alex stared around in awe. Bright-colored gowns glided across the greens. Music and laughter, mingled with voices, floated through the air. She was amazed to see so many guests milling about this early in the afternoon. The dance area and refreshments stood about ten feet from the left side of the house. Music swelled around them as they drew closer to the antebellum home. The two-story monolithic structure rose grandly between majestic magnolia trees. It took her breath away.

Not like she could really breathe. Alex pulled on the bottom of her corset. "Do I have to wear this ridiculous thing?"

"Yes," grumbled Trey. He took her elbow and guided her toward the refreshments.

As much as she resented it, she obeyed. She felt like a trussed-up turkey. The corset was so tight she could barely breathe, but everyone insisted that it would be improper for her to go without one. If only she could remove a few of the stays. Trey nudged Alex out of her thoughts by an elbow. Focusing on her surroundings, she noticed Mrs. Woods approaching.

Lulabelle, dressed in a bright canary-yellow gown, looked like Big

Bird. Alex couldn't help but grin. She watched as Rose embraced her old friend.

"My dear, you look lovely," said Rose.

Alex saw the look Rose shot at Trey to warn him against contradicting her.

So she wasn't the only one who thought Lulabelle could have chosen a better color.

"Why thank you, Rose. I see you have outdone yourself again." She inclined her head toward Trey and Alex. Dressed in all their finery they made a stunning picture.

Rose smiled, as she leaned on her cane a little more. "Are you going to keep me standing while you prattle on? This old leg must keep moving or else it will get mad and stop working altogether."

Lulabelle blushed. "Rose, I'm sorry. Please, come this way."

Rich green grass cushioned their steps as they moved.

As they followed, Alex turned to Trey. "Is she like this with everyone?" Indicating Rose. His nod made her grin again.

Alex realized Lulabelle had asked her the same question twice when she felt Rose's cane thump against her leg.

"I'm sorry, Miss Lulabelle. What did you say?"

Lulabelle opened her fan. "I commented on your lovely pink dress."

"Thank you. Trey helped pick out the color." Alex smoothed the front of the box-pleated skirt.

"This is just what you need," Lulabelle stated, looking at Trey.

He halted for a moment, stunned by what Lulabelle said. "Wonderful," he grumbled. "Another matchmaker." Trey slipped an arm around Alexandra and gave her a squeeze. "I know. I can't figure out how I survived without her."

Lulabelle smiled as she walked up and linked arms with Rose, who was several feet ahead. "I am so glad you could make it. This is the perfect opportunity for Miss Alexandra to meet all of Trey's neighbors."

Rose nodded in agreement as they walked.

Mrs. Woods slowed down for a moment allowing the younger couple to catch up. She smiled as she waved to a young man who approached. "My nephew is here from New Orleans for a visit. Since you're from the city too, I was hoping you could help keep him occupied, Alexandra."

Trey stopped in his tracks again. "I'm sorry, Miss Lulabelle, but my fiancée will be with me this evening."

It took a hard tug from Alex to get him walking again.

"Of course, I meant the two of you," Lulabelle replied, not taken aback by the gruff tone in Trey's voice.

"Be nice," Alex hissed. "I don't think Miss Lulabelle meant anything by it."

"I know," he mumbled back. "But you don't know who her nephew is. I don't want you to associate with him."

Alex's brow arched. "Who died and appointed you king?"

A deep red blush climbed up his neck as he grumbled deep in his chest. "He's dangerous. That's all."

"I can't be rude," she said softly. She wondered what was so dangerous about Lulabelle's nephew, and what did this man Trey hated so much do?

As the man in question approached, he looked vaguely familiar to her. She wondered why. He fawned all over Rose, who loved it. He bestowed a kiss on his aunt's cheek before looking at Alex.

She recognized the eyes. They stared back at her in the mirror every morning. This man had to be her great-great-great-grandfather. She remembered seeing photos of him in her grandmother's album.

"Andrew, you remember Trey Dalton? This is his fiancée, Alexandra Thibodaux."

"Ma'am," replied Andrew as he bent over her hand and kissed it. Next, he looked Trey up and down.

"You haven't changed much, Dalton."

"You haven't either, Leroux." Trey put a possessive arm around Alex.

"True." He finally extended his hand out to Trey. "Good to see you."

Trey hesitated for a few moments before shaking Andrew's hand.

A soft breeze made the ribbons on her bonnet flutter. Alex wondered what made Trey dislike her ancestor. Her grandmother's stories painted Andrew Leroux as a hero. She tried not to stare at her great-great-great-grandfather, but it was hard. "So, Mr. Leroux, your aunt tells us you're from New Orleans. Which part?"

"Please, call me Andrew. I live near Jackson Square. You are from the city too, no?"

"Yes." Of course, her knowledge was a little more than a hundred years too late. Just how much of the city had changed in that time? "The cathedral is beautiful."

He smiled. Taking his aunt's arm, they all resumed walking. "Yes, it is. Someday it will be a national monument."

Alex smiled back. As the oldest cathedral in the United States, it was. She glanced up at Trey, noticing the grim set of his mouth, but she wasn't going to let him ruin her chance to talk to her great-great-great-grandfather. "Did you come back just to visit your aunt?"

Andrew nodded to friends as they passed. "I've got some business to attend to locally as well, and I always look for excuses to see my aunt." He turned his smile on her. "And I am glad I did, or I wouldn't have met you."

"Thank you." She blushed at the complement.

One of Mrs. Woods's servants approached them.

"Ah, your rooms are ready. Matthew, show Miss Rose, Mr. Trey, and Miss Alexandra their rooms," instructed Mrs. Woods. "Please feel free to rest if you'd like. Dinner will be served at seven, until then you're free to do whatever you like."

Alex followed Trey and his aunt up into the antebellum mansion. People were still arriving, the sound of neighing horses and creaking carriages mingled with the steady hum of voices.

A young maid led the two women into the house, up the stairs, and to the back of the house. Trey's room was farther down the hall. Alex heard the scrape of metal as the maid slid the key into the lock on the door of her room. Accidentally, she heard the young valet helping Trey, apologizing for putting him in this wing, but the rooms where the other bachelors would be staying were full.

She walked into her room slowly. Someone had already turned back the crisp ivory linens on the massive four-poster bed that dominated her room. The opened windows allowed a gentle breeze to circulate. It helped to keep the heat from becoming too stifling.

She took in her surroundings. Her room was done in green. From the thick oriental carpet, in a deep forest tone, to the light green borders painted on the wall. Mrs. Woods did a wonderful job of picking out the right accent colors to bring the room to life like the peach kerosene lamp that sat on the marble nightstand next to her bed. Yellow roses, placed in a crystal vase above the fireplace, perfumed the air.

Her hat lay on top of the pale green bedspread that adorned the mahogany bed.

She spied her trunk sitting at the foot of the bed. Some poor soul had to lug that heavy thing into the house. Accustomed to packing light, Alex couldn't believe it took a trunk to carry a couple of days' worth of clothes.

Humming, she opened her trunk, and proceeded to hang her dresses up. Once her unpacking was done, Alex placed her hairbrush on the dressing table along with the rest of her toiletries. The large oval mirror stared back at her. She couldn't believe what she saw. Daddy's little tomboy all grown up. She didn't really pay that much attention to her body, but her waist was almost nonexistent in the damn corset. As much as she hated the stupid thing she had to admit it was making her look good.

A timid knock sounded on her door. Alex opened the door to find a frightened young black girl on the other side.

"Ma'am, I'm here to help you with your…" The young girl swallowed hard as she said, "I have come to unpack your things and help you dress, ma'am."

"Good." Alex smiled. "Perhaps you can help me decide which dress to wear. I can't make up my mind."

Two hours later, fully dressed in a dark turquoise gown, Alex stared at herself in the mirror again. Stiff white lace accented her bodice and sleeves. Although she'd had to fight to keep the design of the taffeta gown simple because of the rich color, Alex was glad she did. The young maid did an exquisite job of blending the hairpiece she acquired a week ago with her own, and piling her hair atop her head, while interlacing it with baby's breath and tiny seed pearls. Alex didn't recognize the beautiful woman in the mirror. "Oh Grams, if only you could see me now."

Two quick raps against the door interrupted her thoughts. Turning from the mirror she crossed to the door and opened it. Trey and his aunt stood on the other side. The sconces on the wall backlit the breadth of Trey's broad shoulders. Her breath caught in her throat. He wore a deep green jacket with matching trousers, and brown boots. Those deep green eyes were even more vivid than before. Dashing came to mind as she stared at him.

Trey didn't do any better. Alexandra had been transformed into the most ravishing creature he had ever laid eyes on. He thought she was pretty before, but in this dress, she took his breath away. His chest puffed up a bit, knowing he was her escort for the evening. He knew all the men would be envious.

Seconds ticked by as they continued to stare at each other.

"I...ah." Trey cleared his throat. "I noticed your maid had left, and I, we thought you'd like to go for a walk before dinner."

She glanced at Rose, who smiled back at her. A coy smile came to her lips. "I'd like that."

When the dinner bell sounded an hour later, they turned and headed to the ballroom, which had been converted to the dining room to hold all the people Miss Lulabelle invited.

Alex's heart fluttered when she found she was not seated next to Trey, but across from him. The thought of staring into those deep green eyes made her heart beat faster. She sat next to Andrew Leroux, who spent the entire meal talking about how he planned to rebuild the south back to its illustrious prewar days. At one point, Alex wanted to stand up and shout. She knew that the war changed the south forever, and after the war many moved west instead of trying to rebuild. One glance at Trey's face kept her mouth shut. A small vein pulsed in his jaw, revealing his barely contained temper. They'd just think she was crazy anyway.

Trey came around to her chair after the meal was finished.

Alex smiled up at him.

"Come, my dear." His darkened mood made him ignore her bright smile.

She stood as she took his hand.

"Are you enjoying your stay at the Dalton plantation?" Andrew asked as he rose with her.

"Yes." The sound of violins playing in the background caught her ears just as Trey tightened his grip on her.

"Excuse me, Andrew, but my fiancée promised to dance with me," he said.

Once they were out of earshot she snapped at him. "Now that was downright rude."

"You didn't look like you were enjoying his conversation." He drew her onto the dance area set up outside. "Besides, I didn't like the way he kept looking at you."

Alex hoped that the steps Rose had drilled into her wouldn't fail her now. "How was he looking at me?"

"Like you were a ripe Georgia peach and I was invisible," he growled.

She glided along with him. "Are you jealous?"

"No."

"Really?" One of her delicate brows arched. "Then how would you feel if he came up to us now and asked to cut in?"

Just as she said the words Trey felt someone tap him on the shoulder. "May I cut in?" he heard Andrew ask.

He flashed Andrew a debonair smile. "Forgive me, Andrew, but I must decline. I wish to spend a few moments alone with my fiancée. Hope you don't mind." He whirled her to the edge of the dance floor before sweeping her off into the darkened evening.

"You are jealous," she said in wonder.

"If you want to be with him all you have to do is tell me," he snapped.

"Trey Dalton, you're the most irritating man." Alex emphasized this by stamping her slippered foot, which found a rock in the ground. "Ow!"

Trey grinned as he bent down to examine her foot. His big hands caressed her delicate ankle. "It's all right. You might have a slight bruise tomorrow, but nothing's broken."

"Nothing but my pride," she said softly. Shivers shot through her body at his touch. As deftly as she could, she disengaged her foot from his warm hands.

He held up her shoe, balanced on the end of his fingers. "Won't you need this?"

Big blue eyes captured green ones. "Yes."

Trey knelt at her feet, gently cupping her foot to glide the shoe back on.

Alex rested a hand on his shoulder for balance as he slipped it on. She never knew a man sliding her shoe on her foot could be so erotic, but the body contact had all her senses firing. How would she make it through this weekend in one piece with him constantly at her side?

"Thought you already proposed," drawled a deep male voice.

Trey stood up. "Manning, what are you doing sneaking up on me like that?"

"Don't know." He shrugged. "Maybe I was hoping to see just how deeply in love you were."

Beauregard bowed gallantly toward Alex. "Miss Alexandra, it is a pleasure to see you again."

She eyed the man warily, as she nodded. "Mr. Manning."

"Please, my dear, call me Beau, everyone does." He took her hand, leading her away from Trey. "Except, of course, your future husband."

"Beau." She glanced over her shoulder at a now fuming Trey. Turning back to the man she walked with, she gave him her best smile. "You know he hates this."

"I know." He smiled back. "That's why I do it."

"Ah, I see. You try to steal all of the women he has dated." They rounded the veranda, heading back toward the dance area.

"No. Only the ones he cares for. And you, my dear Alexandra, are the first one in a long time."

"What makes you say that?"

"The stunt he pulled at my room in town," replied Beau. "That's the first time he's ever accused me of hiring a woman for him. Normally he would just shrug it off, send you packing, and pull some sort of prank on me." As the music from the next song filled the air, he bowed gallantly and escorted her onto the dance floor.

Alex felt a little stiff at first, but as she relaxed she started to enjoy herself. When she got a chance, she'd have to tell Rose what a wonderful teacher she was. Wait until her grandmother learned she could... Her home was more than a hundred years in the future. She started to bite her bottom lip. Somehow, she had to find her way back home. Getting too comfortable in this era would cause problems she didn't need to face.

"Are you all right?" asked Beau. "Would you like to sit down?"

"No." She gave him a weak smile. "I'm fine, really."

"You're a little pale. Why don't we take a break?" His worried brown eyes searched her face. Beau spotted a bench under a nearby tree. Gently, he guided her to it. "I'll be right back."

Alex blew a few loose strands of hair out of her eyes. It had gotten hot on the dance floor, but she couldn't understand why everyone treated her like a china doll. Was it the way all men treated women, or did she really look that bad when she thought about her predicament. Personally, she wanted to give herself a slap on the back. So far, she hadn't had a mental breakdown. As long as she didn't dwell on what happened to her she could almost pretend it didn't happen. Almost. Until she went to reach for her Waterpik shower nozzle or try to heat a cup of coffee in a microwave that wasn't there.

The warmth of a hand resting on her shoulder startled her. Instinctively she grabbed the thumb and forefinger—whoever it was would be sailing over her shoulder in a second.

"Alexandra."

Her free hand came to her throat as she released his fingers. "Trey, you scared me. I must warn you to never sneak up on me. It could hurt."

"What could you possibly do to me that would hurt?" He smirked at her.

"Don't tempt me." She gave him a dazzling smile.

Beau came back with a drink for her. He gave her a relieved smile. "You look much better."

"Thank you." She took the offered drink.

"Why? What's wrong with the way she looks?" questioned Trey.

"Nothing." His friend gave Alex an appreciative smile. "She looks exquisite tonight. She just looked a little faint earlier. I brought her out here for some fresh air and voila', she is beautiful once again."

"Another fainting spell?" he asked accusingly.

"I don't have a history of fainting." Alex crossed her arms under her bosom angrily.

"Well, I've seen you do it twice."

She stood up to face Trey. "That is a lie!"

"Oh?" One brow arched. "My servants found you on the floor after you fainted, no doubt. And you did it again when you first saw me."

Both ignored Beau's avid attention.

She looked down at the lace that edged her dress. "Okay, so maybe once or twice, but I really don't faint at the drop of a hat."

"Come on." Trey offered her his hand. "If you'll dance with me, I promise not to drop any hats."

Alex laughed. "Deal."

Neither noticed Beau's surprised look.

Trey wondered about his own sanity. He was starting to get used to her strange talk. It really did seem to fit her.

～

*A*lex sighed as her head hit the pillow. The soft tick mattress molded around her body like a lover, easing away the busy night. A soft smile played on her lips as she remembered how much she enjoyed this evening, although she and Trey still had a few spats, they dissolved quickly. Almost like neither wanted to be too far from the other.

Trey's attentiveness made her giddy. His quick wit and devastating smile melted any resolve she had to keep her distance from him. Tonight, she realized how attracted she was to this headstrong male.

Snuggling deeper into the bed, she drifted off to sleep.

A noise near her head woke her. She sat up quickly. The darkened room showed nothing out of the ordinary. Hesitantly, she lowered herself back down on the bed. Her mind had just started to drift off again when she heard a floorboard squeak. Both eyes opened wide. Someone was in her room.

A slight movement caught her attention. From the quick glimpse she got of the intruder's outline, it wasn't someone she knew. With a deep exhale, she prepared for whoever to make their move. Alex didn't have to wait long.

A strong hand roughly covered her mouth. She could smell alcohol and sweat on her attacker.

Instincts kicked in. The metal tang of blood filled her mouth as she bit fingers. Her attacker swore, confirming that he was male. When he pulled his hand away, she lunged up off the bed, causing the bed to bang against the wall, and shoved.

The loud groan made her smile. She had knocked him off balance. She watched warily as he rose to his feet.

"A fighter, huh? I like a woman with a little spirit."

"I think you'll find I have more spirit than you can handle," she said, her body poised.

When he came at her again, Alex sidestepped him, giving a swift chop between the shoulder blades.

He crashed against the wall, groaning louder.

Another loud crash made her jump as she whipped her head toward the door. The doorframe splintered and broke away as the door caved in.

In the doorway, stood Trey, fire iron in hand. "What's going on?"

CHAPTER 7

*A*lex stared at Trey. He knocked down the door to protect her, like some sort of hero. Something she didn't expect from him.

Her assailant used those few seconds to dash for the window. Just as she turned around, he leaped out, landing on the rose bushes below.

She felt the heat of Trey's body as he came up behind her to look over the balcony. Damn, if only her hero had waited a few more minutes…she might have figured out her assailant's identity. By the way he limped off into the night she knew it wouldn't be too hard to figure out who attacked her. He'd limp for a while.

"Are you all right?" he asked, gently touching her face.

"Yes, Trey. I'm fine." The way his eyes searched hers made her heart stop for just a second. When it started back, it beat quicker than it should. She swore it would pound its way out of her body if Trey continued to look at her that way.

Suddenly, chaos reigned in her room. Rose came tearing into her room, via the balcony they shared, brandishing her cane. The Woodses and several guests crowded through the busted doorway.

"Any clue who it was?" asked Trey as he lowered his hand from her face.

"No." The deep timbre of his voice made her blood quicken. She glanced up at him. "What were you doing in the hall, anyway?"

He glanced around before continuing in a lower voice. "I couldn't sleep. When I can't sleep, I wander the corridors at home. I thought about going to the kitchen when I heard some commotion coming from your room."

She turned toward the gaping hole that used to be her door. A soft smile played on her lips as she knelt down before what was left of the door. Trey knocked the whole thing down to protect her. Her fingers glided across the smooth wood around the lock. "Um."

"What?"

She looked up into his green eyes. "The door wasn't jimmied."

"Jimmy who?"

Her smile deepened. "Jimmied isn't a person. It's a phrase. He didn't force his way in so he got into my room with help." She looked up at him with wide eyes.

Mrs. Woods came over to her. "You can't stay here. We'll have a cot set up in Rose's room."

"Oh no. I don't want to inconvenience Aunt Rose."

"There, there, my dear." Lulabelle patted her hand. "It's all right. Then we'll move you into another wing. I believe we can empty the room next to Andrew's."

"No," said Trey.

Alex cut him off. "Miss Lulabelle, I really am fine. Whoever that was only wanted to frighten me. I don't think they expected Trey to come to my rescue. I doubt seriously if they'll try this again."

"Oh, of course, you've had a frightening experience." Lulabelle looked at her husband for support.

Trey spoke first. "We can brace the door back up until it can be repaired. That way Miss Alexandra can get some rest."

Mr. Woods nodded.

Fifteen minutes later, Alex sat on her bed staring at her makeshift door. Why would someone sneak into her room? It just didn't make sense.

Quietly, she stepped out onto the balcony. No one knew her here.

She couldn't have enemies. So what was the man after? A quick roll in the hay? It didn't make sense. She stared up at the stars she loved so dearly. They always relaxed her.

A couple hours later a yawn slipped out as she headed back to her bed. The sun began to peak up over the horizon as she drifted off to sleep.

Her eyes didn't open again until noon. She stretched as she sat up in her bed.

"It's about time you woke up."

The deep voice startled her. She leaped to a defensive standing position on her bed before she realized the voice belonged to Rose. "What are you doing here?"

"Keeping an eye on you," Rose replied, trying to keep a straight face. Alex made quite a sight standing on her bed, in a long white linen gown, her hair still mussed from sleep, looking like she'd box the next person who touched her. "Why don't you come down from there and we'll have a late breakfast. Mrs. Woods promised to keep something for us."

"Okay." She climbed down and stepped behind the screen in her room and proceeded to change.

"Rose?"

"Yes?"

"Why would a man break into my room?" She slid the silk stockings up her leg.

"Do you really want an answer?"

She just stared at the corset in her hand. "Yes. I want more than an answer. I want the truth."

"You might not like it." Rose's cane started to beat out a pattern. "There are some who don't believe that you are Trey's fiancée."

Her head popped out from behind the screen. "You're the one who started that rumor in the first place."

"True. But some think of you as a whore. That gentleman could have been trying to see if you were."

Her fingers got caught in the laces of the corset. An exasperated moan came from behind the screen as the corset came sailing over the top. "I think he learned the answer to that question."

The corset landed at Rose's feet. "Is there a problem?"

"I hate that thing. The man who designed it should be shot." Alex pulled her dress over her head and proceeded to button it up.

"You are not going without it, are you?" Rose asked as she picked it up.

"Yes. I'll start a new trend right now." Alex came out from behind the screen fully dressed, minus one corset.

"Oh no you are not. I will not have people talk about you."

"Rose, they already are." She laughed. "If the fact that I've been living in your nephew's home isn't enough fuel for them, last night should fan the flames. What's one little corset?"

"The line you cannot cross. They might gossip, but it's harmless right now. They know you're engaged, and you show yourself to be a proper lady. This will change all that." Rose indicated the corset.

Placing the corset on the bed, Rose crossed the balcony and walked into her own room.

Alex stood in her room in confusion. Should she follow Rose?

A few minutes later Rose came back with the young maid in tow assigned to Alex. Handing the corset to the girl, Rose explained. "Miss Alexandra needs help with her corset. She would have snuck out of her room to look for you if I hadn't have gone after you."

The young girl paled at the implications.

Alex went behind the screen humbly, allowing the young girl to fit and tighten the corset and then help her redress. "I won't say anything to Miss Lulabelle about this. And I will speak to my aunt as well. Thank you for coming when you did."

The young girl nodded and slipped out of the room quickly.

"Rose." Alex let her know she was now ready.

Rose smiled as she stood up. She thumped her cane on the floor once. "It is time to join everyone."

"Yes, ma'am. But first I want to…"

"I would never say anything to Lulabelle."

Alex relaxed. "Then you heard me."

Rose moved away from the chair she stood by and walked toward the balcony doors. "Alexandra, the only reason I said anything was to make sure that you never left this room without being properly attired. That young lady will now watch you like a hawk."

Alex followed her through the doors that led them into Rose's room. Her curiosity made her ask, "Why do you care?"

"You remind me of myself. I was a wild hellion like you when I was your age. But I was trained properly."

Alex smiled. "And you plan on making sure I have the same proper training."

"Of course," Rose replied as she opened the door to the hallway.

Trey stood there waiting for them.

He gallantly offered his arm as he led both women through the hallway and down to the dining area.

The sharp tang of the cold cheese combined with the warm fresh bread they ate for their breakfast. The strong aroma of freshly ground coffee filled the room. This breakfast reminded her of the late nights she sent at the observatory. Alex sighed as she took her first sip of the heavenly brew.

Trey and Rose remained at her side the entire day, giving her no privacy. Every time she tried to indiscreetly pull a stay out of some section of her upper body she felt a sharp jab from a cane. She was starting to become annoyed.

She also had to give Rose credit. Rose was right about the gossip. Although she knew everyone heard what happened, most showed her sympathy. People wanted to know who would do such a thing.

What worried her most was no one showed any of the injuries she knew she inflicted, plus the fall into the rose bush should have cut her assailant up pretty bad. She watched him hobble away, yet none of the men milling about showed signs of injury.

She smoothed the front of her evening dress. It was a beautiful gown, but Alex wasn't used to changing her clothes so often. The deep blue silk brought out the color of her eyes. It came off both shoulders, with a daring décolleté. The light blue gauze that edged the bodice of the dress didn't really conceal anything from probing eyes.

Her mind drifted as she thought about Trey. She wasn't sure what to think anymore. The more she learned about him, the more her attraction grew.

A shadow crossed her path. "Miss Alexandra?"

She looked up into piercing blue eyes. It amazed her to know she saw the same eyes in her mirror every day. She nodded her consent, flabbergasted that her great-great-great-grandfather asked her to dance.

What could she talk to him about? Sneaking a peak up at his face she was caught by his dazzling smile. Her father's smile. This was getting a little eerie.

"I hope you are enjoying yourself, Miss Alexandra."

"Um." Alex closed her eyes in humiliation as her voice cracked. She acted like a lovesick schoolgirl. "Yes, I am, Mr. Andrew. Your aunt has a beautiful home."

"Yes, she does."

Well so much for witty repartee. Alex glanced around the dance floor. She caught sight of Trey, standing on the edge of the dance area glowering at them. As they moved she lost sight of Trey for a few moments, but not long, she spotted him heading toward them, waves of anger radiating from him. Alex wondered why.

He rudely cut between them. Swinging her away before either could say a word.

Her eyes widened. "You sure have a way with people."

"I don't want you to have anything to do with that man."

Alex laughed. "Right."

Trey gripped her arms hard. "I'm serious, Alexandra. He's dangerous."

She turned to look at Andrew, who had found another dance partner, and twirled the woman across the floor. "He looks harmless to me."

"Looks can be deceiving."

She rolled her eyes. "Trey."

He narrowed his eyes at her. "Let's get some fresh air."

"Why do you defend him?" He gripped her arm as he led her away from the dance area.

"Why were you so rude to him?" Her hands went to her hips.

"Is he the one who hired you?"

Alex froze for a moment. How ludicrous. She tried to take a deep breath, but the corset restricted her. "So what are you going to ask next, if we're lovers?"

"The question did cross my mind."

She stepped up close to Trey. A loud slap rang in the air. "You are a jerk!"

Before she could walk away, Trey snagged her hand.

"Mr. Dalton, please release my hand."

"I'm sorry, Alexandra."

She looked up at him, surprised that he apologized so easily. Then it dawned on her. He only did it to save face. A couple in love shouldn't argue.

"Oh no, Mr. Dalton, no need to apologize." She spoke softly, but her anger showed. "I have dealt with men like you before. Arrogant, insufferable—"

"Male chauvinist?"

"Yes." Alex gave him a cross look. "Rude and obnoxious."

"A pig?"

"Yes." She frowned. "Where did you hear that?"

"From you. What is a male chauvinist pig?"

Alex stared at him. She wanted to remain mad at him, but his innocent look made it too difficult. "It's an insult."

"I thought so." Trey paused for a moment. "Are you attracted to Andrew?"

Alex sighed, knowing her anger had dissipated. "No. Trey, he's like a brother."

"Are you saying he's related to you?"

"Yes." Alex looked up into his angry face.

"How?"

"You won't believe me," she replied.

He took a step closer to her. "Try me."

"He's my great-great-great-grandfather."

Trey looked at her for a few seconds with a straight face. He really tried to remain solemn, but he couldn't stop the laughter as it bubbled to the surface.

She continued to speak calmly. "In 1885 he will marry a Elizabeth Boudreaux. Not related to your friend Jacques Boudreaux but a popular New Orleans name. They will have four children. One will die in childbirth. The oldest of the remaining three will be named Joseph. He will marry Katherine Donnelly in 1911. They will have a total of nine children. The third child will be a boy. His name will be Patrick. He will get married in 1938 to a Miss Betsy O'Sullivan. They will have four boys, the second boy, Michael, will marry Janine Manning just before his thirtieth birthday. Seven years after they marry, they will have a daughter, Alex."

Trey's laughter stopped. "You meant to start in 1785."

She shook her head. "No, I didn't."

"You can't honestly want me to believe…"

"The truth?" she asked. "Yes. I do. Trey the evidence is there. Look at the money, or my watch. Check out the clothing I wore that first day. Have you ever seen anything like it?"

"It is just a hoax. When Boudreaux returns …"

"What are you going to do when he says he didn't hire me?" she asked, lifting her skirt to take a step closer. "When are you going to believe what is in front of your eyes? What do I have to do to convince you?"

CHAPTER 8

A hot, humid breeze stirred the curtains. Alex welcomed anything that would help cool her. God, she hated the heat. It was one of the reasons she left New Orleans to go to college in Boston.

MIT, renowned for their science programs, was the perfect place for her to find what she liked doing best. Once she started her studies it didn't take her long to find a niche in astrophysics and a love for cooler temperatures. Her friends couldn't understand why she wanted to lock herself up in a cold observatory. If only she could go back to that cold building right now.

A bead of moisture rolled down her throat, over her collarbone and into the front of her blouse.

Sitting back on her heels, Alex stopped scrubbing the floors to wipe her face with a handkerchief. The sharp tang of ammonia rose from her hands and made her eyes water. She closed her eyes against the fumes.

When she opened her eyes again, Fleurette stood in front of her, holding a tall glass of lemonade.

"Oh Fleurette, you are a lifesaver."

Fleurette just stared at her.

She decided to try again. "Thank you."

This time Fleurette smiled. "You're welcome. I just made a whole pi'ture if you'd like some more."

Alex smiled as she struggled to get up from the floor without stepping on some part of her dress. She'd never get used to so much clothing. She needed a break, from her work as well as her thoughts.

Since Mrs. Woods's party last week, she'd been trying to come up with some way to prove to Trey that she did travel through time. He wouldn't believe her, but she'd overcome this type of attitude before.

He refused to examine her money, or her watch again. Trey just wrote it off as too much wine. When she tried to broach the subject afterward, he would switch the topic. It frustrated her. Somehow, someway, she had to get him to believe her.

∾

*F*rustration! That was what he felt, frustration. The woman must be daft, spouting off about some sort of lineage that goes to the end of the twentieth century. She said it so calmly that he almost believed her. What really bothered him was that he couldn't let it go. Every time he looked at her he wondered if she could be telling the truth.

He shook his head savagely. No, she had to be a very good actress. That's all. Time travel was nothing but a faerie tale.

His foreman arrived, interrupting his train of thought.

"Mr. Dalton, you better come see this."

∾

*T*wo hours later Trey came slamming through the house. Alex took one look at the mud on the floor she just scrubbed and screamed.

"What do you think you're doing?" She came up behind him and started to shove him back toward the door. "If you think I just scrubbed those floors so you can make them dirty you have another think coming, mister. I spent all day working on that floor."

She pushed him out onto the porch and shoved him into one of the rockers sitting there. Bracing one foot against the chair she grabbed a boot and pulled. "From now on, you will remove your boots before entering the house, do you hear me?"

Trey loved the way her eyes lit up in anger. "And if I don't?"

She wrenched the boot off his foot and sent it sailing into the yard. "The next time that will be you."

"That I'd like to see."

She spun around toward the new voice. Beau sat astride his horse, grinning at them. "How long have you been there?"

"Long enough," he replied.

"Good. I won't have to repeat myself." Alex turned and walked back into the house. Once out of sight of the two men, she sagged against the wall. What possessed her to behave like that? She touched her hands to her hot cheeks. The calm Alex Thibodaux, reduced to behaving like a six-year-old.

She pushed off the wall to notify Fleurette and Rose of their guest. Straightening her shoulders, she knew how she would handle it. Just like Trey would. She'd pretend it didn't happen.

When she stepped back out onto the porch with lemonade and some cake, she found the two men deep in conversation. Trey had abandoned the rocker for his favorite chair. Beau sat on the steps.

"Well who do you think did it?"

"Anyone could have," replied Trey. He nodded his head in thanks as he took a lemonade glass from the tray Alex carried.

Beau gave her a dazzling smile as he took his glass. "But the destruction of those wagons cost you. You're lucky that they didn't get all your equipment."

"Most of the equipment was in the field. The new wagons can be replaced."

"Why do you think they went after the wagons?"

"It was a warning." Trey sipped his drink.

The tartness of the lemonade made his lips purse. Alex made a mental note to add more sugar.

"A warning against what?" Beau sat his glass on the top step.

Alex felt like a piece of furniture. Both men totally ignored her.

"That I don't know." Trey rocked his chair back. "Many are angry that I was able to rebuild after the war."

"Many are angry because you didn't fight in the war," remarked Beau. "They don't understand how you could have stayed in Europe the entire time."

"We were out at sea most of the time. I didn't even hear about the war until after it had been raging for two years. By then I knew going back wouldn't solve anything. My vow to my father wouldn't allow me to return until I had made my own fortune, like he did and his father before him. I had to honor that." His chair slammed down on the porch. "If they don't understand that, then I have no use for them."

Beau stood and placed a restraining arm on his friend as Trey rose from his chair. "I do understand, so don't take your anger out on me."

Alex looked from one man to another. She now understood his aloofness toward his neighbors. In their eyes he cared more about himself and wealth than he did about the South.

"I know." He let out a deep sigh. "But I came back to rebuild. Why can't they see that?"

"Because they're jealous," mumbled Alex.

"Why do you say that?" asked Beau.

Alex jumped. She didn't think anyone had heard her. "Well they are. Trey went to make his fortune while they lost theirs. The war cost many of these people loved ones, priceless possessions, and a lot of money."

"But I lost the same things," snapped Trey. "My parents, their home, most of our family heirlooms."

"Yes, but you had the ability to rebuild. They didn't. Most live beyond their means, pretending that they can pick up right where they left off, but they can't. War causes more scars than just the ones you can see. The war left not only physical, but mental scars that will be felt well into the next century," Alex said.

"Well," she continued, wondering how far she overstepped her boundaries. "I'll go and check on dinner. Beau, will you be staying?"

"Of course," he replied.

As Alex headed back to the kitchen, she heard Beau remark. "That woman is wise beyond her years."

"That's what she'd have you to believe," replied Trey.

~

*A*lex took a deep breath of the magnolia's that scented the night air. Trey had planted a dozen bushes near the house when he built it, several directly under her windows. She loved them. They reminded her of her grandmother's house. Her grams had the small bushes around her house too.

The light from the moon lit up her bed, making it easy for her to start the journal she decided to write.

May 17, 1878

   Dear Grams,

   From the moment you made me go to the Dalton plantation and touch the painting, my life has been turned upside down. Somehow, I was transported back in time. The reason I am writing this journal is because you knew this would happen to me. I am assuming that you have this journal that I am now writing.

Alex proceeded to explain everything that happened to her so far. Including the destruction of the wagons Trey bought.

Grams, I don't know what to do. How will I get back home? I don't fit in this society. Every time I open my mouth I seem to put my foot in it. For example, Trey saw his first bicycle today. You know the funny one with the really big front wheel. His amazement made me laugh. I didn't have the heart to tell him that I own two, a mountain bike and a beach cruiser. Besides, he'd never believe me. There is some reason I want to prove that I'm not some raving lunatic to him, don't ask me why.

After writing for several hours Alex felt better. Pulling her mosquito net tight around her bed, she slipped off to sleep.

She woke to Fleurette's humming in her room. Alex sat up, stretching and yawning. Glancing out the window, she could see the sun just beginning to peak over the horizon.

"Well, you're in a good mood today," she remarked as she slid off the bed. The wooden floor already felt warm to her feet, and the day hadn't even started yet.

Fleurette smiled. She pulled a dress out of Alex's wardrobe. "Mr. Dalton asked that everyone be ready by seven this morning. We have to hurry if'n you want to eat before we leave."

"Leave? Where are we going?" Alex slipped into her undergarments and presented her back to Fleurette to help with the ribbons of her corset.

"It is Sunday again."

Wow. The days ran together. She had been here over a month and still hadn't adjusted yet. Alex gasped as Fleurette tightened her corset.

"Can't you loosen it a little?" she wheezed.

"No," Fleurette replied, as she helped Alex into her dress and hooked the buttons on the back of Alex's dress. "Today we go to church and then into town." She patted Alex's back. "There, all done."

Alex turned toward her bed. She slid her feet into the shoes that sat at the foot of the bed. "Oh." Into town was new. The last time she saw it was when Trey dragged her to Beau's apartment. When she remembered how she rode home a flush filled her cheeks.

Fleurette hustled her downstairs and gave her breakfast. Bread and cheese with a cup of coffee.

Coffee was the one thing Alex had to have in the morning. Without it, she couldn't function. She barely choked down the cheese before Trey barged into the kitchen. "Everything ready?"

Fleurette nodded.

"Let's go."

"Can I finish my coffee?" Alex asked, holding up her cup.

Trey reached out, grabbed her cup and dashed the remaining amount into the fireplace. "You're done."

She grumbled under her breath as she followed everyone outside. Her mouth opened at the frenzy of activity she found when she stepped through the door. All the commotion caught her off guard. She stood near the doorway, just staring. Fleurette darted in and out of the doorway, handing Trey and two other men a wide variety of things, including a picnic basket. Their outings to church were never like this before. Once everything was packed, they started an inventory.

Trey finally noticed her standing there, awed. "Come here."

She came to the top of the stairs.

"Can you read and write?"

Alex nodded.

"Good." Trey thrust his ledger at her. "We'll get this done a lot faster if I help the men."

Alex wrote as quickly as she could, but she still had to stop Trey several times. He seemed to have everything memorized, but still insisted that she write everything he said down. She ended up sitting on the porch steps, scribbling quickly to keep up with him. Before she had a chance to pull the pencil from the page, Trey snatched the ledger from her and closed it. She frowned in confusion. If he wasn't going to look at it, why did he have her write everything down?

Rose came out of the house with a flourish. With the help of Trey's foreman and two hands that went into town with them, she climbed into the second wagon and waited.

With the ledger still under his arm, Trey helped Alex stand up before helping her into the second wagon as well. His foreman, Fleurette, and the two hands were in the first wagon.

Several hours later, after church, they rode into town.

Alex swayed with the wagon, glad she didn't get carsick or she'd be in trouble. Once they made it to the open road, Trey handed her the ledger.

"Read me the third line from the top," Trey asked as his gaze swept the landscape in front of them.

"Of what I wrote?"

"No."

She shrugged, adjusting herself a little, and settled the book in her lap. She began to read aloud. "Oat grain for horses, five hundred pounds…"

Trey cut her off. "Fine. How much is two plus two?"

"Four." Alex swatted at a fly. "Why?"

"What's twenty-five minus seventeen?"

"Eight."

"Good. I need someone who can read, write, and do math handling the books today." Trey clucked to the horses to pick up some speed.

"All you had to do was ask me."

Trey turned his head toward her. "Many have tried to fool me."

"Oh, that's right, and I forgot. I am supposed to be a great actress," Alex snapped at him. "How many actresses do you know who can read and write?"

He looked at his aunt. "More and more women are learning."

"How many of these gentle ladies know how to read or write? How many blacks?"

"My Aunt Rose can." The wagon swayed sharply again. He looked at her. "Why do you call them blacks?"

"What do you call them?"

"Colored."

"Fine." Alex crossed her arms across her chest. "Your employees, how did you get them?"

Trey glared at her. "They're not my slaves, if that's what you're implying."

"No! It's just that I heard you and Beau talking last night. You weren't here for the war and your parents passed away before you could return home. If I remember correctly didn't most of the freed slaves leave the plantations they had lived on to find their own land and futures?"

"Some did. True." He still stared at her hard before speaking. "Jessie belonged to my father. Fleurette is his daughter. They hid from the soldiers and the looters for several years, living off the wild crops that grew in my father's fields. When I came back, they were waiting for me. I gave them a couple acres as payment for work when I first started to build this place. Although I work all the land here, I make sure they get the money brought in by their crops."

Alex paused. "Where's their plot?"

He narrowed his eyes. "The northwest corner."

She turned to look at him. "Isn't that where the wagon was destroyed?"

"Jessie and Fleurette would never do that."

"That's not what I meant. I'm wondering if someone tried to get you to blame him or her. That parcel of land is the farthest one out, right? They could sabotage you, not get caught, and throw the blame elsewhere."

Another dip in the road had them swaying again.

"But why you?" she asked.

Trey looked into her eyes before studying the road once again. "I don't know."

Alex thought to herself. Trey did know something but didn't want to reveal it. She would have questioned him further, but the center of town loomed ahead. Excitement filled her. Why, she wasn't sure.

Downtown in the late eighteen seventies wasn't exactly the high life.

The wagons drew close to the general store. Assailed by the sights, sounds, and smells Alex felt like gawking. Sweat from horses mixed with fresh mud from the last rain. Alex couldn't keep from wrinkling her nose. Children's cries could be heard as they played and argued nearby. Bright colors of women's gowns had her staring around. These women were dressed in their Sunday best. She absently smoothed the front of her plain yellow dress. One of the dresses Fleurette altered for her.

"You look fine," Trey murmured as he helped her down from the wagon.

A slight blush tinged her cheeks. How did he know what she was thinking? She smiled as Trey, always the gentleman in public, tucked her hand into the crook of his arm and guided her to the general store. Once inside a new odor struck. One that brought back wonderful memories. Tobacco.

Her father smoked a pipe. As a child she found the smell of his pipe very soothing. When she couldn't sleep because she was sure there was monsters in her closet her father, pipe in hand, would come into her room and scare those monsters away. Alex thought the pipe smoke had a lot to do with ridding her closet of monsters.

Then, as she got older, on those melancholy rainy days when she couldn't go outside, she would bring a book and join her father in his study. While he worked on his ledgers for work, she read. That was when she learned of all the fascinating worlds that lay between the pages. The first few books had been about fictional worlds, but then she found astronomy. She remembered many times, lying on her stomach on her father's study floor staring at star charts.

The first set she ever bought was the set that was based off the Star Trek television program. They were still her favorites. Her eyes misted for just a second before she shook her head. She couldn't cry. If she allowed one tear to fall, they'd all fall and she'd lose the control. She had clamped down on the predicament she was in.

Trey signaled her to follow him back outside. "Please write down every quote he gives you. Then tell me how much cash it should be," he murmured.

Alex nodded. Numbers were shouted and argued over. She watched the proceedings from the front of the wagon. The men were having fun carrying on like this. Bartering was something she had heard of, but never saw.

Out of the corner of her eye she noticed someone walking up to the wagon. One glance told her it was Andrew Leroux. Looking up in Trey's direction she knew he also saw Andrew. Trey's features were taut with anger.

CHAPTER 9

Trey reached up to help Alex out of the wagon, anger etched on his face. He ignored Andrew as he drew her toward the back of the store, where the owner waited with his money. Once it was pocketed, Trey turned to face Andrew Leroux, who followed them. "Why do you plague me?"

"I came to say good morning to your fiancée, Dalton." Andrew bowed to Alex, taking her hand and bestowing a kiss on it.

"She has nothing to say to you," Trey snapped.

"Well, why don't you let the lady speak for herself?" Andrew asked.

Alex felt their eyes resting on her. "Oh no you don't. I won't be dragged into your duel." She pulled her arm from Trey Dalton's strong grasp and walked away from them.

Stepping through the same door she saw the storeowner enter, she left them alone, and ran directly into the man just mentioned.

"Oh! Excuse me, sir! I'm sorry!" She had never been so embarrassed.

"Ma'am?"

"They were fighting, and…" Why was she telling a stranger her problems? "I slipped in behind you without thinking. I'll leave."

"Don't be silly, child. I've known those boys since they were children.

They've always fought. Why don't you wait for Mr. Dalton in the shop? I believe his aunt is already in there."

She smiled. "Thank you, Mr.... I don't even know your name. You must think I'm bold."

"Smart is more like it. When Trey and Andrew get started no one wants to be around." He led her down a corridor that opened into the shop. "Name's Boudreaux, William Boudreaux."

Alex stopped in her tracks. "Do you have a daughter named Elizabeth?"

"Yes." One bushy, gray brow rose. "Do you know her?"

"I've heard of her. Isn't she seeing Mr. Leroux?" she asked innocently.

"That rapscallion? I think not!" He then proceeded to sweep the floorboard furiously with a nearby broom.

A cloud of dust rose quickly around them. She covered her nose and mouth with her handkerchief to keep from coughing.

"I'm sorry. I didn't mean to imply..." Didn't anyone like Andrew? "When I was in New Orleans, a friend told me she had relatives here. When she mentioned the name Elizabeth, she neglected to give me a last name. I thought it might be your daughter."

William harrumphed. "There are several Elizabeths in this town. I wouldn't be surprised if it was that Elizabeth Deveraux. She's not getting any younger. Her parents can't be as particular."

Alex nodded, but kept her mouth closed while she went in search of Rose. She had caused enough damage.

She looked around in wonder as she moved through the store. Bright bolts of cloth rested next to canned goods. The sharp tang of pickles filled the air as she passed by the pickle barrel.

Rose stood near the register, eyeing the peppermint sticks. Alex walked up to her side, her mind reeling. The man she had just spoken to was her great-great-great-great-grandfather. How did Andrew win his approval? Mr. Boudreaux didn't seem to care for him right now. Her heart stopped for just a moment. What if she just ruined any chance for them to be together? She knew she had to be more careful in the future. Anything she said or did could have major repercussions.

A small bell rang when Trey came back into the store rubbing his shoulder.

Alex smiled. Served him right. "Strain yourself?"

"No." He dropped his hand to his side, then gestured for them to go outside. "It is time for lunch."

She nodded her head. After quietly telling Mr. Boudreaux goodbye, she followed Trey and Rose out into the street. Across it, in a well-kept field, Fleurette had set out their lunch.

Trying to maintain an image she knew was false, Alex demurely took Trey's arm and allowed him to escort her and Rose across the street and over to their friends. She lowered herself onto the blanket Fleurette had laid out.

Taking the plate heaped with food from the young woman, she ate her chicken in silence, preoccupied with the events that just took place. She didn't know what to think. Why did she continue to run into her ancestors? It just didn't make sense.

What if she happened to change the future to where she never existed? Or was she back there to make sure that the future she knew would be there, if and when she ever made it back? It was all so confusing. She suddenly realized that someone spoke to her. She looked up into Trey's concerned face. "I'm sorry, what did you say?"

He frowned. "Would you like to go for a walk?"

She nodded. First, she made sure she didn't stand on her skirts before she stood up. Rose had explained earlier that there was a way to arrange her skirts so she wouldn't fall, but she hadn't figured out a graceful way to do that yet. They took a leisurely pace out of the field onto the main road and walked in the direction of the church. Alex remained silent.

"I want to apologize," Trey began.

Alex turned and looked at him. "Why?"

"You're obviously upset with me…"

"No, I'm not. I do understand that males feel a need to dominate each other. I just didn't want to be in the middle of it." She glanced at the general store as they passed it by.

"What did you just say?" he asked.

She studied the dirt road for a moment. Maybe a simpler comment would work. "Boys will be boys."

"We're not boys," he retorted.

"When you behave like you and Andrew did, you are," she said.

"So, you're on a first name basis now?"

Alex stopped walking. "Look. I have only met the man twice in my life. Just because I use his first name doesn't mean I've slept with him."

Trey stared at her. What the devil was she on about now?

"Why is everything I say met with that look?" She stamped her foot. "I'm sorry if I don't know how to talk the way an eighteenth-century Southern woman should! I'd like to see you try to fit into my society."

Before she could whirl away from him, he caught her arm. "What is your society like?"

"Another test?" she asked. "Fine. My world has fast moving horseless carriages, except we call them automobiles. Every house has electricity, you know, Thomas Edison's wonderful device. We have something called a computer that holds all our information. All we have to do is press a few buttons and a wealth of information is at our fingertips. Then there's telephones, thanks to Mr. Bell and his associates, so we can talk to anyone in the world whenever we want. Plus, fax machines that can send copies of printed paper electronically to another location, whether it is two miles down the road or halfway around the world.

"We have air as well as train and ship transportation. I can travel from New Orleans to Boston in three days by car, in hours by plane. There's something called films, and TV. Then there's radio. Films are moving pictures. Something else Thomas Edison developed. From there other people developed TVs, short for television. Moving pictures and sound are broadcast over airwaves, picked up by an antenna and converted into picture and sound again for us to view. Do you want to hear more?" She pulled her arm upward and broke his hold. Angrily, she stomped away, not really knowing where she headed.

He chased after her. "Alexandra. Alexandra, stop." He grabbed her arm again to stop her quickened pace. "You honestly expect me to believe you?"

"Yes, I do. Have I done anything to make you believe that I would lie to you? Do you know anyone who could come up with such a wild story? And as far as Thomas Edison, I believe he's making his inventions right now. You could probably write to him and learn about his work." Alex stepped around him, this time heading back to the picnic.

Their ride back to the plantation was in silence, which Alex didn't mind. In anger, she told him things she shouldn't have, like contacting Thomas Edison. What if… She shook her head. No, she wasn't going to second-guess herself. If she did, she'd end up going crazy.

What she needed to do was find a way home. Since that painting hadn't been done yet she'd have to find another way. A small laugh escaped her lips. Yeah. Right.

"What is so funny?" Trey asked.

Alex turned and looked at his profile. So aristocratic, and very distant. He looked like he didn't want to be sharing the same wagon with her. "Nothing."

The silence that stretched between them became a tangible thing.

She sighed in relief when the plantation loomed into view. At least now she could put some distance between herself and Trey. It might not be a bad idea to think about moving somewhere else until she figured out a way home. Alex glanced at Trey again. Would he stop her from moving now that he was sure she was crazy?

When the wagon pulled in front of the house, Alex jumped off before Trey could even get down. She busied herself with retrieving some items they bought for the kitchen. Everyone followed suit. The wagons were unloaded quickly.

Fleurette and Rose exchanged glances, noting the silent wall that had grown between Trey and Alex.

~

The next morning, after having a cup of coffee to fortify her, Alex stepped out on the front porch and grabbed the broom leaning against the outside wall. Rose sat nearby, enjoying the morning sun.

"Good morning, Alexandra."

"Good morning, Rose." The straw broom scraped against the wooden porch floor. Her brow crinkled as she tried to find a delicate way to broach the subject she wanted to discuss. She stopped and scratched her head. "Um, Rose, is there a women's boarding house?"

"Why?"

"I think it would be a good idea if I move to one." So much for subtlety.

"What has that boy done now?" Rose started to stand up. "I'll straighten this out."

"No. Rose, please. This farce has gone on long enough. It would be smarter for me to move into town."

"I won't have it."

Alex couldn't stop the smile that spread across her lips. "Rose, this is something I have to do."

"Well, I disagree."

Alex rolled her eyes. Leaning on the broom she sighed. "You won't talk me out of this. I've already made up my mind."

Rose's cane banged on the wooden floor. "No! I won't allow you to start the gossip mills again."

"How? Just tell everyone that there is an emergency at home. We know I can't stay with Trey alone, so I'll move into town. Problem solved."

"And when I don't leave?"

"By that point I'll have already rented a room. Wouldn't it make sense for me to stay since it's already paid for?"

"How do you plan on paying for it?"

Alex started to sweep again. "By working."

"Working?" Rose got halfway out of her chair before she realized what she was doing. "Are you mad?"

"No, Rose. I'm sure I can find something to do. How difficult can it be to find a job?"

"Proper ladies don't work!" Rose stared at her aghast.

"Are you saying a teacher isn't a proper lady?" Alex placed one hand on her hip.

She blushed. "Of course not, but Alexandra, you're not a teacher."

"I could be. I have a very strong education. English, math, and science would be easy for me to teach." She shocked herself. Up to this point, she had never even thought about teaching. This might be exactly what she needed. "Is there an opening for a teacher here?"

The deep resonance of a throat clearing made her jump and drop the broom. Although her back was to the front door, she knew who stood there. Without turning around, Alex retrieved the broom. The soft clicking of boots on the hard wood let her know Trey moved toward her.

She tried to ignore him, keeping her eyes on Rose. When she felt him grip her arm, Alex closed her eyes. After taking several calming breaths, she spoke. "Look, I know you don't believe me, and that's fine. As soon as I—"

"Alexandra," he said softly. "Please, come into my office."

She looked up into his face. The compassion she saw there surprised her. She nodded.

Once they entered, she busied herself with her skirts. She learned, after falling several times, to rearrange her skirts so she wouldn't step on them when she started to move. Standing up without tripping herself up was the one she still worked on.

"Alexandra, are you serious about teaching?"

Her head snapped up. "You were eavesdropping?"

"I walked up in time to hear your last comment."

Alex bit her lip. She could be smart and tell him no, she was acting, but lying didn't work for her. "I do have the education."

"Then you can teach the children on the plantation."

"I can?" Not if she moved into town. "Thank you, but I'll have to decline."

"Why?"

"It would be too far to travel."

Trey's eyes narrowed. "If it's too far for you, I'll have the children come to you."

"You'd send them all the way into town?"

"Town? What the devil for?"

Well, now she knew he didn't hear the entire conversation. "I thought you'd be more comfortable if I move into town."

"Me? Oh, I see, this is about that silly business with the time travel."

"It is not silly," she snapped.

"If you really did come from the future, how did you get here? Have the people of your time learned how to travel through time?"

Alex spread her fingers out on the soft silk of her gown. If she hadn't, she would have laughed in his face. Ever since she was a child, she used laughter as an emotional outlet. Her mother was mortified when she laughed at her grandfather's funeral. "No. Time travel is one of the most sought-after theories, but no one has found the answer yet. Too many variables."

"Then tell me about my home, in your time."

"Oh boy. If you think that I've been fabricating this whole thing, you'd better sit down. This will seem like the biggest whopper you've ever heard."

"Whopper?" he asked, as he did as she asked.

"One of Grams's words. It means a fib or a lie." She sat down in the Queen Anne chair in front of his desk. "Okay. In nineteen ninety-seven your plantation is a historical landmark. It is now open to the public on certain days."

"Why would my family allow that?" he demanded.

"I don't know," she replied. So he did believe her, or at least pretended he did. She couldn't tell him the story her grandmother told her. "In my time, owning land is very expensive. It would cost millions in the upkeep of this plantation and the amount of land you have. A lot of families open their homes to help defer taxes or donate their properties to the government. That way it's protected." That answer seemed to satisfy him.

"My grandmother has photos from the late eighteen... I mean this time zone. I saw one of you." She smiled at the memory. He stood very straight, but the twinkle in his eyes let the real man show through. The man who was working his way into her heart, even if he annoyed her. "Grams wanted to come to your plantation to show me a painting. That painting is how I got here. I touched it, and somehow, it teleported me back here."

He rubbed his hand across his chin. "You do come up with the most bizarre stories."

"I knew you wouldn't believe me." She hung her head. Standing back up, she smoothed the front of her gown. "I'll ask Jessie to prepare the buck board."

"I didn't say I don't believe you, but I do need time to think about this."

Alex watched him for a moment.

"Please stay."

Her eyes widened. "Why?"

"Because…because I want you to." Trey rubbed a hand across his face. "And the children here need a proper education."

"All right." She lifted her skirt and glided to the door. "When can I start classes?"

"When would you like?"

"Monday?" That would give her four days to come up with a curriculum.

"Then Monday it is."

Inclining her head, Alex opened the door and exited.

Trey stood and crossed to his window. Was the woman a terrible liar or telling a strange truth? He crossed back to his writing desk, knowing one thing. He couldn't wait for his friend to return from France now. Boudreaux could be there for years. He'd have to write for the answer.

～

A gentle breeze stirred her curtains. After finishing the first set of lesson plans for the students, Alex retired to her room for the night. Her mind knew what she needed to make everything work. She just didn't know if supplies would be that easy to acquire, or if Trey would be willing to pay for them.

She sat on the windowsill and looked up at the stars. Everything was so clear and bright. It would be easy to make star charts, and sketches of the night sky. All she needed was paper and pen. Her journal! Excitement hummed through her veins, she hadn't done this since she was a child.

Grabbing a wrap, her book, a pen, and an inkwell, she snuck down the hall and out into the yard. For a while she just lay on her back and stared up at the stars. The darkened sky looked like someone took diamonds and tossed them across a velvet backdrop. She also had to adjust to a different alignment of the constellations she could see. First, she located the North Star, from there she found the Big Dipper, Venus, and Sirius. A sigh escaped her lips as she picked up the pen and began to sketch. These stars were like family to her. She knew more about them than her own ancestors. The pen she used paused, her mind wandering back to the scene in the mercantile.

Did she really screw up the future? Her future? Or was this the way her ancestors' relationships started. Right now, she could kick herself for not listening closer to her grandmother's tales of her heritage. Perhaps giving fate a little nudge wouldn't hurt.

It was late. She should get back inside before anyone realized she was gone. As she picked up her things, she thought of how she could bring her ancestors together without causing a disaster.

It took three more nights of sketching, giving her an outlet for her frustrations, before she thought of an idea to bring her ancestors together, but first she'd have to talk Trey into it.

The next day, Alex found that she didn't need to do anything. In the middle of the afternoon another invitation arrived. This time it was just for her and Rose to come to the Boudreaux's for afternoon tea.

Trey came up in time to see a mischievous glint in her eyes. "What are you up to now?"

She jumped at his voice, clutching the invitation to her breast. She smiled at him. "Oh, nothing. Your aunt and I have been invited to a tea."

Trey took the invitation she thrust at him. A quick glance told him what she already announced. He looked back up at her. "I take it you'd like to go."

"Well, yes." Her smile widened. "I have been cooped up here for a while, and you did say that I had to play the dutiful fiancée. The tea is on a Saturday afternoon and won't interfere with the children's education."

He looked back down at the invitation, before meeting Alex's eyes again. "I can't see any harm, but you will behave yourself."

Her eyes narrowed. "Oh, I promise. Heaven forbid I forget myself and tell them the truth," she said sarcastically. "Do you think I want to get thrown into an insane asylum?"

He handed back the invitation. "I wouldn't put anything past you, but I'll drive you. And Fleurette can accompany you if you like."

She paused for just a moment. Fleurette would probably enjoy the outing. "All right, I'll ask her."

"Ask?"

"Is there a problem?" Alex knew she said the wrong thing again.

"No." Trey shook his head. "Go and ask her, I'm sure she'll agree."

Her steps weren't as sure as she'd like. Would asking Fleurette to join her instead of telling her show that she didn't fit in this society? If Fleurette hadn't come around the corner at that time, Alex probably would have talked herself out of it. Instead she rushed in. "Um, Miss Rose and I have been invited to a tea in five days, when I told Trey, he recommended that I bring you with me, if you're not too busy. If you are, I understand, I hadn't thought about bringing any kind of companion. But isn't that something ladies do here?"

"Miss Alexandra, hush."

Alex blushed. "I do have a tendency to ramble when I'm nervous."

Fleurette blushed too. "I'm sorry Miss Alexandra, I don't know what came over me. I do know better than to talk to a lady that way."

"Me?" Alex's eyes widened. A giggle bubbled up out of nowhere. "A lady?"

Fleurette nodded.

The giggle turned into laughter. "I can't even walk through a door with a hoop skirt and maintain any kind of dignity."

Fleurette fought the smile that threatened. She remembered Alex fighting with the hoop skirt when she first arrived.

"And my table manners are atrocious."

Fleurette started to laugh. "At first, maybe, Miss Alexandra, but you are a fast learner."

Alex wiped a few stray tears from her eyes. That felt good. "Photographic memory."

"What's that?"

"Have you ever seen a photograph, Fleurette?"

She shook her head no.

"Okay. But you have seen paintings." They hung all over the walls of the house. "My mind is like a canvas. I can look at something for just a second and it is committed to my memory. In my mind I can pull out that image over and over again and examine it."

Fleurette nodded, but Alex knew she didn't quite understand. "Would you like to go with me?"

"Yes. Thank you, Miss Alexandra, I'd like that very much."

*A*lex stood at the front of her newly formed class. There were nine children, in all, ranging from about five to eleven years old.

"Jebidiah, where's your brother?" she asked as she started to hand out the supplies that Trey had bought for her to give her students. Each child received a small chalkboard and a piece of chalk.

"He ain't comin.'"

"Why not?"

Jebidiah shrugged. "He said he too growd up for schoolin.'"

"Not if he talks like that," she murmured, as she walked up to the front again. Alex smiled, as she watched the children pick up each item and examine it thoroughly. "Since today is our first day together. I thought we could get to know each other first. Please stand up."

The younger children were on their feet quicker than the other ones.

She waited patiently until all of them stood. "I'd like each of us to say our names and tell everyone what their favorite thing is. My name is Alexandra and I like watching the stars the best."

One of the younger boys spoke next. "My name's Jebidiah, and I like Miss Fleurette's praline cookies the best."

"Very good, Jebidiah. Is there anything you like to do as well?"

He shook his head no.

The little girl standing next to him tugged on his arm. "What about your drawins?"

"Hush, girl!"

The little girl ducked her head.

Alex spoke quickly to defuse the moment. "It's okay, Jebidiah. Is this your sister?"

"Yea, this here is Delila."

"Hello, Delila. What do you like to do?"

She glanced up at her big brother for a second. "I likes to watch him draw. He makes some pretty pictures."

"Really? I'd like to see some of them." She looked up at Jebidiah. "If that is okay with you."

He frowned but nodded his assent.

Each of the children in turn told everyone who they were and what they liked to do. From this, she learned that two of the boys were sprouting scientists, two of the three girls liked to sew and cook, one boy liked to build things, two others would probably follow in their daddies' footsteps and work the plantation, Jebidiah was an artist, and little Delila was a dreamer. "Well, let's dig right in. First, I want to show you the letters of the alphabet."

Four hours later she sat behind a desk updating her notes on each child, trying to figure out how she could help develop their interests further and make it fun. A soft knock made her look up.

"So how was your first day?" Trey asked as he stepped into the room he had worked hard to convert into a classroom. The chalkboard he had spent three hours hanging displayed the alphabet.

A soft inner light started to glow in Alex's eyes when he asked that question.

"It was wonderful! Thank you so much for giving me this chance, Trey."

The smile she gave him was infectious. He couldn't help but smile back.

She gathered her papers and slipped from behind her desk. "Nine showed up today. I have hoped for more, but it is a good start. They aren't sure about learning their letters though. Jebidiah couldn't understand what is so important about learning how to write."

"He's a bright boy. I'm sure you'll be able to convince him soon enough." Trey offered her his arm.

"I'm sure I will." She linked her arm with his. "Did you know he draws? His sister let it slip."

"Yea." Trey drew her out of the room and out into the bright sunlight. "His papa thinks it's a waste of time."

"Oh dear. I was hoping to get him interested with our classes by using some of the great works of art. Leonardo Da Vinci was a great scholar as well as an artist. If his father doesn't want me to encourage him, I'll have to find another way."

"Why don't you let me talk to his papa about it. He felt the same way about this school idea too, but I was able to talk him into letting his two youngest to come."

"You would do that for me?"

Trey looked down into her hopeful face. "Yes."

"Why?"

"Because…" *Because I'm falling in love with you*, he thought. Trey glanced away from Alexandra. He wouldn't dare reveal that to her yet. "Because I know you really want to help these children, and I believe they need the education. Our world is starting to change before our eyes. They'll need all the help they can get."

"Spoken like a true visionary." She tugged on his arm to get him to stop walking. "Thank you." Alex stood up on her tippy-toes, leaned on his arm, and planted a feather-like kiss on his cheek.

CHAPTER 10

The door opened for Rose on the third knock. Fleurette followed Rose and Alex into the Boudreaux home. Introductions were given, while Fleurette took Alex's gloves and parasol. A rustle of crinoline made Fleurette look up at the young woman who walked into the room.

Alex's head snapped up when she heard Fleurette's gasp. Poised in front of her was Elizabeth Boudreaux, young, beautiful, and except for hair and eye color, Alex's twin.

Alex stared at her great-great-great-grandmother. Chocolate-brown eyes stared back at her.

The only photo her grandmother had of Elizabeth Boudreaux looked nothing like the vibrant young woman in front of her. They shared the same chin and aristocratic nose. Elizabeth's chestnut-brown hair shone with auburn highlights. Now Alex knew where her red highlights came from. Alex never considered herself beautiful, but this woman, who looked like her twin, was stunning. She could only say the one thought that came to mind. "Oh my."

Elizabeth suddenly found her voice too. "I'm sorry, I didn't mean to stare, but you look, well, I feel like I'm staring in a mirror."

"Me too." Alex smiled. "They say that everyone has a twin in the world. You must be mine."

"They do?" murmured Elizabeth. "How wonderful." She shook her head, sending ringlets of hair bouncing around her face.

Alex watched Elizabeth as she walked around the room. Her great-great-great-grandmother couldn't be more than sixteen years old, still more of a girl than a woman.

"I've heard you met Mr. Dalton in Paris. It must be so romantic to travel like that," said Elizabeth.

Alex looked over at Rose. How could she answer this one when she didn't know?

Rose snapped open her fan. That fan started to flutter vigorously.

"Yes, it was." Alex arched a brow. Slowly, she spread out her own fan. She brought it up to her face as she started to fan herself, blocking her smile at Rose's blatant lie.

Elizabeth continued to chatter away. "You must tell me about what Paris is like. I've never been there."

Alex leaned toward Rose. "What do I say now?" she whispered from behind her fan.

"Elizabeth, please," said her mother. Her tone indicated that she wanted her daughter quiet. "Perhaps everyone would like to retire to the veranda for tea."

Alex followed Rose through the parlor to the back porch of the Boudreaux home. Intricately placed flowers and plants among saplings took her breath away. The scent of pine and magnolias filled the air. Strategically placed trees tickled her memory. She rubbed her forehead.

This was her grandmother's backyard. She tried to keep her face passive as she looked around. The new saplings that the Boudreaux's just planted were soaring trees in her grandmother's yard.

Rose's cane connected with her calf as the tea tray stopped in front of her. She jerked her attention back to her hostess. "Thank you," she mumbled to the young maid as she grabbed a cup.

Silence. Alex could almost hear every head turn toward her. A young black woman stared at her with wide eyes. Alex sighed inwardly. She did it again. "Thank you, Mrs. Boudreaux, for your wonderful hospitality," she continued. "You have a beautiful home."

Too bad it would burn to the ground in the next few years and her grandma's house would be built in its place.

She took a sip. The hot tea had cooled. What she would love would be a few ice cubes but wouldn't dare ask for them. When was iced tea created anyway?

"Would you like to see Mama's prize roses?" asked Elizabeth.

The voice broke through her thoughts. Alex nodded as she stood up. She looked over at Rose.

"No dear, you go ahead. These old bones need a rest."

She gave Rose a knowing smile, wondering what Rose wanted to talk to Mrs. Boudreaux about. Following Elizabeth wasn't easy in yards of material. No wonder women didn't run away from their husbands too much during this time. The skirts wouldn't let them.

The fragrant aroma of roses enveloped her as they drew closer. Perfect deep red blooms exploded all over the bushes they approached.

Elizabeth looked up at the canopy above them. Sunlight filtered through, casting golden red highlights in her brown hair. "Do you think we really look that much alike?"

"There is a strong resemblance," Alex said, strolling along the path touching a velvet petal here and there. "Your father didn't mention I met him on Sunday?"

"You were at the store? Papa never said a word." Elizabeth scuffed her foot. "But that's Papa's way."

"Ah." Alex bent to smell a rose.

"You have one of those too?" Elizabeth picked up a pair of shears lying nearby to cut the rose for Alex.

"I did," Alex said, taking the rose from Elizabeth. She proceeded to break the larger thorns off the stem. "But passed away a few years ago."

"Then you are very lucky to have Mr. Dalton in your life."

Alex started to move along the path in the garden again. Elizabeth sure did change the subject fast.

"Yes."

"Does he make your heart flutter?"

"His kisses do," Alex murmured. Since she really didn't want to think about what Trey Dalton's kisses did to her, why did she say that?

"What is it like?"

Alex pushed a stray hair out of her face. "What?"

"Kissing. Mary Margaret says it's divine," said Elizabeth.

She smiled as she looked at Elizabeth. "Haven't you ever been kissed?"

"Oh no." A blush bloomed on Elizabeth's face. "Papa wouldn't approve."

More like Elizabeth's papa wouldn't let her out of his sight long enough, Alex thought. "And you do everything your papa tells you to."

"Of course." Big brown eyes looked at Alex.

"Is there anyone you want in particular?" A devilish twinkle entered Alex's eyes.

The girl's brow creased.

"Want?"

Alex racked her brain for the right word. "Shine? Is there a gentleman you have taken a shine to?"

"Oh. Well, yes." Her eyes cut to the porch where her mother and Miss Rose sat. Elizabeth's voice lowered as she answered, "Mr. Dalton's friend, Mr. Manning, is very handsome. So is Mr. Leroux." A sigh escaped her lips. "But Papa refuses to have me introduced to them."

"Why?"

"Elizabeth? You and Miss Alexandra should come back up on the porch. Roberta is ready to serve our guests her famous beignets," said Mrs. Boudreaux.

A sigh of resignation escaped Alex as they made their way back to the two older women. She'd never get the answer to her question now.

As she sat down, she heard Mrs. Boudreaux say, "I don't think I've heard the wedding date yet."

"That's because we haven't set it yet," Alex said. When she realized how that must have sounded she continued. "I mean the actual date, but it will be two weeks after harvest."

Rose's smile made Alex give her a scathing glare. Somehow Rose manipulated Mrs. Boudreaux to ask that question to force her to answer it. Trey was going to kill her.

~

*A*lex nervously pulled on the ribbons on her bonnet on their carriage ride home. She tried to come up with a safe way to tell Trey that she inadvertently set the date. Rose staring at her the entire way home didn't help.

"Is there something wrong?" Alex finally asked.

"No." Rose leaned back against the cushions. "Should there be?"

"No." Alex ran the end of the satin ribbons through her fingers.

As they neared the house, Alex leaned forward to look out the window. Trey's silhouette could be seen. She slumped back in the carriage wishing he were still in the fields. Even time was against her. After alighting from the coach, Alex lingered on the porch.

"Is there something wrong?" Trey asked.

"Could be," Alex replied. "I inadvertently said something I shouldn't have." She didn't like the feral smile that spread across his face. "Mrs. Boudreaux forced me into revealing a wedding date."

Color drained out of his face. "I thought we discussed this."

"We did. But I was pushed into a corner."

Trey blinked. "Mrs. Boudreaux would never do that."

"It's a figure of speech." Alex rolled her eyes. "She manipulated me into revealing a date."

"What did you tell her?"

"Two weeks after harvest."

"Which harvest?" he asked.

"There's more than one?"

Trey smiled as he escorted her into the house. "There is now."

~

*A*lex sauntered into Trey's office, determined to get her way. "Trey, as an engaged couple aren't we supposed to entertain?"

"Yes. Why?" Trey asked, not looking up from the ledgers he worked on.

"I think we should have a dinner party."

"That's fine."

"Oh good." She wandered about the room as she talked out loud to herself. "Let's see, I know I want to invite Elizabeth Boudreaux, but if we invite your friend Beau and Andrew Leroux, I'll need another female."

"No."

"What?" she asked absently.

"Not Andrew."

Alex stopped dead in her tracks. The main reason for this party was to introduce her ancestors to each other. "But, Trey, I..."

"I said no!"

Alex crossed her arms in front of her. "Why not?"

Trey rested his face in his hands for a moment. Arguing with her gave him headaches. "Because I said so."

Alex leaned her hands against the large oak desk he sat behind. "Don't you pull that macho crap with me. I deserve a straight answer."

"You?" Trey braced his hands on the desk as he rose. "What right do you have to make demands on me, woman?"

"I will be your future wife."

"Only because of my meddling aunt."

"Oh right, I forgot. I'm just some trollop who performs on the stage. And you are the most pigheaded, egotistical maniac I have ever had the misfortune to meet." Five angry steps had her at the door. She turned and glared at him. Too exasperated to speak she grabbed the door and slammed it behind her.

The sound reverberated through the house.

Rose and Fleurette came out into the hall at the sound of the door. They watched as Alex climbed the stairs.

"I wonder what that was all about?" questioned Rose.

Fleurette looked around before shrugging as she picked up the empty tray in front of her. "But it's sure been lively around here since Miss Alexandra showed up," she said as she headed toward the kitchen with Trey's leftover snack.

Trey came out of his office a few seconds later. "Where did she go?"

Rose pointed up the stairs with her cane. A smile spread slowly across her lips as Trey went up after Alex.

Trey rounded the corner, listening for some sound to tell him Alexandra's location. A loud crash nearby told him she was in her room.

"Alexandra," he said from the doorway.

"Oh no you don't. You're being a jerk and I don't want to talk to you."

Expecting to feel the weight of his aunt's cane on his back at any moment, Trey took a chance and stepped into Alexandra's room. "Why does this upset you so much?"

She looked at him with those large blue eyes glistening from unshed tears.

"I will not allow Andrew Leroux to step into this house." He ducked as her hairbrush sailed by, barely missing his head. The woman had good aim. She also caught him off guard. Alex had almost swept past him before he realized it. Instinct made him grab her arm.

"Will you please move?" She struggled against him. "I have work to do."

"Work be damned! What does Andrew mean to you?"

Her body tensed. Bright angry eyes glared at him. "You don't want to talk about it."

He stepped toward her. "I do. I will not be cuckold…"

The pain that exploded on the right side of his face told him she also packed a wallop. He let go to shield his face from another blow.

She took this chance to scoot past him.

Trey turned to watch her retreating back. "Damn, woman."

Descending the stairs two at a time, he chased her toward the back of the house. He didn't want to think about the odd knot in his stomach. There was no reason for him to be jealous.

He found her on her knees, pounding at the dirt around some flowers in the garden. The poor flowers didn't stand a chance.

Alex's head snapped up when she felt the vibration from his step as he drew closer. Without saying a word, she got up off her knees and walked toward the clothesline at the other end of the garden. She jumped when she heard his voice close to her ear.

"Running away from me isn't going to keep me from getting answers. What is he to you?" Angry blue eyes looked up into his. Somehow, he hurt her, and it tore at his heart.

"You won't believe me," she said.

He looked startled, and it gave her the chance to get away from him again. In three long strides he walked beside her. "Why won't I believe you?"

"Because the truth is too fantastic for you." Alex stopped walking and watched him continue on.

Once Trey realized this, he backtracked to stand in front of her. "Are you going to start talking about this time-travel nonsense again?"

"No." She rubbed her hands against the soft linen of her skirt.

"Then tell me."

"No."

His brow furrowed. "Why?"

"Because you won't believe me." She started walking again, this time, toward the barn.

"And if I said I did believe you?" He called to her.

She stopped and turned to face him. "You'd be lying." Then she headed into the barn before he could say anything more.

~

*A*lex punched her pillows for the tenth time, trying to relax enough to fall asleep. A cricket chirped. She rolled over. After midnight, she gave up and looked out the window. There were a few clouds out, but it wouldn't stop her from stargazing. Maybe it would relax her enough to sleep.

Her stomach rumbled, reminding her that she didn't have any supper. The last time she ate was at the Boudreaux's home earlier that day, before she tried to convince Trey to have the dinner party.

What a fiasco that turned out to be.

She tiptoed past Trey's office. A light came from under the door and she didn't want to face him at this point. Heaven forbid he caught her running around in just her shift, but it was too hot to wear anything else.

She entered the darkened kitchen; her only light came from the quarter moon that peeked out from behind the clouds from time to time. At one such instant, she spied several pieces of bread, cheese, and an apple. A relieved smile eased itself across her face. "Thank you, Fleurette."

Biting into the apple, she held it in her teeth as she eased out the back door with the rest of her food.

Every sound she made frightened her. She felt sure she'd wake the whole house. Finally, after she reached the copse of tress closest to the back of the house, she slid down to the grass to stare up at the stars.

Inside, Trey cursed at himself. Someone wanted his crop to fail this year, but he didn't know why. There had been another attempt. This time they blocked up his irrigation system. If his foreman hadn't caught it he would have lost everything. He crossed to the window, hoping to catch a small breeze. Instead, he caught Alex running through the yard. What the devil was she doing? Then it dawned on him.

She's probably going to meet whoever hired her, and he planned on following her. His heart constricted at the thought. She wore next to nothing, so it was obvious what she planned to do.

When he made it to the lawn he didn't see her, so had no clue which direction she went in. He guessed, going around back near the garden she cared for so diligently. A flash of white made him jump behind a tree. One brow furrowed. Alex lay on the grass, staring up at the stars while eating the last remains of an apple. As he watched, she started working on the bread and cheese she brought with her too.

His back slid down the trunk of the tree. If she had to wait, so would he. An hour later, he still waited. He stretched, and then slowly, he stood up. No reaction from Alex eased the tension he felt in his body. Inching closer for a better look, he heard a branch break under his foot. Now she'd know she'd been followed. Still no movement. Softly, he called her name. No answer. He came closer.

A soft snore drifted to his ears.

She was asleep. Of all the daft things. He knelt beside her and gently scooped her up. There were a few moments of fear that she'd wake up, but she settled into his arms without opening an eye.

Once back in the house, he carried her up the stairs to her room, eased the door open with his boot, and carried her in.

Her bed was a wreck. Covers strewn all over the floor. The sheets lay half off the bed. He shook his head. This wouldn't do. Never setting her down, he turned around and headed down the hall to his room.

At least she'd be comfortable, and he wouldn't have to wake Fleurette to make the bed.

He lowered his burden to the crisp linen sheets. After tucking her feet in, he pulled the covers up to her bosom. He stared at her for a long time. She had him so confused. Part of him couldn't believe her story, but part of him did.

There were things she did he couldn't explain, like reaching for something on the wall in the evenings when she walked into darkened rooms. It was a natural habit for her. She'd always mumble to herself about forgetting her lamp. She'd look for things or use words that no one understood. When she realized what she had done, she'd act embarrassed. She tried so hard to fit in. If she was an actress she was the best.

He leaned down to blow out the candle on the nightstand beside the bed. His bed would be down the hall tonight. Why he didn't put her there instead of his room he couldn't fathom. The thought did cross his mind to join her, but he wouldn't dare. No matter what Alexandra claimed to be he knew one thing for sure. She was a lady. Anyone could tell just by the way she carried herself.

Before he had a chance to straighten up he found himself grabbed roughly around the neck. He felt his body become airborne as he flipped over onto his back and landed with a thud on the hard wood floor.

CHAPTER 11

A loud groan escaped his lips when his head banged against the wooden floor. He tried to sit up but found himself pinned down. Someone's knee pressed into his throat, cutting off any air to his windpipes. Wedging his hand under the knee, he pushed. For his effort, he got a harsh blow to the neck. The knee, only inches from his face wouldn't move. The longer he stared at the offending appendage, the more he realized that the knee looked awfully delicate to be putting so much pressure on him. How had she accomplished it?

"Alex," he croaked. Some of the pressure eased, allowing him to get air.

"Trey?" She leaned down to get a better look at his face. A blush bloomed on her cheeks, as she quickly released him. She clambered to her feet. "Oh God, I'm sorry." She glanced around. "What are you doing in my room?"

Sitting up a little, he rubbed his throat, eyeing her. "It's not."

One delicate brow arched. "What's not?"

"Your room." He gestured at the furniture.

A quick glance at her surroundings had her blushing deeper. "How did I get here?"

Trey saw a wary look enter her eyes. "Before you judge too quickly, I found you outside, sound asleep. When I brought you back to your room, your bed wasn't fit to sleep in, so I brought you here."

Her arms crossed over her chest.

"Oh, now you don't believe me? I'm sorry, my sweet Alexandra, but you were asleep. Until I blew out the candle." He rubbed his neck again. "What was that?"

"A defensive move." His confused look made her sigh. Everything that was second nature to her was questioned here. Turning her back to him, she looked out the bay window that dominated his room. She would never fit in here. Too many things she took for granted would constantly show how different she was.

The moon chose that moment to come from behind another cloud. Its gentle beam enveloped Alexandra, outlining her body through the linen gown she wore. Trey didn't want to stare but couldn't help himself. She was beautiful. His body reacted instinctively to her curves.

"Um…" He forced himself to his feet. Hoping a different angle would help his libido. It didn't. The moonlight revealed the curve of her hips.

As if she instinctively knew where his mind wandered, Alex placed her hand on that hip as she turned toward him.

He forced his eyes up to her face. "Why were you out there?"

She shrugged. "I like to star gaze. It helps me relax." Alex turned to look out the window again, giving him a view of her beautifully sculpted throat.

Trey stared at her silhouette. "Then you know a little about the night sky?"

She smiled as she glanced back at him. "A little."

"Which one do you recognize?" As she started to rattle off about a half a dozen stars his jaw dropped. This woman knew more about the heavens than any man yet couldn't ride a horse. One thought leaped to the foreground. Could her story be true? He shook his head. It wasn't something he was ready to accept, yet. "In nineteen ninety-three…"

"Ninety-seven," she corrected him.

"Yes." He couldn't catch her on that. "What did you do? Were you married? Have a family?"

"No. I'm not married." She gave him a wry smile. "Marriage is not the most important thing to a lot of women where I come from. Women are allowed to have careers."

"And you had a career?" He didn't believe her for a minute. No man would force his wife or daughter to work unless they were very poor. Besides, she had hands of a pampered woman, all soft and delicate. "What was it?"

"I'm an astrophysicist." Her smile widened as she watched his face.

He locked eyes with her. Trey wouldn't even try to pronounce it. "And what is that?"

"A fancy name for an astronomer." She didn't know how to explain what she really did.

"You study the stars for a living?"

"Yes. I have several degrees to prove it." She could tell by the tone of his voice that he didn't believe one word. "Of course, they're more than a hundred years in the future, but that is life in the big city."

"Life in the big city?" he mimicked.

Why did she keep throwing these idioms at him? Her frustration welled up. "You think I'm crazy, don't you? I could smack you upside your head with my PhD and you still wouldn't believe me. If only I had been a historian! If only I could tell you something that would prove to you I was from the future."

"You're not crazy, but maybe I am." He rested his hands on her shoulder. "As strange as your tale is, I'm starting to believe you."

"Really?" Large blue eyes looked up at him with hope.

"Yes." He traced the outline of her cheek. His gaze slid from her eyes to her rosy lips, full, sensuous ones that begged for his kiss. When his gaze finally returned to her eyes once more, they had darkened.

His hands slid from her shoulders to her waist, rapping around her and pulling her close. He lowered his head, brushing his lips against hers. Their tantalizing softness made him want more. He gently nipped and tugged at her bottom lip as he deepened the kiss.

When his lips touched Alex's, she felt a bolt of desire crash into her. Their drugging warmth relaxed her. Her body molded itself against his. She couldn't think beyond this moment. His tongue raked against her teeth, demanding entrance. With a sigh she yielded.

His grip tightened as she opened her mouth to him, allowing him to explore the warm recesses of her mouth. The feel of her body pressed against his was heaven. A soft groan escaped him when she started to return the kiss with the same amount of passion.

A loud banging penetrated Alex's ears, causing her to stiffen in his arms.

Trey tore his lips from hers. The banging persisted as he stared at her for a long moment. He didn't want to stop, and by the look in her eyes, she didn't either. Crossing to the offending portal he flung the door open.

Shielding Alex from his foreman, who stood on the other side, he demanded, "What?"

"I'm sorry, sir, but fire. One of the barns is on fire."

Without a backward glance Trey followed the man down the hall.

Alex stood there in a daze for a few seconds before racing to her room. Digging through the drawers, she found her jeans and shirt. The nightgown was already halfway off as she threw her clothes on the bed.

Her jeans didn't want to zipper properly, but with a few colored words she had them on, along with her blouse, and boots. She ran into Trey's room for a moment. His shirts might be huge on her, but they would protect her much better than her thin poet's blouse.

Flames climbed high, lighting the night sky. Trey could feel the heat from it as the flames consumed something he built with his own hands. The pounding of shoes on the ground caught his attention. He turned around to see Alexandra running up to him. His brow arched at the sight of her in pants, and one of his shirts. "What are you doing here?"

"You're going to need all the help you can get, right?" The hot flames illuminated one side of her face.

He curtly nodded.

"What do you want me to do?" A spark landed near her.

"Stay out of the way."

Hands on hips, she faced him. "No. I can help."

"I don't want to be worried about you while we are trying to put out the flames." Sweat trickled down his face from the heat of the flames.

Frustration welled up in Trey. He was going to lose this barn. How much more would he lose before he caught the saboteur?

Alex watched as the men lined up between the barn and the well, trying to douse the walls with water, while the wives and daughters of Trey's men worked on the flames with blankets.

The flames were consuming the building quickly. Too quickly to be natural. Alex walked to the back of the barn. The doors stood wide open, revealing Jessie struggling to release animals tied to their stalls.

Covering her face with a sleeve from Trey's shirt, Alex dodged in and grabbed the ropes from Jessie.

Three properly angled tugs had the ropes loose. Alex led the animals out while Jessie went to retrieve the last two animals.

Once the animals were secured in a coral nearby, Alex touched Jessie's arm. "What else?"

Jessie just stared at her. Thick black smoke coiled around them.

"What else is in the barn? We can still save a few more things," she said.

"The tack is still in there."

Alex ran back to the barn. Smoke snaked up her nostrils, sending her into a coughing fit. Heat from the flames made her very cautious. They probably could only go in one, maybe two more times before it would be too dangerous.

Jessie signaled, pointing out a saddle to her left. He went to the right.

As she picked up a small saddle, Alex noticed a much larger one across one of the gates. Shouldering the smaller one, and thanking her parents for broad shoulders, Alex lifted the second saddle, only to have it land at her feet with a thud.

A giggle escaped her lips when she heard it. The thud sounded like the noise Trey's body made when it landed after she knocked him down. She chastised herself. Now was not the time for this. A load crack and falling ambers got her moving again. Just as she sat the two saddles down on the grass near the barn, the roof caved in.

Alex examined the leather of the finely tooled saddle and found no damage. Strong arms wrapped around her before lifting her up. "Trey?"

"Thank God!" He hugged her then gave her a resounding kiss.

She blushed. Trey released her enough to allow her to slide down until her feet touch the ground.

"When you disappeared..." He hugged her to him again. "Don't do that again."

Fleurette and Jesse led the band of people who had helped back to the plantation house. After their hard work, they all deserved a hearty meal. It didn't take long before Trey and Alex were alone near the remains of the barn.

He ran his hands up her back, pausing about midway. "What do you have on under this?"

Uh-oh, in her haste earlier she didn't want to fight with a corset, besides it wouldn't have worked well with the jeans. She also didn't want to fight with her bra, so she went without either. Alex knew he'd be angry. She remembered the last time, but she wouldn't lie to him. "Um, nothing."

"Nothing! Are you crazy?"

"No," she snapped, pulling out of his arms. "There wasn't a lot of time. I wasn't thinking about modesty here, only your barn. No one knew, the shirt was too big, and I made sure it was fastened tight. You didn't notice it until now. No one else did either."

"I will not have people talk about you like you're some sort of harlot." His anger flashed in his eyes.

Her heart fluttered at his words. He was worried about what people thought about her, even though he had accused her of the same thing.

"But I must admit that the thought of what you don't have on underneath is quite thought provoking." His slid his arm around her waist and pulled her close. "Now I know why you felt so good earlier when I picked you up. It was all that softness."

This time she blushed deeply. Pretending to fan herself, she said in her best Southern drawl, "Why, sir, I think you flatter me."

He laughed. There was a lot more he'd like to do to her, but knew he had to take his time.

~

*T*he next morning Fleurette threw open the curtains on Alex again. Fleurette clutched her throat when she saw the shape of the bed.

"I know, I'm sorry." Alex gave her an apologetic smile. "I tossed and turned last night. I thought I'd take care of it before you came in, but I guess I overslept."

Fleurette laughed. "You always oversleep, Miss Alexandra. Mr. Trey asked me to make sure you woke up early today."

"He did?" Alex stifled a yawn. "Why?"

"Now, I don' go asking Mr. Trey questions like that." Fleurette clucked her tongue. "If'n you want to know you'll have to get up and find out for yourself. He did ask me to make sure you wore one particular outfit though."

Alex stepped behind the screen to put on what she had deemed her torture device. She presented her back to Fleurette, so she could lace up the corset. Several strong tugs, and a yelp from Alexandra let Fleurette know it was tight enough.

Fleurette presented her with a short blouse, followed by a long riding skirt, a short bolero jacket, and a jaunty little riding hat.

When Alex saw herself in the mirror she didn't know whether to laugh or cry. The outfit was beautiful, a deep blue velvet that accented her coloring. But in ninety-degree weather? Trey must plan on putting her on a horse, and probably on a sidesaddle since she wore a dress. She closed her eyes, thinking that if this really were a dream, then now would be a good time to wake up. She really didn't want to prove she'd never been on a horse. It would be too embarrassing.

Just as she tried to come up with some excuse to get out of her lesson, Trey knocked on her door.

Fleurette opened it, and the excuse died on her lips. His face glowed with excitement. It melted her heart a little more.

Trey waited impatiently as she ate a light breakfast. She tried to gulp everything down. Knowing that if she took too long he probably would do like he did the last time he was in a hurry when he threw her precious cup of coffee away.

He snatched up a basket Fleurette had prepared for them, grabbed her hand, and half dragged Alex out the door.

The remnants of the barn loomed ominously in front of her. The scent of burnt wood still filled the air. She skidded to a halt at the sight of the two horses in the coral near the barn's remains. The first horse she saw was a huge black stallion. She prayed that wouldn't be her horse. The next horse slowed her heartbeat a little. It was a little dapple-gray mare, already saddled. That she could handle, she hoped.

Trey led her to the second animal. Placing his hands around her waist, he lifted her up into the sidesaddle.

"Place your feet here and here," he instructed her quietly. "Hold onto the pummel. I'll lead your horse out."

Alex released a sigh of relief as she did what he told her. She watched with pride as Trey vaulted into his saddle and started them out on a sedate pace.

"Are we going too fast?" Trey called back as they cleared the plantation and headed into a small copse of trees where he liked to ride.

Sunlight flickered down on her through the leaves. "No," she said. "And thank you."

"Are you ready to try to do this on your own?"

"No," she answered quickly. She didn't like the gleam that entered his eyes. What was he up to?

They rode on like this for almost an hour before Trey stopped the horses. He placed his hands on both sides of the saddle. "Now, I brought you out here to learn to ride. Since you don't want to learn on your own, I guess I'll just have to give you a little help." With that he released the lead he had on the mare, slapped it on the rear, and sent it galloping off, with Alex screaming at the top of her lungs.

CHAPTER 12

"Trey Dalton, I'm going to kill you," Alex screamed at the top of her lungs as she flew down the wide path. "How do I stop this thing?"

"Try using the reins," he shouted back.

She stared down at the pieces of leather in her hand. Gripping the flimsy straps, she pulled, hard. The poor mare skidded to a halt so fast she found herself face down on the dirt road. She came up sputtering.

As she dusted herself off, she heard the pounding of Trey's boots coming toward her. Just before he touched her, she spoke. "Don't you dare lay a hand on me."

Although she didn't look at him, she held herself stiffly, pulling away whenever he tried to move closer. Her anger was so strong it acted like a shield around her.

"Alexandra," he said.

"Don't you Alexandra me," she snapped as she pulled off her gloves. "You knew I didn't know how to ride a horse."

This was one time when she wished she didn't have good peripheral vision. When she saw him look away, she knew he felt guilty. It fired her anger more. "So! You thought to trick me by putting me on a horse! You didn't believe me when I told you I couldn't ride? Of all the insufferable..." She proceeded to beat him with her fists.

"Stop," he commanded, as he tried to keep her hands from striking him. She did get a couple of good blows in before he wrestled her to the ground and sat on her to stop her.

Alex gave him a hateful glare. She didn't care how handsome he looked with the sunlight flickering through the canopy, illuminating his black hair with blue highlights.

He grinned at her.

"So this is how you control women?" she snapped. "By sitting on them?" Her legs came up behind him, wrapped themselves around his throat, and pulled him backward.

Trey landed with a thud.

Alex crab-walked backward enough to be able to regain her feet. "This woman won't be controlled."

Trey looked up at her. "How did you do that?"

"My legs," she said. Turning her back to him, she started to walk back toward the house.

The slight vibration coursing through the ground told her he ran to catch up. When she was sure he stood at just the right distance, her left foot shot out, hitting him directly in the chest, knocking him to the ground again.

"That is for being a jerk."

Sitting up, he rubbed his chest. Amazement lit his face. How did she do that? "And the other?"

"For not believing me." She stood over him. "Now you have a choice. Believe me, and I'll stay. Don't, and I'll leave."

"Where would you go?" he asked.

Her shoulders drooped. So he didn't believe her. "I don't know. Perhaps I'll join the circus. Become a gypsy and tell fortunes. Or become a teacher." The children she worked with the last two weeks brought a glow to her face. "I'm sure I'd qualify for that. It's the diploma I'd be without. If only I hadn't touched that stupid painting."

"You mentioned a painting before. Why?"

Alex sank to the ground near him. "There was a painting hanging in your home in my time. The portrait was of me. Grams dared me to touch it. Somehow, she knew what would happen. When I did, I ended up here."

Tears welled up in her eyes as she looked at him. "This is no place for a twentieth-century woman. I have no rights. Nor can I live on my own. Too many people would talk. There's no family to turn to. I don't exist to them. But I'm stuck with no way home."

"Alexandra, don't cry." Trey watched as tears slipped from her eyes. His heart lurched in his chest. He tried to move closer to her.

"Don't." She stood up.

As she moved away from him, he frowned. "Where are you going?"

"To get my clothes. Once I change, I'll head west." She took a few steps before stopping. She kept her back to him as she said, "If it's okay with you, I'd like to take two dresses with me. I'll send you money for them as soon as I find a job."

He stood up. "You're not leaving."

"I am not wanted here," she said quietly.

He stepped up to her. Taking her arm, he swung her around. "Yes, you are."

Tears threatened to fall again. "You don't believe me."

The hurt he saw in her eyes sliced right through him. "It's hard for me to believe your wild tale."

She pulled her arm free. Turning, she continued to head toward the house.

"Alexandra, give me time."

She turned at his words. "You've had plenty of time. What are you waiting for? Me to sprout three heads? You and Rose have already said I talk differently, several of your friends have noticed it. So have your workers. I came here with just my driver's license, a couple of bills, and the clothes on my back. If I was an actress wouldn't I have had a lot more props?"

She stomped a few more feet, then turned around again. "And just how many Thibodauxs are there in the world?"

Trey shook his head. One thing was for sure, Alex was full of fire. He pulled himself into the saddle, and if he wanted to keep her around, he'd have to do something drastic.

Alex felt the pounding of hooves. She cursed her luck in having to wear long shirts that hampered her movements. "Oh, the hell with it." She grabbed the back hem of her dress, along with the front, and pulled it forward, then up. Then she ran as fast as she could in a corset. A grin split her face when she realized that she outmaneuvered Trey. Just as the house loomed in the distance she knew she couldn't go any farther. Her lungs burned, her knees shook, and her feet hurt.

Placing her hands on her knees, she gasped for air. "And ... to believe ... that I ... exercised. Next ... time I'll ... do it with ... twenty pounds of ... clothing on."

The sound of thunder penetrated past her ragged breathing. She looked up too late. The rider and horse that charged at breakneck speed was headed straight for her.

"Oh Lord." She spun on her feet, took two steps, and then noticed that her feet no longer touched the ground. A vice-like grip circled her waist.

Trey knew the moment Alex realized he held her. She started to fight like a hellion. He concentrated so hard on maintaining a grip on her that he lost his seat. Both fell to the ground in a heap.

"Damn it, Alexandra," Trey yelled when she struck him across the face. He grabbed her hands, pinning them behind her. "Calm down."

Wild blue eyes looked up at him. "Calm? I am calm!"

"If you don't behave yourself, I will tie you up." Warily, he released her.

She stood up and dusted herself off. "I'd like to see you try."

"Is that a challenge?" A cold glint entered his eyes.

Alex became wary. She didn't like the look he gave her. Her eyes narrowed. "Why?"

Standing, he whistled for his horse. As it cantered up, he responded, "I never back away from a challenge." From his saddle, he uncoiled a rope that hung from the pummel. Snaking it out, he proceeded to wrap it around his hand and elbow. After tying a secure knot, he started to swing it overhead.

"Did I ever tell you that I learned how to rope steers and cattle?" The rope continued to loop over his head.

She slowly started to back away. "Don't you dare!" Unfortunately, she knew he would. How did this happen? How did she lose the upper hand with such a bizarre twist? Alex knew she shouldn't run. Logic dictated that if she stayed put and faced him, he'd have to back down, but logic didn't win. The rope snagged her before she got one hundred feet.

Trey grinned as he slowly pulled Alex back toward him. Now that he had her captive what was he going to do with her? His eyes darkened at the thought of what he would like to do with her, and to her.

But not now. First, she needed to be taught a lesson.

"I could tie you to that tree," he said as he pulled her in closer. "And send someone out to get you."

Alex spied the tree, a grand old oak. It wasn't one she could escape from. "And how would you explain that to your aunt?"

Totally ignoring her, he continued. "Or I could tie you to my horse, and make you walk back to the house." Then a wicked gleam entered his eyes. "Or I could tie you to me."

She started at his last statement. "To you?" she sputtered.

"Yes." He pulled Alex up against his body. He tilted his head down toward hers. "Of course, it would cause quite a scandal," he said, using his free hand to trace her jaw.

She swallowed hard. The heat of his fingers on her jaw and throat sent flickers of desire through her. She couldn't stop the shiver that racked her body when he bent his head closer to hers. She could feel his breath on her neck.

"If anyone saw us, we'd have to marry immediately," he softly said in her ear. "I wonder where Aunt Rose is."

"Marry?" She pulled back. "Wait a minute…" A rock tripped her up as she tried to back away from him. Instead of putting distance between them, she pulled him down on top of her. His weight knocked the air out of her.

Trey stared into her eyes. The rest of the world disappeared for the moments they stared at each other. His fingers rested against her throat, feeling the erratic tempo beating there. "But," he murmured. "I'll let you off with a kiss."

"A kiss?" she whispered. Her heart beat faster. "Okay." She quickly pressed her lips to his. "There."

"No, no. A real kiss." He brushed his fingers against her lips. "One with meaning."

"Meaning," she mimicked as she licked her lips.

"Yes, chère, meaning." He dipped his head toward hers.

Alex gasped as she felt his tongue trace an erotic line against her lips. His tongue surged into her mouth, licking and probing her recesses. White heat filled her veins. His lips slanted across hers, becoming more demanding. He coaxed her tongue to join with his. A soft groan escaped her lips as she complied.

While he worked his magic against her mouth, his hands caressed her throat. His molten touch slid down her neck to the swell of her breast. Tracing the neckline with his fingertips, his lips moved to her earlobe. Trey could feel the quickening tempo against his fingers. He slid his thumb beneath her neckline and brushed it against her nipple. It pebbled up at his touch. His blood pounded.

No woman had aroused him like this. It was always a game for them. A game he decided he didn't want to play. But Alex wasn't playing any of the games. If he wanted to, he could take her right now. He nipped at her collarbone then raised his head.

Her eyes revealed her confusion.

Trey gently traced her cheek. "This is not how I plan on seducing you."

"Seduce me?" Her voice didn't want to work.

He grinned at her. "Oh yes. I have plans for you, my dear. When we make love, and we will make love, you'll be like putty in my hands. But first I must work the clay. Loosen it up first. Make it soft, and pliant."

What was he doing to her? Instead of being angry, she wondered how his hands would feel on the rest of her body. She suddenly felt very overdressed.

Standing, he offered her his hand. He untied the rope from her waist.

As he recoiled it, he watched the rise and fall of her chest. Realizing his eyes seemed to be stuck there, he forced his gaze up.

Her neck had a small love bite. Her lips were still full from his kiss. He liked the sparkle he put in her eyes. Trey smiled deeper. Yep, he was going to enjoy seducing her. Especially if she was going to look like that afterward.

~

*A*lex slipped into Trey's study and found him working on his ledgers. "Trey, I was out by the burnt barn today."

He looked up from his journals and stared at her. "What were you doing all the way out there?"

"I took the children there to help explain how chemistry worked. Visual reinforcement works better than numbers." She placed something on his desk. "While we were there I found this."

"You shouldn't have brought the children there. They could have been hurt." Trey looked at her instead of the object she sat on his desk. Her teaching methods were definitely different, but he hadn't heard one complaint yet.

"They were in no danger." She rolled her eyes. It figured he'd react this way.

A sigh escaped him as he picked up and rolled the charred piece of wood in his hand. "What is it?"

"I believe the top of a cane."

Trey arched an eyebrow as he got up and took the charred bit to the window. Although badly burned, he could see some design on it. It looked vaguely familiar, but it was too damaged to really tell anything. "You're right. It is. Where did you find it?"

"I think I should show you."

The putrid smell of burnt wood and hay still hung in the air as Trey surveyed the area where Alex found the evidence. "Here?" he questioned. "You found the head of the cane here?"

"Yes."

He scratched his head. "This is more than forty feet from where the blaze started."

"Sniff," she said.

"What?"

"Sniff," Alex repeated. "What do you smell?"

"Kerosene." Trey's eyes grew wide. "Then I was right. This was no accident."

"The fire was set all right," Alex said. "But I'm not convinced that the person who owns this did it."

His eyes narrowed. "Why do you say that?"

"It's a little too obvious."

"So you think someone put it here on purpose?"

She nodded her head. "Yes, I do."

"For what reason?" he asked as he knelt down to get a closer look.

"To throw the blame away from the real culprit and onto someone else."

He frowned. Who could be doing this to him? Who hated him that much?

CHAPTER 13

*A*lex fanned herself while she rocked on the back porch, avoiding the late afternoon sun. She couldn't understand how the women of this time handled the heat in all the clothing they had to wear. Sweat trickled down her neck. What she wouldn't give for a pair of shorts and some air-conditioning. Her eyes were half-closed when she sensed someone standing beside her rocking chair. An ice-cold glass against her throat jolted her fully awake. Her instincts made her grab the hand holding the glass.

Five seconds later she wore its contents.

Alex stood up, sputtering. When she looked down, she noticed that the contents of the glass soaked the bodice of her dress. Slowly her head rose. "I am going to kill you."

Trey looked embarrassed. "I'm sorry, but...but you startled me, Alexandra."

Alex rolled her eyes. "It's Alex. And you didn't think a cold glass against my throat would startle me?"

He rubbed the wrist she grabbed so hard. "Well I didn't expect you to react so violently. Most women wouldn't have done what you did."

"Ah, but I'm not most women, am I?" she asked, placing her hands on her hips.

Trey smiled. "No, you're not." He sat down the empty glass. Instead of wondering where the ice cubes from the glass nestled now, he cleared his thoughts so he could say what he came to talk to her about. "I came out here to tell you we were having a guest for dinner."

"A guest?" Her anger faded as curiosity took over. "Who?"

"That is a surprise." He held up his hand to stop her from questioning him. "You have just enough time to get ready before they arrive."

"But…"

"The longer you pester me, the less time you'll have to get ready," he taunted.

She stared at him for a few seconds as she lifted her skirt a little. Then she swept past him. Calling out Fleurette's name, she headed into the house.

Fleurette came into the hallway wiping her hands. "Yes, Miss Alexandra?"

"Mr. Dalton just informed me we'd be entertaining tonight. I could use your help."

"Of course, Miss Alexandra." Fleurette headed up the staircase behind Alex. "Mr. Dalton had me get your clothes ready earlier."

Alex stopped halfway up the stairs. Turning to face Fleurette, she asked. "And you didn't tell me?"

Fleurette looked confused. She stopped a few steps below Alex. "Was I supposed to?"

Alex continued up the stairs. "Oh yes. There are two things I've learned. Men can't be trusted, and we women must stick together."

~

Two hours later Alex emerged from her bedroom. She smiled to herself when she saw Trey at the bottom of the stairs. He looked very handsome in his tan trousers, white shirt, and green vest. Her heart beat a little faster as she descended the stairs.

Since that first riding adventure several days ago, he had become very attentive. Every evening that he had free time he took her out riding. She felt confident on a horse now. At least she wouldn't fall flat on her face the moment it took off. Alex began to see a side of this man she could care deeply for.

He had the same look now as he did when she had finished her first lesson, a combination of hope and pride. She was dying to know what he was up to.

He bowed to her before offering his arm. He walked her down the hall to the foyer. "You look splendid."

"Thank you, I think." She noticed his brow lift. "Well you did tell Fleurette which dress to press."

He looked at the floor. "I only made a few suggestions. Fleurette picked out which dress you'd wear."

"Then I will make sure I thank her later."

Trey paused before the door to the sitting room to let Alex enter first. Most people wouldn't think twice about what their servants did for them. It was expected. "You don't need to thank her."

She looked up into his eyes. "I know. I want to." Then she heard Rose's cane thumping against the floor.

"'Bout time you two showed up," Rose said.

Alex smiled as she looked up at Trey again. They did look good together. Her heart skipped a beat at the thought.

"Why Miss Alexandra, you look smashing. Where did you get that dress?"

Alex gazed about the room to find out who spoke to her. A smile lit up her face when she saw Elizabeth Boudreaux, and Elizabeth's chaperone standing in the living room. "Why, Miss Elizabeth, what a wonderful surprise!"

She looked up at Trey once again. He gave her a quick grin. With a gentle nod he let her know she could approach her friend. As she walked to her new friend's side, Alex realized she always looked to Trey to make sure she didn't break any code of etiquette. Her grandmother would laugh if she knew this. Alex had always done the exact opposite of what anyone wanted.

Even though her father and grandmother expected her to go to Tulane University, Alex went to college in Boston. She rebelliously picked MIT instead of a college close to home in New Orleans. Her father wanted her to get married and start a family. She locked herself away in an observatory instead. Her father would be amazed at the transformation his daughter had gone through.

Trey watched the two women chattering away. He shook his head. His hand pressed his pocket, finding his pipe where he stored it earlier. Leaving the women to themselves, Trey stepped out onto the front porch. One foot propped up on the banister that edged the porch; he lit and proceeded to puff on his pipe.

In the distance he saw a dust cloud. He waited patiently as it came closer. Trey's mind wandered while he waited.

Aunt Rose was right. Elizabeth and Alexandra could be twins. Yet he found when he compared them he saw a lot of differences. Alexandra's smile was more open, not as shy as Miss Elizabeth's. Her blue eyes had the most amazing flecks of gold in them. She carried herself with more confidence. He loved watching her move. Each expression so vibrant, every gesture full of life. She had a lot of passion, and he wondered how far that passion went.

His stopped his thoughts before they got him into deep trouble. Stretching, Trey noticed the cloud was close enough to discern a man riding a horse.

Beau Manning reined in his horse just before the stairs to the porch. "Evening, Trey."

Trey narrowed his eyes at Beau. "Why are you here? Could it be because Miss Elizabeth is here, without her father along?"

Beau laughed as he slid off his horse. "Come now, am I that obvious? She is very pretty, but that father of hers…"

"Keeps you at arm's length." Trey tapped his pipe against the heel of his hand to empty it. "She is my guest this evening. If you try any of your normal shenanigans, I'll throw you out on your ear."

"I promise to be on my best behavior," Beau said.

Trey sighed. He didn't believe his friend for one minute. "Come on, it should be time for supper about now anyway."

The aroma of fried catfish filled the air as they stepped inside. Just as they entered the hall, the women exited the living room.

"Oh good. Fleurette just announced that supper was ready," Alex said to Trey just before she noticed Beau. "Why, Mr. Beau, what a pleasant surprise."

"Miss Alexandra," he said as he took her hand. After placing a chaste kiss on her hand, he turned to Elizabeth. "And who is this enchanting creature?"

"Beau Manning this is Elizabeth Boudreaux. Elizabeth, this is Beau, Trey's friend," said Alex. Then she looked at Trey realizing that he probably should have introduced them.

Trey slipped his arm around Alex and grinned.

If she did overstep her boundaries neither man called her on it.

Alex noticed the blush that blossomed on Elizabeth's cheeks as she offered her hand to Beau. Beau bowed elegantly, gently kissed her hand, then took her arm and guided her into the dining room.

Alex watched the couple throughout the meal, curious. She couldn't tell if her great-great-grandmother was infatuated, or intimidated. Elizabeth never made eye contact with Beau and barely spoke during dinner.

Spearing a small morsel of catfish, she looked up, under the impression someone watched her. It surprised her to know that she had Beau's attention. "Beau, is there something wrong?"

His smiled, picking up his wineglass. "No. I just couldn't help but notice how much you two look alike."

Alex blinked. How could she explain this right? No one would believe the truth. To her amazement, Trey came to her rescue.

"Beau, our friends say you and I could pass for brothers. Alexandra and Miss Elizabeth do resemble each other but notice all the differences. They have different hair color and eye color. Notice the shape of their lips and eyes. The size of their noses."

Alex opened her fan, and gently moved it up and down. She didn't realize Trey had paid attention to her features so closely. It flattered her. She noticed Elizabeth fidgeting under Beau's scrutiny. She pushed her fish around on her plate.

Beau leaned back in his chair and pulled out his pipe.

Before Alex could open her mouth, Trey spoke. "Beau, let us leave the women for a few moments."

He dragged his friend outside with him.

The moment the men went out to smoke their pipes, Alexandra turned to Beth.

"So?" Alex asked, keeping her voice low enough that their chaperones wouldn't hear.

Beth blushed. "What?"

Fleurette peeked in the doorway. After Alex waved her in, she proceeded to fill the ladies' teacups.

Alex glanced at Rose, who was still deep in conversation with Elizabeth's chaperon. "He seems quite infatuated with you." Something she didn't like, but only because Beau wasn't her great-great-grandfather.

"Me? No, I think he is more interested in father's land. Besides, a gentleman would call on my father first."

Fleurette picked up several plates from the table. Her sidelong glance at Alex didn't go unnoticed.

Alex took a sip from her cup of tea. She grimaced, realizing she forgot to sweeten it with a dollop of honey. "Why would he be more interested in land than something as pretty as you?"

Beth blushed deeper. Her cup clanged against the saucer as she picked it up. "I don't know, but he never requested to be introduced before."

"Are you sure?" Alex asked. A second sip brought a sigh. It had just the right amount of honey.

"Quite. He has always limited his conversations to Father."

"Perhaps your father has denied him an introduction," Alex said, setting her half-empty cup down for a second.

Elizabeth's look turned hopeful as her fingers surrounded the small cup. "You think so?"

"You did say your father was very protective of you, Elizabeth."

She touched Alex's wrist. "Please, call me Beth, Alexandra."

"Alex. Please call me Alex."

Beth pressed her hand to her chest. "That is a man's name, Alex."

Alex grinned. "I know. Isn't it scandalous?"

Beth grinned back. "Very."

Fleurette filled Alex's and Beth's cups with more tea before turning to the other two ladies.

Alex stood up. "Why don't we go out on the back porch for a few minutes?"

Beth nodded before following her.

n the front porch Beau filled his pipe. "So why did you push me out here?"

"Alex doesn't want any smoking in the house, and I didn't feel like arguing the point." Trey glared at Beau. The rich flagrance of tobacco filled his nose.

Beau cupped the pipe in his hand, struck a match, and took a long pull. "So Miss Alexandra has already started putting down rules. I thought you wouldn't allow any woman to rule you."

Trey snorted as he filled his own. Beau hadn't dealt with Alexandra yet. "You like to antagonize me."

"True." Smoke circled Beau's head.

Trey hesitated lighting his pipe for a second.

Beau grinned. He banged the bowl against his palm. Pulling out another match, he relit it. "So, you and Miss Alexandra getting along okay?"

Trey's teeth clamped down on the stem of his pipe. "Yes. Why do you ask?"

Beau shrugged as he flicked his match away. "Don't know, just thinking about the way you dragged her to my door that day. You didn't seem too happy with her then."

"Everything is fine," Trey snapped.

An amused grin tugged at the corners of Beau's mouth. He took a puff of his pipe. "So, when is the wedding?"

Trey almost choked on the smoke from his pipe as he turned to glare at his friend. "What are you talking about?"

"Rumor has it that you and Miss Alexandra plan on marrying right after harvest." Beau took another puff, watching a plume of smoke rise.

Trey started paying close attention to his pipe, stirring the powder around in the bowl. "I see you've heard."

Beau leaned against a post beside him. "Then it's true?"

"What is true?"

"That you really are going to marry her. I thought you didn't believe in marriage," Beau asked. Another lazy curl of smoke rose from his pipe.

Trey bit on his pipe stem in anger. Jerking it from his mouth, he tossed most of the ashes onto the porch. "I never said I didn't believe in marriage."

"But you've never considered marriage before." Beau watched Trey as he wrestled with his tobacco pouch.

"You really are enjoying this too much." Trey pounded more tobacco into the bowl.

"True, but I've never seen a woman effect you this much." Beau tapped his pipe out.

Trey brought his pipe to his lips and lit it. "Why do you say that?"

"Because you seem to be going through with it."

"I have to keep up appearances."

Beau laughed. "Really?"

"Of course. You really think I want to marry?"

"Right now?" Beau studied his friend for a minute. "I'm not sure."

Trey ignored the sound of the thump of a cane on the floor that floated out of a nearby window.

~

"Where are you ladies going?" asked Rose.

"To join the men," said Alex. She had enough of waiting for Trey and Beau to rejoin them.

"Don't you want to show Miss Elizabeth your dress?" Rose leaned on her cane.

Alex glared at Rose before glancing out the front door, wondering what the men were up to, and if they could hear this conversation. "Show her my dress?"

"Yes." When she noticed Alexandra wasn't paying attention she continued. "Your wedding dress."

Alex turned around. "Oh, oh, my wedding dress. Of course, um, well…"

"Your dress is up in the attic, where I told Fleurette to store it, Alexandra," said Rose.

"Oh, thank you." She kept her apprehension to herself. "I've been so busy lately I haven't had a chance to ask you."

"It's all right, chile," said Rose.

"Can we go see it?" Beth asked.

Alex turned to Fleurette. Her unspoken question obvious.

Fleurette smiled.

"Of course, but it still needs to be altered, unless you've already finished with that, Fleurette."

"Yes, ma'am, jus' like you asked."

A dress she had never seen had already been altered to fit her. This should be good.

"Then lead the way," Alex said. She saw the odd look Beth gave her, but since she had no clue where Fleurette had put this fictitious dress she ignored it.

They had just cleared the first landing when the screen door creaked. Trey and Beau stood at the bottom of the stairs. "What are you ladies up to?"

Alex jumped. She didn't want to tell Trey.

Beth had no problem. "Why, Alex has graciously promised to show me her wedding gown."

One of Trey's brows rose. "Really, Alexandra?"

Alex hid her hands deep in the folds of her skirt to keep her from wringing them together. She didn't like the twinkle in his eyes. How could she answer this honestly?

Trey didn't give her a chance.

"We'll go with you," he said as he started to climb the stairs.

"Oh no," Elizabeth said. "It is bad luck for the groom to see the dress before the wedding."

"Only when the bride is in it," said Beau.

"Oh," Elizabeth said. "I never did pay much attention to those old wives' tales."

Fleurette led her small group up to the attic. Alex entered first, followed by Beth, Trey, and Beau bringing up the rear. Rose and her companion stood near the ladder.

In one corner, a mannequin stood with a breathtakingly beautiful white dress draped over it.

Alex stepped up to examine the intricate beadwork. The dress had a high collar and sweetheart neckline. The sleeves were long, mutton shaped, with a point that would extend down to her index finger. A full skirt, its train wrapped around the mannequin on the floor, set off the drop waist. It was exquisite. Alex could guess how many long hard hours Fleurette had put into it. She turned toward Fleurette to thank her and noticed paper scattered across the floor. Bending down, she picked up several.

She stared at beautifully drawn dress sketches. Several with Xs through them. Alex looked up at Fleurette. "Did you draw these?"

Fleurette stared at the floor. "Yes, ma'am."

"Fleurette, they are beautiful," exclaimed Alex. She watched as Fleurette raised her head so she could look at Alex's face. "You have a real talent. Please show me the rest."

Fleurette started to race out of the attic when Trey stopped her. "Later, Fleurette. First, I would like to speak to my fiancée, alone."

Alex felt the fingers of dread wrap around her heart as everyone filtered out of the room. Lifting her chin high, she waited.

CHAPTER 14

Trey glared down at her, his fists on his hips. "Where did that dress come from?"

Alex's brow creased. Just because he stood a head taller than her, he couldn't intimidate her. "How do I know?"

"Did you buy it? Smuggle it up here somehow?" One arm gestured around the room.

Her jaw locked as she closed her eyes. She wanted to shout at him that he should ask his aunt Rose, but she refused to lose her temper.

"Are you going to answer me?"

"That's it. I have taken all I can." She knew he wouldn't believe her so she swung around him, and headed toward the door.

In two long strides Trey blocked the door, cutting off her exit.

She placed her hands on her hips, blue eyes flashing angrily, Alex worked on maintaining her composure. "If you want to know where the dress came from I'd ask your aunt, but since you probably won't believe her either I'm leaving and you aren't stopping me." In one swift movement, she stomped on his foot. As he reacted, she grabbed his arm and threw him over her shoulder.

He landed with a thud. Alex hoped he hurt himself as she descended the attic ladder. Seething, she turned from the ladder and found five sets of eyes staring at her. She hooked her thumb over her shoulder. "He fell."

Alex brushed her hair out of her face. "I um, I'll be in my room."

She walked into her room and got as far as pulling her shirt and jeans out of the drawer before Trey burst in, forcing the door to bang against the wall. The heat from his gaze burned her as he watched her place her clothes on the bed.

"What do you think you're doing?" he demanded.

Alex looked up. She saw a small audience gathering around him. Great, just what they needed. Looking back down at her belongings, she sighed. She only had two choices. Either back down and hate herself or follow her heart. Her heart told her she couldn't stay here any longer. Not if Trey didn't believe her.

She crossed the room and opened her wardrobe.

"I asked you a question," Trey said.

She stopped to glare at him. "What does it look like I am doing?" Alex picked up her boots from the bottom of the armoire.

"Making a scene." He took a few steps into the room.

"No." She pointed behind him. "I think you're the one making a scene bursting into my room like this. What will your friends think?"

He turned around to find everyone watching them. Trey grabbed Alex's wrist.

"Fleurette, take our guests downstairs and give them some refreshments. Aunt Rose, please make sure the ladies are comfortable." Then he proceeded to drag Alex out of her bedroom and down the hall toward the stairs.

He kept a strong grip on her wrist while he spoke to her softly. "We need to talk. If I have to, I'll throw you over my shoulders, and carry you down the stairs."

"This strong-arm tactic isn't going to win you any friends. Where are we going?" she whispered through gritted teeth. Alex dragged her feet, trying to slow him down.

They started down the stairs.

He shook his head. Alex definitely had a way with words. "Out on the porch."

She stopped resisting, although she didn't go along willingly. The front screen door banged shut behind her. Her eyes bright with anger, she demanded, "What do you want?"

Trey let go of her wrist, turning her so that she'd face him. "You can't go thundering through the night."

"I can do anything I damn well please!" She stomped her foot.

"Stop swearing! Ladies don't do that." He grabbed her hand and pulled her down the stairs that led to the yard. The night air carried the scent of magnolias.

Alex remembered how many times she heard those exact words from her grandma. She allowed Trey to lead her away from the house. She sensed their audience crowding around the front windows. Even though she couldn't see them she knew they were there.

"What is wrong with you?" He lowered his voice. "I thought you didn't want anyone to know the truth about you."

"I don't!" Alex took a deep breath. "But...but it's hard knowing no one believes you." Alex walked away from him. She had never felt so terribly alone, even when working alone for hours on end with her calculations and computer data she had never felt this isolated.

"Why should I believe you?" He ran his hands through his hair.

She turned back to face him. "Because it's the truth. You know it too, but just won't admit it."

Trey stiffened. "What are you talking about?"

Alex rolled her eyes. "You don't even realize you're doing it, do you? You constantly come to my rescue, like tonight. Why did you contradict Beau? Everyone can tell that Elizabeth and I look alike."

"I don't know." Trey paused for a moment. "Why do you look alike?"

"You're not going to like the answer." Alex paused long enough to get Trey's attention. "She's my great-great-grandmother."

"Not the time travel again!"

"Yes, the time travel again." She grabbed his arm. "You might not want to, but you have to admit I don't fit in, do I? Trey, you should know, you've watched me enough. What have you learned?"

"Women don't behave like you." He started to pace back and forth. "They don't treat servants like close friends. They'd never be caught in pants. When I saw you in your jeans and shirt it shocked me, but you wore them like a second skin. Hell, they fit you like a second skin."

Alex blushed. A smile tugged at her lips. He was attracted to her or he wouldn't have noticed how her jeans fit.

"And your driver's license, I've never seen paper so hard."

"It's plastic," she corrected him.

"Plastic?"

"A man-made product. Doesn't break like glass. We use it everywhere," she explained.

"And the color picture?"

"Color became popular in the early sixties."

He stopped pacing to look at her intently. "Sixties?"

"Nineteen sixties." She rubbed her hand across her forehead. "Look, I can stand here and spout off about the wonders of my time all night long. The real question is, do you believe me?"

Trey looked at her quietly. He really didn't want to believe her. It was too fantastic. But the things she said, and the things she did, had him questioning his own sanity because he had started to believe. Now she wanted him to admit it out loud.

A heavy sigh broke the silence.

"I don't know what to believe, Alex. The whole idea is crazy, but you're right. You don't quite fit in here. I have figured out you're not an actress. There is an elegance about you that can't be faked. Yet, there are common things you know nothing about, like ballroom dancing or which fork to use when eating. You know about the stars and can have an intelligent argument with any man, and normally be right. You walk like a lady and talk like a…a sailor. And that tae—"

"Taekwondo."

"Yes. I've never seen the likes of it before." His hands lightly gripped her shoulders. "You're different, and I like that. You listen to me, argue with me and make me think. Not many women will do that."

One corner of her mouth turned up a little more. "Except your aunt."

He laughed. "True." Trey offered her his arm.

Alex slipped her arm in his. He didn't come right out and say he believed her, but he did seem headed in the right direction. At least it was a start.

~

*T*he next morning Alex carried a cup of coffee to Rose's room. Rose's habit kept her in her room in the morning before the sun worked its way over the house and made the upstairs unbearable. Eleven o'clock was still cool enough to catch up on her letters and do a little sewing.

A swift knock on the door was all Rose heard before the door opened.

"I trust you are comfortable," Alex said.

"Very," said Rose. She took the cup Alex held in front of her. "Thank you."

"So, when were you going to tell me about the dress?"

"I wondered when you'd ask that." A sly grin spread across Rose's face. "There was no need to tell you about it unless we're really going to have a wedding. I just needed something to stop you from joining the men and that was the perfect excuse."

"Why?"

"It's just not done."

"You could have told me that instead of bringing in a dress I knew nothing about," came Alex's reply. Her skirt rustled as she crossed to the window and looked out.

"Miss Elizabeth wouldn't have understood why I had to point it out to you," said Rose. Her cup chimed softly as she sat it down on a small table beside her chair. "Most women still make their dresses, especially their wedding gowns. It would seem odd that you didn't have it completed by now since you came here to marry Trey."

Alex gave Aunt Rose a sidelong glance. Why did Rose say "still"? There was no way Rose could have figured out she had traveled through time, could she? Then she shook her head, deciding it was impossible for Rose to know the truth. "But I didn't come here to marry Trey. That's something you made up."

"For your protection," Rose said. "You must keep up appearances."

Alex mumbled something under her breath as she turned from the window to face Rose. "Why must I keep up appearances?"

"A young woman doesn't live under a man's roof without a proper chaperone. Our neighbors already have jumped to their own conclusions about you, even with the engagement."

"What kind of conclusions?"

Rose just stared at her.

"Oh." She paused as what Rose hinted at took root. "Oh!" Alex tapped her foot on the floor. Challenges always got her attention. "Well, then I'll just have to prove them wrong, won't I?"

~

Three days passed. Trey heard Alex talking but couldn't figure out from where. Following to the sound of her voice led him to the attic.

"This is great. All the pants need are drawstrings in the waistband."

Fleurette held up the white jacket. "How do you keep this closed?"

"With the sash." Alex held out the strip of cloth she spoke about.

Fleurette gave her a dubious look.

"I swear it works," Alex replied. "How many can you make of these?"

"How many do you need?" She neatly folded the jacket up.

Alex started to count on her hands. "Well let's see. I'll need one, Mr. Trey, you."

"Me?" Fleurette squeaked.

"Yes. Every woman should be able to defend herself. Besides, you are doing all the sewing." Alex watched as Fleurette's hands glided across the white material.

"Is there anyone else you can think of?"

Fleurette paused. Then shook her head no.

"Okay, then three. Let me know when they are ready."

"When what are ready?" asked Trey.

Alex's head snapped up. "It's a surprise." She quickly crossed to the door and led Trey back down the hall.

"What are you up to now?" he demanded.

"You'll know in a few days." Alex saw the stubborn look in his eyes. "Please? I promise to explain everything to you, but you have to be patient."

"All right." Trey studied her. "Two days. That is all you get."

Alex smiled at him; hoping two days would be enough time for Fleurette to complete her task.

~

Two days later, Trey found a note pinned to his bed. "What in tarnation?"

After reading the note he crumpled it and yelled. "Alexandra?" No answer. He raced down the steps and charged outside.

"Was that you bellowing?" asked his aunt, who sat in a rocker on the porch. She snapped open her fan. "If you're looking for Alexandra, I believe she's gone to Fleurette and Jessie's cabin."

"What is she doing there?"

The slight breeze from Rose's fan rustled a few tendrils of hair. "I don't know. Why don't you go out there and ask her?"

Trey looked at his aunt while she innocently fanned herself. "What are you two up to?"

Her fan moved faster. "Why, Trey Dalton, what are you accusing me of?"

He let out a sharp breath. "Nothing." He shook his head as he took the front porch stairs two at a time. After saddling his horse, Trey headed to Fleurette and Jesse's.

The door to their small cabin stood wide open. He slid off his horse in time to hear Fleurette exclaim, "I will not wear that, it's…it's…no."

Trey walked in the doorway. To the right stood Alexandra wearing a white jacket and white pants.

Although the jacket was large enough to wrap around her and closed tight with a sash, Alexandra's ankle and feet were bare. "Woman, what in blue blazes are you wearing?"

CHAPTER 15

*H*e heard her exasperated sigh and frowned.

"This," she said, placing her hands on her hips. "Is a dobock. It's what you'll wear while learning martial arts."

He stepped closer to study the outfit. "And what are martial arts?"

"Martial arts are the arts of combat. One of those arts is Taekwondo."

"Tae—" His eyes lit up. "Your..." He twirled his fingers in the air.

"Yes, my..." she repeated, mimicking his hand gestures. She handed him an outfit like hers.

He took it from her, noting the soft cotton feel of the white outfit. Trey continued to stare down at it. "You want me to wear this?"

She nodded, her hands clasped behind her.

"Why can't I wear this?" he asked, gesturing at his clothes.

"Too confining," she replied.

"They will do fine."

Alex looked at him. Amusement sparkled in her eyes. How long will it take for Trey to realize she knew what she was talking about? Maybe the first time he split his pants. "Okay."

It took Trey a month and three pairs of ripped pants before he gave in and wore the dobock.

Their lessons progressed pretty smoothly. Trey objected a lot in the beginning, but Alex's logic and his strong desire to learn eventually won out.

~

a sharp pain in the small of her back made her straighten. Alex groaned as she rubbed at the ache. "I hate housework."

The front door banged open, allowing the heat from inside the house to escape out, bathing Alex. Sitting on the wooden stairs that led up to the porch was a mistake. Every time that door opened she felt the temperature rise five degrees. She felt like a wilted flower.

Fleurette picked up the silver she had finished with. "Miss Rose found a few more pieces for you to do."

Alex brushed the back on her hand against her forehead. Why did she volunteer to do this? Her lessons with the children had been postponed so she could help.

She already knew the answer. Because Fleurette couldn't do this all herself and Trey couldn't afford to let any of the workers out of the fields. She nodded as she bent to her task once more.

If Rose hadn't decided the time had come for their formal engagement party Alex wouldn't be going through this at all. She tried to talk Rose out of the party. Trey did too. Alex heard his voice rise several times during that conversation, but Rose wouldn't give in. So now Alex sat in the shade of the porch, polishing silver to help get the house ready for this grand party. One she didn't want to go to. Pretending to be something she wasn't wore on Alex. This had gone on for more than three months.

She sat back for a minute, finding it hard to believe she had been here that long. This way of life had started to feel normal to her. Once she started to teach the plantation children she knew she found her niche. The desire to return to her own time died with the beginning of the lessons. That scared her. What scared her most of all was Trey.

Since she began the lessons in Taekwondo, she started to see another side of him she never noticed before. His human side. None of the

138

overbearing ogre she met when she first arrived. When he made a mistake, he laughed at it. He was eager to learn. Alex found Trey's complex personality intriguing. He was attentive, compassionate, and easy to tease. She found herself enjoying their time together, and she knew she was on the verge of losing her heart to him. Somehow Trey had slipped in under her armor.

The front door opened again. Fleurette came down the steps with several candelabras. "This is the last of it."

"I hope so," Alex responded as she took the candleholders from Fleurette. The metal felt warm in her hands. "If there is any more, hide them from Miss Rose. I think she's trying to be too helpful."

The familiar thump of a cane on the porch preceded Rose's comment. "I heard that."

"Good," Alex said, smiling.

Rose ignored Alex's comment. "We have company coming."

Alex stood up to look toward the lane. In the distance they could see the cloud of dust from someone's horse. "Who do you think it is?"

They had very few visitors. Trey normally knew who planned to visit and gave them some warning. Whoever headed toward the house didn't have an invitation.

Alex watched as Andrew's horse skidded to a halt in front of her. He leaped down, landing agilely in front of her.

He bowed as he took her hand. "Ah, Miss Alexandra, you're as pretty as a flower." He kissed her hand.

Alex fought a grin. She wondered what flower he compared her to because right now she felt like a weed. Most women wouldn't be caught dead looking the way she did. They would have dashed to their rooms to freshen up, but then she wasn't most people. "So, Mr. Andrew, what brings you here?"

She turned and headed toward the rockers on the porch. A slight nod toward Fleurette sent the maid in for a drink for them. Alex sat down in a chair next to the one Aunt Rose sank into, indicating that he do the same.

"My aunt received the invitation to your engagement party." He smiled at her. "I had to bring over our RSVP. We'd love to come."

"Thank you, Mr. Andrew. We will be glad to add you to the list."

Fleurette came out with four glasses on a tray. She offered one to Rose, then Alex, and then Andrew. It didn't take long for Alex to figure out whom the fourth glass was for.

Trey took the stairs two at a time.

A habit Alex noticed he did when angry. She stood up and greeted him, placing a restraining hand on his arm. "Sweetheart, Mr. Leroux came by to tell us he and his aunt will be attending our engagement party."

Trey looked down at her.

She could see the war of emotions that played across his face. Alex hoped he wouldn't do anything rash.

Placing his hand on top of the one she rested on his arm, he drew her closer. Once he had her beside him, he stole a glance at Rose before giving Andrew a feral smile. "Good. Will your uncle attend too?"

"No. He has some business to take care of that evening," Andrew answered.

"Too bad," said Trey. His arm slipped around Alex's waist.

Rose's cane thumped on the floor as she stood. "He will miss a wonderful party."

A tense silence filled the air.

"Well," said Andrew as he stood. "I guess I should be getting back to my aunt's house. I'll see you this weekend." He bowed to Alex, and then nodded toward Trey.

Alex stepped out of Trey's grasp as soon as Andrew rode out of sight. "That was nice and tense."

Trey remained silent.

"Come on, chile, Fleurette has your dress ready for a fitting," said Rose.

Alex nodded as she entered the house. She didn't know what happened between Trey and Andrew, but it had to be something that they wouldn't leave in the past. Or at least Trey wouldn't.

∾

*A*lex fussed in front of her mirror. "But I don't want my ass three miles behind me!"

Fleurette rolled her eyes. She was getting used to Alex's profanity. "Miss Alexandra, a bustle is part of the style."

"I know, along with that damn corset," Alex whined. "Why do people feel these things are attractive? I can't even sit with it on. Can't we start our own trend?"

Fleurette attached the bustle wire as if Alex hadn't spoken. "Trend?"

"Style." She had to stop talking while Fleurette helped her get her dress on. Pulling the sleeves up her arms she continued her tirade. "And I thought hip huggers were ghastly."

Fleurette finished with the last button on her dress. She adjusted the hem of Alex's dress to make sure it centered over the bustle properly, then stepped back. "You're ready."

Alex looked in the mirror at the gown Fleurette created for her. "Fleurette, you amaze me. This is beautiful." The low-cut lavender gown accentuated her slim waist. Although she felt like she had a table following her around in the back, it did add to the design of the dress.

"Any chance you could have made this a little higher?" she asked, touching the bodice.

"You're going to be fine, Miss Alexandra." Fleurette laughed. "You'll see. Most of the ladies will probably expose a lot more than you."

"Please, Fleurette, when we're alone, call me Alex. I sound like a tsar's princess when I hear Miss Alexandra. It's too formal."

"Yes." Fleurette hesitated. "Miss Alex."

Alex beamed. She turned back to the mirror and tugged on her bodice. "Are you sure? I feel like I'm exposing myself. One false move and the girls will come out and say hello."

She leaned forward while looking in the mirror to see if she could fall out of the dress.

"Nice view."

She stood up quickly and spun around. A bright shade of pink started at her breasts and quickly climbed up her face. Even her ears turned red. "Trey Dalton, it's not nice to sneak up on a girl like that."

"I didn't sneak." He sported a wicked smile. "I came to escort you downstairs. Our guests are starting to arrive."

"Okay." Alex took a deep breath. "Let's get this show on the road."

Trey arched an eyebrow as he offered her his arm.

They joined Rose at the foot of the stairs, welcoming each guest.

After an hour she was bored, hot, and itched in places she couldn't scratch. Alex gently tugged on Trey's coat sleeve.

"Any chance we can take a break? I'm dying here," she whispered between introductions.

Trey turned his gaze toward her. "You're what?"

A thump of a cane brought them both back to what was going on.

"Sorry." Alex blushed. "One of my odd phrases."

"Perhaps, your fiancée' needs a drink, Trey," said Rose.

Alex leaned toward Rose. "What I really need is some fresh air. All this stuffiness is getting to me."

Rose snapped open her fan.

Alex saw the smile the fan tried to hide.

An hour later, the couple could finally stroll the gardens where most of their guests were. Alex was grateful for the slight breeze that helped move the stifling air. Her fan just didn't cut it. Her hair stirred with the movement of the fan. It was the first time she didn't know what to say to Trey. With everyone watching them, she felt like they were on stage. Her conversations seemed formal and stiff. She had almost forgotten that their relationship was a farce, but this engagement party brought it all back. Her fan moved a little faster. In a way, she wished his attentiveness wasn't an illusion.

She'd been seeing a lot more of the side of Trey that she liked this evening. He was not the angry young man she saw every time Andrew was around. The thought of Andrew had Alex wondering what happened between them.

When Trey saw her out studying the stars recently, he joined her, instead of yelling at her for being outside late at night unchaperoned. She liked the changes in him.

"Alexandra?"

Her name sounded so elegant when he murmured it. She looked up into his handsome face.

"I'm sorry." A slight blush came to her cheeks. This man always made her blush.

"Are you enjoying yourself?" he asked.

"Oh, very much," she smiled. "Am I behaving properly?"

He smiled back at her. Taking her hand, he drew her closer. "You have been perfect." He raised her hand to his lips.

A voice startled them apart. "I thought I gave you two enough time to be alone, and you're only getting started?"

Trey turned to face Beau. "We do have the rest of our lives, don't we?"

Beau's brow rose up. "Taking it a bit more seriously now, aren't you?"

A throat being cleared made Alex look. Her eyes widened. "Why, Mr. Leroux. I'm so glad you could make it. Did you lose your aunt already?"

"Yes. She's with Miss Rose." He smiled, revealing a dimple. "You look lovely this evening."

She blushed prettily.

He nodded at the two men. "Beau, Trey."

Trey pulled Alex against him. His eyes narrowed as he stared Andrew down.

Alex had her hands clasped in front of her, so a quick jab to his ribs went unnoticed.

Beau draped an arm over Andrew's shoulder. "I want to talk to you about that horse you're selling."

The couple watched the two men head toward the refreshment stand.

"Why are you nice to him?" Trey growled at her.

"Why shouldn't I be?"

"Are you attracted to the man?"

"Is that what you think?" She looked up at him. "Good God, he's my ancestor."

"What?"

143

"I told you my lineage, only you won't believe me." Alex looked until she saw Elizabeth Boudreaux. "I have to make sure they fall in love."

When Trey spied Elizabeth, he found her near the refreshment table. Beau had already finished with Andrew and was trying to draw her into a conversation. Andrew hung back, but he couldn't keep his eyes off Elizabeth. "You want to play matchmaker?"

"She is going to be his wife someday, or else my family line will not exist," Alex said.

"Her father wouldn't allow his daughter to marry Andrew. He plans to send her back to Paris next year to find a suitable husband," said Trey. He gave her arm a gentle tug, guiding her toward the refreshment table.

"Now what is wrong with Andrew?"

"Nothing, unless you want your daughter to marry well." Trey's lips turned up a little. "Her father wants her to marry a man with a title. Andrew has none."

"And her feelings have nothing to do with his decision? How awful."

When Alex became silent, Trey started to worry. She was far too independent to leave things alone. He had already seen evidence of that with her dealings with his aunt and Fleurette. Alex didn't put up with his aunt's interference, yet she coddled Rose. And Fleurette. The woman barely spoke before Alex showed up. Now, she was becoming almost as pushy as Alex according to Jesse. "Don't interfere, Alexandra."

She patted his arm. "What makes you think I will?"

"You've been living here with me, remember?"

She blushed. "Yes. I do."

Someone pushed a glass of champagne into her hand. Glancing over at Trey, she noticed that he held one too.

Beau's voice boomed out, catching everyone's attention. "Tonight," he said. "We're here to congratulate Trey Dalton and Alexandra Thibodaux on their engagement." He turned toward them. "So a toast. May you two find the happiness in marriage that everyone looks for, and I hope I will have a few more years before I have to take that step." He raised his glass as he heard a few chuckles.

"Congratulations."

Alex smiled up at Trey as they touched glasses before taking a sip.

She wondered what these people would think when there wasn't a wedding. Her thoughts died when she grimaced at the taste of the drink. She managed to swallow what was in her mouth, but she didn't want the rest of it.

The band started to play. Trey took her drink and handed his and hers to Beau. Taking her hand, he led her on to the dance floor.

She smiled as they moved, but she couldn't get the bitter taste out of her mouth. If only she had a piece of mint gum. When would that be invented? Her face started to stiffen on her. As discreetly as she could, she tried to loosen the muscles.

Alex blinked several times when she noticed that Trey seemed to float in front of her. What was wrong with her?

She knew Trey spoke to her, but she couldn't understand what he said. Her eyes felt very heavy, like someone had tied lead weights to them.

Trey watched as all the color left Alexandra's face. She stumbled a couple of times but didn't seem to be aware of it. When he asked if she was all right, she just stared at him. He quickly took her off the dance floor and moved her to a spot where she could rest.

Grasping her shoulders, he tried to get her attention. "Alex." He shook her. "Alexandra, are you all right?"

She looked at him with glassy eyes. "Yes, the painting is nice, Grams."

He felt his heart drop in his chest as her eyes rolled up and she crumpled at his feet.

CHAPTER 16

$\mathcal{A}$lex woke to find herself in bed. Fleurette cleared off her nightstand while a kindly man sat on the edge of the bed beside her with a stethoscope about his neck.

"Drink this."

Taking the cup from his hand, she downed the contents. The vile concoction threatened to come back up almost immediately.

The doctor turned toward Trey. "She should be fine now, just make sure she gets plenty of fluids."

He stood up and handed the cup to Fleurette. "I'll check in on her in the morning."

When Alex tried to sit up, she was pushed back onto the feather pillows by Trey, who took the doctor's vacated place on the side of the bed.

"What happened?" she asked. She couldn't remember how she got back to her room.

"You gave me quite a scare." Trey took her hand. "The doctor thinks the excitement got to you."

"Excitement!" She tried to sit up again. "I'm not a fainter."

"There has been a lot going on." Trey pushed her back down as he tried to calm her down.

"Fleurette told me you haven't eaten today. It's okay to faint."

"It's not okay," she snapped. "And I didn't faint."

Fleurette crossed in front of the bed and went out the door with a heavily laden tray in her hand.

Trey searched Alexandra's face, making sure she looked all right.

Those large blue eyes filled with anger. "I don't faint."

He stroked her cheek. When she turned so pale before fainting in his arms, he thought his world had broken apart. Thankfully, she was all right.

"Trey..." Alex felt her heart do a flip in her chest. She wondered if he realized that he was so easy to read, at least to her. Her eyes lovingly watched him as he stared at her mouth. As his head dipped toward hers, Alex let out a sigh she didn't realize she held.

His lips were tentative at first, gently nibbling on the corners of her mouth.

Her arms curled up around his neck to pull him closer and deepening the kiss. Fire blossomed in her stomach, heating her blood, making her bolder. Just as their tongues started to touch Alex heard the distant thump of Aunt Rose's cane.

Trey sighed as he broke the kiss. He leaned his forehead against hers while he brought his passions under control. If it weren't for his aunt, he wouldn't have stopped this time.

"Is the party still going on?" Music floated up into her room.

"Yes." Trey gave her a half a grin. "I dragged you off the floor so fast that no one really knows what happened."

Rose banged into the room. "Trey Dalton!"

Trey stood up and faced his aunt. "Aunt Rose, let me explain."

"You don't have to explain." Her fan moved furiously. "I can see what's going on here. And I thought you two were better than this. Alexandra, I can't believe you...well, a lady wouldn't be up here alone with a man. It's scandalous. What if someone saw?"

Trey tried to interrupt her again, but Rose ignored him.

"To think I trusted you. I wanted to believe that you weren't a ..." The sound of someone clearing their throat stopped her in mid-sentence.

"I'm sorry," said the doctor. "Please make sure Miss Alexandra isn't left alone tonight. Just in case."

"Thank you, Doctor," Trey said. He guided the doctor out this time, leaving his aunt alone with Alex.

Rose leaned heavily against her cane as she glanced from Alex to the door. "Doctor? I don't understand."

Alex slid her feet off the bed. Standing made her feel a little light-headed, but no one was there to stop her.

"Rose, it's okay. Come, sit down." She led Rose to one of the chairs in her room. Alex took the other.

"What happened?" asked Rose, her fan forgotten.

"I guess I fainted," Alex said. Her stomach lurched. "Excuse me." She hurried behind the screen to the chamber pot, which wasn't there. Looking around, she found it by her bed. She barely made it back behind the screen in time, embarrassed to be seen like this.

When Trey walked in he didn't see Alex he accused his aunt. "You didn't make her leave, did you?"

Rose shook her head and pointed behind the screen.

Chamber pot in hand, Alex stepped from behind the screen. "No. She didn't make me leave."

Trey reached for the pot, but she pulled it out of reach. He took her arm and guided her back to her bed. "You should not be up."

"I feel fine." The light shade of green of her face, her glassy eyes, and pale lips contradicted her statement.

"You don't look fine." He led her back over to her bed.

Fleurette came back into the room carrying a tray with several glasses and a pitcher of water, some linens, and a new chamber pot. She took the used one from Alex.

Alex looked down at the new one as she sat on the bed, grateful Fleurette noticed the pallor of her face earlier. Smacking her lips, she wondered why her mouth tasted like tin. "Has anyone else gotten sick?"

Trey looked at Fleurette.

"No, Miss Alexandra. At least no one we've heard about," Fleurette answered as she tidied up the room a little more.

Alex's brow furrowed. There must be another reason. She pushed herself up off the bed and onto her feet again.

"What do you think you're doing?" Trey demanded.

"Going back to the party," she replied.

"No, you're not." Trey would make a great football blocker. He crowded her back toward the bed.

She placed her hands on his chest and pushed. Alex knew she must be weak if she couldn't budge him at least a little.

"You need to rest," Trey grounded out. Just as he stooped to pick her up, he felt the blow of a fan against his arm. He stared at his aunt. "Aunt Rose."

"She's right."

"Have you gone daft too?"

"How will it look if I bow out early?" asked Alex.

"Normal?"

"No. What will the neighbors think if we were to leave early? I thought you didn't want to give the gossipers any more ammunition."

He grumbled as he allowed Alex to remain standing. Then, rubbing his temples, he thought about what she said. Unfortunately, she was right, but his instincts told him to protect her.

He stopped rubbing. Since when did he want to protect her? When did she work her way into his heart? "All right, but you do not leave my side."

Alex smiled up at him as she nodded yes.

∽

Several hours later, Alex wished she hadn't talked Trey into letting her come back. Most of the smells made her stomach roll, including one guest's heady perfume. She continued to get sick, which made things awkward when conversing with someone. It came on suddenly. Thankfully, it had only happened twice, each time she had been lucky enough to be alone, and her noxious spells came less frequently now.

She sat on a bench, braced up against a huge oak, listening to the musicians play a waltz. Her fan moved lazily up and down, giving her some breeze. It helped keep her stomach settled.

Trey came back from the kitchen with a glass of water for her.

"Thank you," she said as she took the cool drink.

"Are you feeling any better?"

"Yes. I guess I must have eaten something I shouldn't have." It made more sense that she ate something tainted than just fainted. She didn't faint but arguing the point with Trey would get her nowhere. "Where's Beau? I haven't seen him since I came back down."

"Beau had to leave early. Something to do with cargo coming in," Trey said. "Are you up to walking? We should circulate."

She nodded. After placing her glass on the bench, she took his hand and rose to her feet. As they started to move, she noticed Lulabelle Woods. "I see Miss Lulabelle is making the rounds."

"Darling woman, she has monopolized all of Andrew's time this evening." Trey gave her a smug smile. "I'll have to thank her for that."

Alex rolled her eyes.

Mrs. Woods disengaged herself from the people she talked to and moved toward Trey and Alex.

"There you are! I've been looking for you for almost an hour. Andrew regrets that he had to leave early, but he had some urgent business that he had to take care of. He does wish you well."

"Thank you, Mrs. Woods." Alex smiled. "That's very kind."

Mrs. Woods smiled back. "Yes, well, you are going to be my friend's niece soon."

"Lulabelle, where have you been? I've been looking for you for at least a half hour."

Lulabelle turned at the sound of the voice. "Rose, I've been waiting by the gazebo. Right where you left me earlier when you went charging toward the house. Did you catch whoever it was stomping in your garden?"

"Ah, well, no." Rose reddened. "I found out I was mistaken. No footprints. Come, I need a refreshment."

Once they were out of earshot Alex turned to Trey. "What do you suppose that was all about?"

Trey shrugged. "I don't know. Aunt Rose doesn't go near the gardens here. She hates them."

"Then what did she see that would piss her off enough to lie?" Alex questioned.

"Piss her off?"

"Yea, you know, rattled." At the negative shake of his head she added, "Anger." She stumbled over a small root.

Trey tightened his grip. "Are you all right? Perhaps you should sit down again."

"Trey, I'm fine. I haven't gotten sick in a while, and my head's clear now."

He led her over to the gazebo. "Still, you should rest a bit more."

She sighed her acquiescence. "If it will make you happy."

Alex sat on the top stair that lead up to the gazebo. Opening her fan, she tried to reassure him. "Trey, I'm fine, really."

As he began to explain why she needed to rest, Alex did what she always did when someone lectured her. She tuned him out. Looking around, she noticed how nice and quiet it was around this side of the house. All she heard was the chirp of a few crickets. No wonder she liked this side for stargazing. Movement inside the house caught her attention. The rooms on the second floor were highly visible from here.

"...Alex, are you listening to me?"

"Huh, oh yeah. Um, whose rooms are up there?"

"Yours, Aunt Rose's, several guest rooms, why?"

Alex looked at him, laughter dancing in her eyes. "I think I know what garden your aunt meant."

He tilted his head a little to the right. "Excuse me?"

"Look." She pointed toward the room. The lamp in her room was still lit. Alex and Trey could see Fleurette as she walked past Alex's open door as she headed down the hallway.

"She saw me carrying you into the bedroom."

Alex nodded. "But she must have headed toward the house before she saw the doctor."

Trey started to laugh. "No wonder she came in mad as a March hare."

Alex looked at him oddly. Then she shook her head. Some of this century's colloquialisms seemed strange, but then most of what she said was strange to everyone here. "March hare, huh?"

"And what would you say? Pissed off?" he asked.

She smiled. "You remembered."

"I wonder if Mrs. Woods and Andrew Leroux saw anything," Trey said.

Alex ran her fingers over her silk dress. To her, Trey was reaching for straws. "What is it between the two of you?"

"Nothing." Trey stood up. "It's history now."

Alex looked up at him. "The man is your rival. Although I can't understand why."

"That is none of your concern." Trey took a few steps before turning around. "I'm going to get myself a drink. Would you like one?"

"No, thank you."

Alex watched his retreating back. Whatever went on between Trey and Andrew made a deep scar. It was obvious Trey wouldn't tell her. She wondered who would.

CHAPTER 17

Trey ran his fingers through his hair as he poured over the numbers one more time. Something just wouldn't add up. Engrossed so deeply, he didn't notice anyone enter his office. The soft click of the door didn't penetrate his thoughts either. A large vellum envelope thrust under his nose did. "What is that?"

"I had the same question," responded Alexandra.

He sat back in his leather chair to stare up at her, running his fingers through his hair again. His heart skipped a beat when he noticed how pale she looked. It had only been two weeks since their engagement party, and although the doctor gave her a clean bill of health, he still worried that she might have a setback.

"Go on. Open it up."

His thumb slid under the flap, lifting it from the broken wax seal. He pulled the card out of the envelope. It was an RSVP card. "To our wedding? When did you send these out?"

Alexandra fanned herself with five other envelopes baring a striking resemblance to the one Trey held. Loose tendrils of hair moved in the breeze they made. "I didn't."

Trey stood up. Now he understood her pale face. "Aunt Rose."

As Alexandra followed him up to Rose's room, she asked, "Why would she do this without our permission?"

"You haven't been around my aunt long enough. She does whatever she wants, always has." Trey wanted to burst through the door. Instead, he took a deep breath to calm himself before knocking.

They heard Rose humming to herself as her cane tapped its way across her bedroom floor to the door. Leaning heavily on the doorknob, she smiled at them both. "And what brings you two up to my room at the same time?"

Trey handed Rose the one envelope. "Oh good. They're starting to arrive."

"Good?" questioned Alex. "This is not good." She held out the five other envelopes.

Rose took them and slipped them into a pocket. "Of course it is."

"Aunt Rose, you had no right," said Trey. He gestured for Alexandra to sit in one of the two chairs in the room.

"Now you listen to me, Trey Dalton. If I waited for you two to come to your senses, this wedding would never take place."

"This wedding isn't supposed to take place," blurted Alexandra, still standing next to the chair he indicated earlier. Her cheeks heated up when she felt two sets of eyes on her. She looked from Trey to Rose, then back to Trey. "Are you saying you changed your mind and want to get married now? To me?"

"Your eyes light up when you're angry." Trey grinned.

"I don't care if my whole body catches on fire!" Alex stomped her foot. "I thought the invitations angered you too!"

Trey's eyes darkened at the thought of her on fire, but not in anger. He'd like to be the one to set the match. These thoughts were dangerous for him to think. Already, the desire to make these ideas a reality grew strong. He turned back to his aunt. "She's right. You shouldn't have sent out the invitations."

"I had to." Rose crossed her arms over her chest. "Even with me here, you two have been living under the same roof for too long. If the invitations didn't go out quickly enough people would begin to talk. There's been enough of that about this family."

Trey knew she meant the vicious talk that circulated when he first returned home after the war. Many hated him. He found animals poisoned, and crops destroyed those first few years. He thought everything had finally calmed down. Until Alexandra showed up. Perhaps Aunt Rose had the right idea. He grabbed Alexandra's arm. "I'll talk to Alexandra."

As he dragged her out of his aunt's room, Alexandra protested. "Talk to me about what? You aren't seriously considering this. Are you?"

He stopped in the hall. "All I know is that Aunt Rose could be right. Perhaps someone, not happy with our living arrangements, is the one doing the sabotage."

"They'd burn a barn over this?"

"I don't know. That piece of the puzzle doesn't fit, but the rest does. Perhaps they hoped to scare you off or force me to take drastic measures to protect you."

"Like making me your wife?" Her brow creased. "That doesn't make any sense."

"If we marry, the saboteur might stop," Trey said.

"And what if it doesn't," she asked.

"Hopefully our marriage will appease whoever is doing this and I won't have to answer that question," said Trey.

~

A light breeze stirred the netting around her bed. Alex just finished another entry in her journal. She sighed. It was the first evening in weeks where she didn't have her gown plastered to her body. Her mind drifted off slowly.

She could feel hands on her. What were they doing? She tried to fight them off but found her arms wouldn't work. The voices she heard were garbled. They sounded like bees buzzing in her ear. A giggle escaped her lips.

"She's still with us," someone said.

"Oh, thank God." That voice belonged to her grandmother.

"What happened here?"

"She fainted," said her grandmother after she paused for a moment.

Alex knew why she paused. These people probably wanted to know what she was doing behind the rope that blocked the picture. Her eyes fluttered open. "Grams?"

"I'm right here, Alexandra."

"Grams…" Her voice faltered. "I've been having the wildest dream. I went back in time and met Trey Dalton. He's the sexiest man I've ever seen."

"Are you sure you're dreaming?" Her voice sounded strange. Like she was a million miles away.

"I…I don't know. I don't think so. Am I dreaming?"

"Can't say, just enjoy yourself. Follow your heart, chile. I'll be here waiting for you."

"When do I get to come home?"

"Soon, Alexandra, soon. You have a job to do first."

"Okay, Grams what… Grams?" Everything turned gray on her again. Flashes of light exploded behind her eyelids. Alex opened her eyes, expecting to find herself in a hospital room. Instead, she was back in Trey's house, more confused than ever. What exactly did she just see? Evidence that this was only a dream after all, or a snippet from her own time. Alex sat up in her bed.

Thinking on the conversation she had with her grandmother made Alex realize that her grams questioned her about this being a dream. The only time she did this was when she wanted Alex to see the truth. Alex had been right all along. This was real. What should she do now?

Grams told her to follow her heart. Her heart wanted to be with Trey. She wasn't quite sure when her feelings for Trey had deepened, but at least now she had her family's consent. Her grandmother knew her future.

She had the diary.

JULY 25th, 1878
Dear Grams,
I'm getting married in a couple weeks…

The next morning, she woke early. After donning her robe, she went down into the kitchen.

"Why, Miss Alex, what are you doing up so early?" Fleurette had just started to beat some eggs. The aroma of freshly brewed coffee filled the air.

"Couldn't sleep anymore." She eyed the coffeepot sitting on the stove longingly. "How long before it's ready?"

Fleurette laughed. "I'll pour you a cup right now."

Alex blew on the hot brew before putting it to her lips. The heat from the coffee burnt her tongue, before it slid down her throat, and warmed her stomach. She drank half of her second cup before Trey came in from the fields.

He stopped in the doorway when he spotted her. "Alexandra! I didn't expect to see you up so early. Did you sleep all right?"

"Oh yes." She smiled over her cup. Trey stepped in and turned toward Fleurette to take the full plate she offered him.

"As a matter of fact, I realized that your aunt's right."

"Really?" Trey turned to stare at Alex. "Then you want to go through with the wedding?"

"Of course." Alex didn't add that her grandma told her to follow her heart, which was exactly what she planned to do. Being Trey's wife was something she secretly desired. Of course she'd never tell Trey that.

"Okay. I'll send word to our priest and make sure that the day Aunt Rose put on the invitation is still open. That gives you two weeks."

"What is expected of me?" Alex cradled her cup. "Or do you know?"

"That is a question you should ask Aunt Rose. She's the etiquette expert."

She took another sip of her coffee. "I'll talk to her once I dress properly."

Alex worked on her third cup of coffee while Trey ate his breakfast. Yawning, she wished she hadn't stayed up most of the night. Normally, two cups would sustain her. After Alex finished consuming a fourth cup of coffee, Fleurette followed her upstairs to help her dress. Properly attired, she approached Rose's quarters. She rapped against the door. "Rose? May I come in?"

The familiar thump of Rose's cane grew louder as she came closer to the door. "Alexandra! Of course you can come in."

The door swung wide.

"Thank you." Alex clasped her hands in front of her. That hateful bustle was in place, as was the corset and whatever else she needed to keep Rose and Trey happy. She stepped into Rose's room. "I need your help."

"Of course, chile. What can I help you with?"

Alex sucked in her breath. "I need to learn everything to make sure the wedding goes off properly."

Rose paused for just a second. "Then you'll wed my Trey?"

"Yes." Alex nodded. She watched in amazement as Rose changed in front of her eyes. She started to pace as she spouted off all the things that they'll need to do before the wedding. "Then we'll have to make sure that your dress is well fit. You seem to have lost a little weight. Well, no matter, I'm sure Fleurette can make the proper adjustments. Do you want any bridesmaids? I know your family and friends are too far away, but if you'd like to invite someone in particular, then we can."

"What about Elizabeth?" she squeezed into the one-sided conversation.

"That is a good idea." Rose stopped pacing for a moment. "You will need two people to stand with you as witnesses. I assume Trey will ask Beau. Elizabeth is a good choice for you. Although you really don't know her very well, she'll understand when she learns that California is too far a journey for your friends and family to make. I'll have Trey talk to her father for you."

"But you have told people that I'm from New Orleans. Aren't they going to expect some of my relatives to show up?" Alex asked.

"Oh no. They know you to be a New Orleans lady, but your father moved you out to California when you were a young girl. His scientific studies sent him out there."

Alex was amazed at how easily everything fit in Rose's fabrication. She nodded absently as Rose went on to talk about the cake, and flower arrangements. The list of things to do grew so quickly, Alex wondered if she made the right decision in asking for Rose's help. No wonder so many people eloped in her time. It took several hours, and a lot of nodding, before she escaped Rose's rooms. At least she knew everything would be handled properly. Rose seemed to be very thorough.

The next two weeks flew by. The day of the wedding, Alex awoke to the sound of Fleurette throwing back the curtains in her room.

"Rise and shine, Miss Alex. Today is your happy day," Fleurette said as she bustled about the room.

Alex groaned before pulling the sheets up over her head. "I've changed my mind. Tell Trey to forget it." Silence. She peeked out from under the sheets.

Fleurette stood, staring as if she had gone mad. "You...you want to cancel the wedding?"

"No." She didn't realize her words would frighten Fleurette so. "I was just teasing. The thought of being the center of attention just gives me the willies."

"Who is Willie?" Fleurette asked.

Alex laughed. Throwing back the covers, she stood up and stretched. "Just a phrase. It means I'm scared."

"But, Miss Alex, you ain't got nothin' to be scared of. Mr. Trey is a good man. He'll treat you right." Fleurette started to lay out the undergarments she needed to wear with her gown.

Alex eyed the corset and bustle balefully. "I know he will."

Fleurette pointed to a tray she had set on a small table earlier. "I brought your coffee, Miss Alex."

"You are a wonderful person," Alex said as she took a cup. Lifting the silver pot that sat on the tray, she poured herself a cup. A cat-like grin spread across her face as she inhaled the aroma of the fresh brew.

Maybe the day wouldn't be so bad after all.

~

*A*lex watched as her carriage drew up in front of the house. She shook her head. The crisp lace pinned to her head crinkled with her movement. "I can't believe I'm actually going through with this."

"Did you say something, dear?" asked Rose, as she came into the room.

Alex turned around, finding herself wrapped up in the long train of her white gown. "Oh no. Just talking to myself."

Rose stopped just inside the door. She rested her hand against her heart. Alexandra looked like a fairy princess in her beaded dress. "I wish Trey's parents could be here. They'd be so proud."

The praise made her nervous. Her heart beat a little harder. She changed the subject. "What's that you have in your hand?"

"Oh, what every bride needs. Something old. This has been in the family for years," Rose said as she pinned an ivory broach to the gown. "It's a likeness of my great-grandmother. Then something new." Rose handed her a new handkerchief. "You might need this later."

Alex tucked it up in her sleeve.

"Something borrowed," Rose continued.

"The broach is borrowed," Alex interrupted.

Rose ignored her. "This is my best fan."

Alex watched as Rose fastened it to her wrist. She couldn't help but open it. It was a beautiful mother-of-pearl and lace fan.

"And something blue." Rose handed her a swatch of cloth.

"Where do I put this?" she questioned.

Rose gestured toward the bodice. Without another word, she headed toward the door.

Alex hastily stuffed it down the front of her sweetheart neckline before following Rose.

The two women sat in the carriage, with Fleurette sitting up top with the driver. Neither said much since both were nervous about what the day would bring.

A loud shout startled both women. Rose put her hand on her heart.

Alex rapped on the roof of the carriage.

"Hang on, ma'am. Someone is coming up fast."

Alex stared at Rose for just a minute, before leaning out the window of the coach. The only thing she saw was a man on a buckboard racing to get by. "It's nothing. Looks like someone wants to get to the church before we do."

She kept looking out the window, watching as the other vehicle caught up with theirs. Another shout caught her attention, followed by a loud bang, and then she felt the whole carriage lurch.

Before she could move, the carriage groaned, tilted, and started to slide into the ditch.

CHAPTER 18

"*A*re you all right, Rose?" asked Alex. She heard a muffled reply. Their carriage had slid on its side into a ditch. Looking out the door, Alex could see the clear blue sky. So much for exiting like a lady. She reached for the door above her but found her arms wouldn't reach. Perhaps if she braced her feet on the walls of the carriage she could climb out. Her cumbersome gown pinned her down. Somehow, it got trapped beneath her, making movement difficult. She slumped against one wall, feeling something bite into her back.

Alex reached behind her. Her hand came across a smooth cylindrical object. She pulled. Then pulled again. When she freed the item, it came flying over her head, whacking it in the process and pulling part of her skirt over her face.

"Great, and it's not the part that was trapped," she grumbled. She stared at what she held. Rose's cane. A smile spread across her face. At least she could now get out with the help of it. Setting the head of the cane against the door, she pushed. Nothing happened.

The latch must have caught. How was she going to turn the knob from her position? The neck of the cane was too wide. She fiddled, and fought, and cursed, which brought a few muffled comments from Rose, but she did snag the handle and forced the door open. After hooking the handle over the side, Alex pulled herself up as far as she could before trying to straighten her legs. A ripping sound made her cringe.

Hopefully that sound came from her petticoat, not an important part of her gown. Both hands gripped the outside of the carriage as she lifted herself out. She lay across the side and looked down at Rose.

"Rose, are you okay?" Absently, Alex patted her head. Her veil had disappeared. She spotted it in the mud at the bottom of the carriage.

"I'm fine." A familiar snap filled the air. "Don't you think it's about time you started calling me Aunt Rose?"

"All right, Aunt Rose. Can you get out on your own?"

"Of course not! I believe I am wedged in here a little too tightly."

Alex drummed her fingers against the side of the carriage. It had slid into the deep ditch, so if she could get Rose out of it she would be able to just slide down to the ground. "So how are we going to get you out of there?"

"I don't know, but you better hurry. Water is starting to seep into the carriage."

"No prob..." A distinct click of a pistol hammer made Alex look up. Her eyes narrowed at the man who held a gun on her. Although tall, and slightly large, his body showed little muscle.

She could take him. "Is that thing loaded?"

"Yes, ma'am," he said. "Now if you'd kindly..."

Alex stuck her head back into the carriage. "Aunt Rose, there's a man up here holding a gun on me."

Alex and her attacker heard her sharp intake of breath. She looked back up at the man who had climbed up on the carriage with her. "Are you going to shoot me?"

He pulled his hat off his head. "No, ma'am."

She glanced back down at Rose before speaking to him. "Then help me get her out of the carriage."

The man hesitantly took a quick glance down though the open carriage door. "I can't. I'm ... I'm supposed to..."

Alex's eyes widened. "You can't let her die in there!"

"Die? Oh no, ma'am, I..." He glanced back down at the opening.

Tears brimmed her eyes. "Aunt Rose can't get out of there by herself. She..." Alex hiccupped. "She can't walk without this cane. Without help she'll die! Look. The carriage is starting to fill with water!"

Before the man had a chance to look into the carriage again, Alex blocked the entrance with her head again and spoke to Rose. "Aunt Rose, you all right? Can you feel your legs?"

"What?" Rose looked at Alex, confused.

"Oh God. Her hearing isn't that good." Alex looked back up at the man. "She probably doesn't even know she's in trouble. Please, you've got to help her."

He crumpled his hat while he thought. "All right, ma'am. I'll help. But you climb down off the carriage first."

She clambered down, knocking the cane into the wheels, and stepped onto the dirt road. "Thank you."

He nodded. He looked around before releasing the hammer and tucking the gun into his waistband. If the man who hired him caught him, he'd probably be dead, but he couldn't let an innocent woman drown because of him. He wasn't that evil.

Alex waited until most of his upper half was inside the carriage before she looked for Fleurette and Jessie. They were nearby, waiting for a chance to help.

～

*R*ose sniffed. Low tide. The odor of mud at low tide made her eyes water. Using her fan didn't help. She snapped it closed, then looked up at the door. How was she going to get out? She tried to stand, but slipped in the mud that seeped in.

A head popped into the window, blocking the sun. "Ma'am? I'm going to help you out, but no funny business."

Rose nodded. Who was he? Not their attacker! How did Alexandra get him to do this? It took two tries before she found herself on top of the coach. She looked out and stared as Alexandra examined the hem of her gown, tsking at the rips in her dress. Alexandra never cared about the way her clothes looked before. Why did she worry now?

"Oh dear. I've torn the lace. Do you think Trey will wait while we repair it?"

Rose looked at Alexandra strangely. What had gotten into her? She thanked the man absently as he helped her down off the carriage.

"Well, I can't marry him looking like this, can I?" Alexandra asked, holding out her skirt.

Her rescuer spoke. "I'm sorry, ma'am, but you're not gettin' married today."

"Oh? Was there a change of plans?" asked Alexandra.

"You might say that," he said.

"Good. That will give me time to repair my dress."

Rose started to open her mouth.

"Are you feeling okay?" Alexandra grabbed her arm. "I know this is a bit much for you? Do you need your cane?"

Rose stared at Alexandra. "I'm fine."

"Perhaps you should sit down. There's a nice shady tree over there. Do you need your cane?"

"My cane?" She looked over to where it had dropped. The wedged cane protruded between the wheels. Alex could have retrieved it while their attacker helped her out of the carriage. Why was she worried about it now? She looked back at Alexandra.

Alexandra's eyes slid to the trees several feet behind the coach where Fleurette and Jessie waited.

Rose's eyes widened in understanding. If they could distract him, it would give them a chance to overpower him. "Of course, I need my cane."

Alexandra lifted her shirts. "I'll get it for you."

Just as she reached the wheel the soft click of a gun hammer being pulled back filled her ears. "Hold it right there, missy."

Alex stared at her rescuer as he pointed his gun at her. Perhaps he wasn't going to be as easy to subdue as she thought. He bent down to grab the cane. "I can't let you ladies have a weapon."

"I don't need one," mumbled Alex as she struck him in the neck. He crumpled at her feet. She massaged the heel of her hand. That hurt. "How far is it to the church?"

"About ten minutes by horse," said Fleurette as she and Jessie hurried up to them.

"Which is when the wedding is supposed to start." Jessie reminded them.

"Oh man," grumbled Alex. "Trey is going to hate me."

"What about one of the horses? We could send a message to Trey. Explain why we were delayed," said Rose.

"They ran off," said Alex.

"Not really, no," said Jessie. He tilted his head toward a nearby field.

Rose shielded her eyes. "It's Buttercup."

One of Alex's brows arched. "Isn't that the one that threw me?"

"Yes, ma'am," said Jessie.

"Great." Alex felt Rose's fan on her arm.

"You're not going," said Rose.

Alex placed her hands on her hips. "I'm the one who's supposed to get married."

"Not looking like that. What would people think? I will go and tell Trey what happened." Rose nodded to Jessie who ran toward the horse. "Fleurette will help you freshen up."

"You? I've never seen you on a horse," she argued.

"Just because you've never seen it doesn't mean a thing." Jessie brought the horse over for her and helped her climb up into the saddle.

Alex felt her jaw drop. That woman was good. She wished she could be there when Rose told Trey what happened. Of course he was going to lose it when he heard they were attacked. That anger she didn't want to see.

Rose clicked at the horse and they took off toward the church.

"Trey is going to go ballistic," said Alex as she watched them disappear from sight.

"Ballistic?" Fleurette asked as she examined Alex's wedding dress.

"Yeah, very angry."

"Ah." Fleurette plucked at the hem of Alex's dress. "I can fix this." She paused for a moment. "Mr. Trey is jus' being a man."

"I know," said Alex. "But Aunt Rose is going to tell him that his bride will be a little late, in front of a church full of people, because someone tried to stop the wedding. I want to see that performance."

"They're goin' to take one look at Aunt Rose astride that horse and be on theirs," said Jessie. "She probably won't have to say a word."

$\sim$

*A*lex marveled at the cloud of dust that moved toward them. "My goodness, Fleurette, that has to be the whole congregation."

Fleurette had her sitting beneath a canopy of trees when people started to arrive. Trey's horse skidded to a halt first. She watched as Trey stopped and stared.

Light filtered through the leaves, tiny beams of sunlight danced in her hair as well as across her face and clothing. "You look beautiful."

A slight blush filled her cheeks. "Thank Fleurette." Alex was amazed herself. Fleurette did wonders with her dress. It showed no sign of damage.

Trey gripped her arm. "What happened?"

What did Rose tell him? She looked at his aunt and saw her fan move slowly. They had tied the man up to the carriage wheel, which was hidden by the trees surrounding her, making sure he couldn't move until they could get him to the jail, but by the look on Rose's face she didn't mention their assailant. What could she tell him? She was saved by the priest.

Father Francis approached them. "Are ye ready?"

"Yes," said Alex.

"Then let's begin." Alex and Trey took their places as the priest opened his bible.

$\sim$

*T*he music was loud, and off-key.

Trey whispered in her ear as he swung her across the impromptu dance floor. "So tell me what happened."

"Sure," said Alex, eyes brimming with mischief. "But you tell me what Aunt Rose told you first."

His eyes narrowed. "Why?"

Alex blinked. "She's your aunt and you have to ask?"

Trey watched her face as he replied, "She said that one of the horses got spooked and bolted, causing the carriage to turn over."

Alex gave him a brilliant smile. "That's what happened."

Trey glared at her. "Why don't I believe you?"

Alex laced her fingers with his. "Walk with me." A gentle tug got him moving again. They moved away from the party, walking around the cove of trees toward the hidden carriage. She wondered how long it would take for Trey to notice the man tied to the wheel. Trey stopped moving a few seconds later when he spotted the attacker Alex had subdued.

Well, that didn't take long.

"Who is he?"

"He won't tell me his name. But Jessie says he works for Miss Lulabelle," said Alex.

Trey shook his head. "Unless he's the foreman, and they've had the same foreman for seven years, a white man wouldn't take a job at Lulabelle's plantation."

"Well he's been seen several times coming from the Woods's plantation. He's either working for somebody there or likes to trespass."

Trey looked at the prisoner one more time before they moved away from the carriage. "How did you stop him?"

"A chop to the neck."

He tried to ease the fear that gripped him. "No flying kicks?"

"Not in this dress." She pasted a smile on her face as they approached the party again. "Are you angry?"

"You could have gotten yourself killed," he said softly. "That thought shakes me to my core."

"My life wasn't threatened, Trey. That man only wanted to make sure that I didn't make it to the church on time. He was very polite otherwise. He even helped Aunt Rose out of the carriage."

Trey laid a hand on her arm, stopping her for a few seconds. "You waited until after he helped Rose out before 'decking' him?"

She smiled at his use of her twentieth-century language. "Yes. Try to imagine Jessie, Fleurette, and myself lifting your aunt out of that rolled carriage. He was a much better choice."

"You're exasperating," Trey said. He turned as Beau walked up with champagne glasses in his hands.

"And you love it."

~

The gentle plopping of the horse's hooves lulled her to sleep, and then a pothole jolted her awake. Alex grumbled. "Sure will be happy when they finally pave these roads."

She snuggled close to Trey's warm body. Sleep overtook her once more before she heard Trey ask what 'pave' meant. When she did reopen her eyes, it was to Trey gently shaking her.

"We're home," he said.

Home. That word had a wonderful sound to it. Right now, all she wanted was a warm bed to curl up in. Yawning, she took a right at the top of the stairs.

She frowned when she noticed the door to her room open. The darkened room looked vacant, like she had never lived there.

"Alexandra."

She jumped at the sound of Rose's voice. "Fleurette moved your things to the master bedroom."

"Oh." It took a few minutes for the words to sink in. "But I thought…"

"We must keep up appearances."

Alex glared at the woman. What did Rose have, a mouse in her pocket?

She yawned again before heading toward Trey's room. As she neared the room, she formulated her plan. She'd talk to him. After all, he agreed that this would be a marriage of convenience. He'd have to see her side.

The door to Trey's room stood open. A soft light spilled into the hallway. Humming came from within.

Alex swallowed hard. She knew who hummed that tune. It was Fleurette, and she knew it meant trouble. No matter what her plans were, Fleurette had a few of her own.

"Fleurette," said Alex, preparing to send her out of the room.

"There you are, Miss Alex. I was beginning to get worried. Please, sit right here." She gestured toward the chair that sat in front of a vanity.

"This isn't necessary."

Fleurette clutched her brush to her chest. "Miss Alex, please let me do this. I want to give you and Mr. Trey a gift. This was all I could think of."

"Oh man." Alex couldn't say no to the pleading look in Fleurette's eyes. She sat in the chair Fleurette indicated earlier. "I know I'm going to regret this."

When Fleurette left, Alex sighed. The simple cotton gown flowed down to her ankles, making sure that she was properly covered, but she'd read enough romance books to know that the lighting in the room would backlight her perfectly. This gown wouldn't hide a thing. Fleurette had painstakingly removed her hairpiece and brushed her hair until it shined, which now reached her shoulders.

She curled up in the bed that dominated the room, but sleep eluded her. Counting sheep didn't work, but she hoped that sleep would give her a little more time. Yet putting off the inevitable would just make matters worse. The few times she had tried to have sex were utter failures. She never knew what to do. In the end, she wouldn't go through with it, losing the man and a little more of her self-esteem.

What kept Trey? The sooner she talked to him the better she would feel. Could she reason with him?

Did she want to?

"What has put such a frown on your face?"

Alex jumped at the sound of his voice. "Trey, I thought maybe you... Um, where were you?"

"Helping Jessie." He undid the top buttons of his vest as he closed their bedroom door. He noticed her nervousness. "Buttercup doesn't care for too many people."

She snorted. Buttercup didn't like anyone. "And the man who tried to stop the wedding?"

"Sleeping in the livery barn." Trey smiled at her. The candlelight deepened the plans on his face. "Jessie will stay with him until I get a chance to take him to the sheriff tomorrow."

The room suddenly got smaller. "Um, Trey…"

His vest slid off his broad shoulders. He hung it on a nearby chair. "Yes?"

Alex swallowed as he started to work on the buttons of his shirt before removing his cuff links and sitting them on a bureau. "Um, we need to talk."

After slipping his suspenders down, Trey peeled the shirt off. "So talk," he said as he worked on the top button of his trousers.

"Okay, um…" Heat filled her cheeks. "Could you stop that? You're making it hard for me to think."

He looked into her eyes. "What is there to think about?"

Alex licked her lips. "This marriage of ours."

One of Trey's brows rose. Deep green eyes pinned her to the spot. "Ah, yes." He stepped close to her and took her hand. "You're my wife now."

"I vowed to cherish you, and I do," he murmured as he kissed the inside of her wrist. "To honor you." He gently cupped her cheek. "To love you, Alex." His hand slid down the side of her neck and dipped inside the gown. "Let me love you."

"I…"

He gently muzzled her neck. "I've wanted you from the first moment I saw you. Let me show you what love feels like."

CHAPTER 19

The moment his lips touched hers, she felt her body surrender. Part of her mind wanted to know what happened to the plan she formulated on her way to their bedroom. The part that controlled her at the moment, though, didn't like the plan and had already trashed it. She felt herself moan as his lips blazed a trail over to her ear, before nibbling their way down her throat. Alex tilted her head back to give him better access.

"God, Alexandra, you taste so good." He emphasized his words by gliding his tongue down along her neck.

She felt her knees go weak. "Trey," she said breathlessly. He recaptured her lips before she could say anything more.

His teeth gently nipped at her lower lip. The feather-like caress of his tongue seduced her into opening her mouth for him.

As their kiss deepened, Alex felt a heat unfurl inside of her. Starting deep within, slowly igniting her blood.

Her hands spread across his chest, stroking the silky thin layer of black hair. A satisfied smile spread across her lips when she slid her hands around him and felt the warmth of the smooth skin on his back. His muscles rippled under her fingers as he loosened her gown and pushed it off her shoulders so it could slide to the floor. Her fingers hooked into his trousers, trying to unfasten them. Zippers hadn't been invented yet. She tried to stifle a giggle as she heard buttons popping against a nearby wall.

"What is so funny?" Trey murmured against her lips.

"Nothing," she murmured back.

Trey pulled back to look at her. "Now, why don't I believe that?"

She melted at the love and desire she saw in his eyes. No one had ever looked at her this way before. Her finger gently traced the velvet texture of his lips. "Trey, I think…"

"Shh," he said, placing a finger against her lips. "Don't think, just feel."

"I'm afraid."

"Don't be." Taking her face in his hands, he rained kisses across her brow, cheeks, and lips. "I'd never hurt you."

"I know that." She placed her hand against his chest. "I just don't want you to be…disappointed."

A soft laugh escaped his lips. "You haven't disappointed me so far. Drove me crazy, yes. Made me mad with desire, very much." He kissed the edge of her lips. "I want to make love to you."

Alex swallowed the lump in her throat. She wanted the same thing, but fear controlled her. Her eyes stared at the floor.

Trey watched her, allowing her to make the first move.

A few seconds ago, she wouldn't have stopped him. If only he hadn't talked to her. Beneath her hand, she felt the rapid beat of his heart. She knew she wanted this. Why fight it? Alex let out the breath she held. She knew why, because this was real.

She looked up at Trey. This was something she wanted. When she tried to be with a man before it always ended in failure, but she didn't love those men. Her heart fluttered. Love? When did she fall in love with him? It didn't happen overnight, but slowly. Her love for him started when he trusted her enough to let her stay. Then each time their paths crossed it got deeper and deeper. Love sure was sneaky. A shy smile spread across her lips. "Trey?"

He brushed a stray hair out of her face. "Yes."

"Make love to me."

His hands cupped her face as he brought her lips to his.

The sensations she felt from his lips overwhelmed her. Her whole body came alive. Alex didn't realize that Trey had lowered her to the bed until she felt the stiff linen sheets against her back.

His lips blazed a trail down her chin and across her collarbone. The heat spread, pooling deep within her. She gasped when his mouth closed over a hardened nipple. The moist heat of his mouth sucked and pulled against the hardened core. Her fingers buried deep in his hair. A whimper escaped her when he released his hold, but a catlike smile slipped across her face when he paid equal attention to her other breast.

Deftly, his hands moved down her stomach, to the center of her desire. A new sensation assailed her as his fingers entered her. Her breath caught. Muscles she didn't know she had contracted against those fingers.

"Ah, Alex," Trey muttered.

"Trey," she gasped. "Now, please!" She tugged at him. Desire made her wanton as she moved beneath him.

He didn't need any more encouragement.

She felt the bed dip when his weight shifted. The fire in his eyes burned her. There was no turning back. A pressure built inside her as he entered. She felt Trey's hesitation when he broke through her virginity. Now was not the time for him to change his mind.

She wrapped her legs around him. A new sensation caught her attention. Feeling him penetrate deeper by her movement caused delightful friction.

He pulled out and slid back in again slowly.

Her eyes widened. That felt good. She clutched him when he did it again. Experimenting a little, she learned that her body knew exactly what to do. In the beginning she was hesitant, but with Trey's encouragement, she started to move with him. Their bodies danced to a music all their own. Slowly she felt a different pressure start to build. She raced with the wind, moving toward the sensation that was building in her, only to feel it move just a little ahead of her. Then, suddenly, it flowed over her.

Fireworks went off in her head. Her body shook from the explosion that took her over the edge.

She lay on the bed, Trey's head cradled against her bosom. "Wow."

Trey kissed the skin where his head lay. "That is a very appropriate word."

Alex smiled. That was the only way she knew how to express what she just experienced. Her girlfriends lied. Chocolate was not better than this. She even saw fireworks, something she thought only happened in romance novels.

"Trey?"

He moved up to give her a gentle kiss. "Yes?"

She searched his face with wide eyes. Perhaps he didn't feel the same sensations she did. "Was I...was it all right?"

She heard him laugh. He nuzzled her neck, leaning his hips into her. "Is that proof enough for you?"

She could feel him harden against her thigh. A slight shift of her leg got a groan out of him.

He kissed her, leaving her breathless. "Perhaps I should show you just how much I enjoy this with you."

"Perhaps you should," she sighed, rapping her arms around his neck.

He did.

~

It amazed Alex how easily she fell into the role of Mrs. Dalton. The days were busy teaching the children and learning how to manage the household from Aunt Rose. Her evenings were filled with making love with Trey. She couldn't get enough, which didn't seem to bother Trey at all. In fact, some evenings they found themselves being reprimanded by Aunt Rose because they wanted to retire so early.

A month passed. At breakfast one morning Rose put her teacup down and announced, "I'm leaving tomorrow."

"So soon?" asked Alex.

Trey started to choke on his egg.

Alex shot him a glare.

"Yes, chile. It's time I returned to my home. You seem to have everything under control." Rose looked purposely at Trey. "You two don't need an old fussbudget like me around."

"We'll miss you, Aunt Rose," Trey said.

Alex shot him another look that asked where his manners were.

She looked at Rose. "Are you sure?"

"Of course, dear." A snap filled the room as Rose opened her fan. "My home has gone unattended for too long now. But I'll come back to visit. Perhaps when I do come back you'll have some more wonderful news for me."

Alex fought a grin. She knew exactly what Rose was hinting at. "We'll see, Aunt Rose, we'll see."

*I*t took her and Fleurette all day to pack Rose's things. Of course, a large part of the day was spent in arguments. Rose felt that Alex shouldn't be doing menial labor now that she was the lady of the house. It took several hours, and a firm I'll do whatever I want to shut Rose up. Alex had no intention of changing just because she married Trey. Despite the fact Rose started the argument by saying she didn't want Alex doing menial things, she actually seemed happy when Alex refused to listen to her.

After a lot of hugs, and a few unshed tears the next day, Trey and Alex stood on the porch, watching Rose's carriage leave. Alex swore she heard Trey sigh.

He pulled his fob out of his pocket, checked the time, and headed back inside to his study.

Alex eased herself down onto the steps. Rose might have been meddlesome, but she would miss her.

*T*he sun sank deeper on the horizon, painting streaks of purple and fuchsia across the sky. Crickets started to chirp as twilight deepened.

"I've always loved this time of day," said Alex. She pointed up to the darkening sky. "You can just start to see the stars fill the sky."

Trey sat in the glider beside her. Putting his filled pipe to his lips, he struck a match and lit the tobacco. Smoke circled his head like a wreath.

The smell of sulfur made her nose wrinkle. As the scent of tobacco drowned out the sulfur, Alex inhaled deeply. "Hmm, is that nice."

"You are a rare woman." Trey palmed his pipe. "You like the smell of pipe tobacco, yet you threaten bodily harm if I try to light up in the house. Something my friends don't understand."

"You mean Beau." She pushed with her feet to start the glider swinging.

Trey just looked at her as he took another puff.

"Well he is the only one who knows about that particular rule. I'm sure he had a few choice words to say about it too."

Trey grinned. "Actually, I didn't give him a chance."

"How did you stop him?"

"I changed the subject." He stretched his arm out on the back of the swing.

She leaned her head against his arm. Her boots scraped across the porch as she gave the swing a gentle push.

"I've arranged to have Miss Elizabeth come to visit you," Trey said nonchalantly.

Her eyes lit up as she turned toward him. "When?" The glider swung awkwardly. She gave him an apologetic look for her sudden movement.

"Tomorrow, if that is all right with you. She'll be here in the morning." Trey couldn't help but add, "Please make sure you've had your coffee before she gets here."

Alex stuck her tongue out at him.

"I can think of better things to do with that tongue of yours." Trey reached over and pulled her into his lap.

Alex felt her insides melt as Trey lowered his head toward hers.

～

he next morning, Alex used a very unladylike gesture toward her second cup of coffee when Trey ushered Elizabeth into the living room. His smile made her sigh. How could she enjoy his outrage if he didn't understand what the gesture meant? One more thing to teach him she decided.

She offered her friend a cup of coffee, and then led her out on the porch. They sipped their coffees in silence.

Elizabeth looked over at Alex. "Married life seems to agree with you."

"It has its advantages." Alex smiled.

"What is it like?" Elizabeth asked.

"What?" Alex sat her coffee down.

Beth looked around for a moment, blushing profusely. "You know, it."

Alex looked around as well and leaned toward her friend. "Well, I found it to be very nice." She picked up her cup and took a sip.

Elizabeth's blush deepened. She took another sip from her coffee. "Mother says ladies don't enjoy it."

Alex started to cough on the last sip she took. "Um, Beth, I'm not sure we should be discussing how your mother feels about this."

She stared into her coffee cup. "Mama doesn't really like talking about it."

Alex placed her hand on Beth's arm. "At all?"

Beth shook her head, her blush still very prominent.

That changed things. If her mother wouldn't talk to her about sex, she knew she had to.

"Why don't we go for a walk?" Alex asked, sitting her coffee cup down again. "The bayou is beautiful this time of morning."

They walked along in silence. She wanted to find out what bothered Elizabeth but wasn't sure how to broach the subject. The sun glistened off the water, making Alex wish sunglasses had been invented.

"You really enjoyed it?" asked Elizabeth quietly.

Alex smiled softly and nodded.

"But Mama said only a strumpet would enjoy it. My friends say that to a real lady, it was painful, and awkward, and that his...his, well, that it looked hideous," Beth blurted out before she clamped her hand over her mouth.

Alex's lips twitched. She waited to be sure she had her laughter under control before she spoke. "The first time can be very awkward, and there is pain involved, but it doesn't have to be that way afterward. Beth, my grandmother was a unique woman, she taught me that love is a big part of the physical union and when you're in love and then share that love with your husband it makes it beautiful."

Beth didn't look convinced.

She swatted at the mosquitoes that buzzed her head. "Let me ask you something. Do your mother and father love each other?"

Elizabeth put her hand to her throat. "Of course."

"Have you come up on them without their notice and seen them kiss, or hold hands?"

"The other day they were giggling about something, and Papa never giggles." Beth blushed. "I tried to find out what made them behave this way, but Papa got mad, and Mama made me scrub the floors in the store."

"I think you came up on a private moment that embarrassed them. I'm going to make a suggestion. The next time you and your mother talk about it," Alex said, stressing the word *it*. "Ask her about love."

"Love?"

She nodded. "Sex is just the physical. Love is the emotion as well. If you ask your mom about love, you'll understand better how it is between a husband and a wife."

"Alex? How come you don't get all flustered and turn bright red like Momma does when I ask you these questions?"

"What kind of questions are those?" asked a deep voice.

Both women whirled around.

"Beau Manning, how dare you sneak up on us like that," Alex snapped at the man on horseback, who had miraculously appeared behind them.

Elizabeth turned bright red, then deathly pale.

Alex grabbed her arm, afraid that Beth would faint.

"I'm all right." Beth placed the back of her hand against her forehead. She straightened herself. "Beau, you were mean when were children, and you haven't changed a bit!"

"Ladies, I'm sorry. Truly I am. You were in such a deep conversation with each other I didn't know any other way to get your attention." He swung one leg over the pummel of his saddle and slid to the ground.

"You could have called to us."

"I did. You didn't hear me." Beau tugged on the reins so that the horse would follow as he walked back to the plantation with the two women. "What were you two discussing so seriously?"

"Roller skating," blurted Elizabeth.

Alex stared at her friend. "Right." She looked up at Beau. "I did a lot of roller-skating in California. When Beth found out, she insisted that we go. We were trying to figure out how to talk Trey and her father into letting us go tomorrow."

"And did you come up with a plan?" asked Beau.

"No," said Alex.

"Yes," said Elizabeth.

"Which is it?" Beau gave them a knowing smile.

"What she said," they said in unison, then started laughing.

Beau shook his head. "I have a plan for you. I'll be your escort, and then neither of you will have any problem. Agreed?"

They both nodded.

"Now all we have to do is talk everyone else into it."

CHAPTER 20

"Roller skating?" Trey asked.

The odd look on his face made Alex wonder if she had suddenly grown a second head. She folded her hands primly in her lap. "Yes, roller skating."

"I need to be in the fields now," he said, picking up his fork.

Alex hadn't planned on asking about this until after lunch, but Beau opened his big mouth before she could stop him. She watched Trey cut the ham on his plate. Adjusting herself in her chair, she started to answer him. "I know."

"I'll escort the ladies, Trey," Beau interrupted. "You know I'll take good care of them."

Trey chewed on the slice of ham, before swallowing. "Beau, I know the kind of escort you will be."

Elizabeth stared at her plate, a slight blush filling her cheeks.

Alex did too. Thin sliced ham lay untouched on her plate. If Trey agreed, Beau would monopolize all of Beth's time. Not something she wanted, but it looked like Elizabeth did.

"No."

Her head snapped up. "Why?"

"Because I promised Mr. Boudreaux that I'd keep my eye on her while she visits. I can't do that if she isn't here. Besides, Elizabeth's father has promised to come calling. Elizabeth should be here when he does." Trey continued to eat his meal.

"But…" They had started a lie that she knew she had to make look good.

"No, Alexandra," said Elizabeth. "Mr. Trey's right."

She looked from her husband to Elizabeth. Neither would make eye contact with her. Alex frowned as she looked back at her plate. She felt like pinching them both. Except for the clanking of silverware, the rest of the meal passed in silence. Well, as long as Beau didn't push it they wouldn't have to go, and she could explain everything to Trey later.

Trey escorted Beau out onto the front porch while the women retired to the back porch, once they finished the meal.

"Why did you have to say roller skating?" demanded Alex, her hands on her hips.

"It was the first thing I could think of." Beth said, as she sat down on a rocker.

"Why couldn't you have said horseback riding?"

"You don't like horseback riding." Elizabeth watched her friend pace back and forth. "Are you feeling well?"

"I'm fine."

"Then is something bothering you?"

She stopped pacing. "Can I ask you something personal?"

"Of course."

"Um, do you like Beau?" Alex started pacing again. "Because if you do I can ask Trey to let us go anyway." She noticed that her friend's eyes became larger as she stared just past Alex's shoulder.

"And just how do you plan on doing that?"

Alex felt Trey's deep voice slide up her spinal cord. Just his voice could arouse her. Turning around, she gave him a sultry smile. "The same way I did two nights ago."

Desire flared in his eyes as the memory of their lovemaking came back to him.

Alex smiled. She could also get to him easily.

"Are you playing matchmaker again?" Trey asked.

"Not sure. She hasn't answered my question yet." Alex turned toward her friend. "Well?"

Beth turned a bright shade of red.

Although Trey could keep his face straight, amusement filled his eyes. "I'll take that as a yes."

Alex wasn't happy but had to agree.

"I'll contact Elizabeth's family and make them aware that we're going on Sunday, after church, that way I can be your escort and if Beau joins us there will be no problem." He wrapped an arm around her waist. "Besides, I'd like to see you roller skate."

Alex smiled. "Only if you'll skate with me."

~

*A*lex stared at the cumbersome boots. What she wouldn't do for a pair of in-line skates. Oh well, as her grandma said, "If wishes were fishes, we'd all have a fry."

Once she secured the skates on, she stood up to take a test spin. It couldn't be that bad. She still had memories of the metal skates that she slipped over her Keds. Those things caused some real damage. Alex still bore a few telltale scares from falling off them. Admitting she even knew what it was like to wear the metal skates over shoes really dated herself.

A giggle escaped. Although she knew that metal wheels were available as early as the 1860s, not every rink carried them. No one here used metal wheels or even heard of plastic, but then again, people from her own time wouldn't dare use wooden or metal wheels. Plastic was the way to go, but that was still about eighty years in the future, or twenty years in her past, depending on how you looked at it. She rubbed her forehead. This could get really confusing.

"And just what are you giggling about?"

Alex smiled as she felt Trey's warm hand encase her elbow. "How much I'm going to enjoy watching you fall."

She pushed herself away from him and moved out onto the floor. It proved to be not as easy as she thought when her skates went out from under her just a few feet away from Trey.

He rolled over to her side to offer her a hand.

Alex ignored his hand as she regained her feet. "So, I'm not used to wooden wheels."

"What are you used to?"

"Plastic," she answered, dusting off herself. When she looked up, she saw the perplexed look on his face. "Sorry. It's that man-made product I told you about. Same stuff my driver's license is make of, very durable. Oh, never mind."

Trey offered his arm to Alex, then guided her over to Elizabeth. Offering an arm to each of them, he asked. "Shall we?"

They slid into the flow of skaters.

Alex spotted Beau Manning first. Her brow creased. Perfect. How was she doing to keep him away from Elizabeth? When they skated by again, she noticed Andrew Leroux. She gripped Trey's arm. "Oh man."

"What?"

She looked up at him with wide eyes. "Nothing."

"What did you see?"

"Beau is here." A bump in the oak floor made her stumble. Her grip on Trey's arm kept her from falling.

"Where?" asked Elizabeth.

"Over, wait a minute." She glanced around. Where did he go? A flash of blue caught her eye.

"Hello," said Beau as he caught up to them. He nodded as he drew up alongside Beth. "Miss Elizabeth."

"Mr. Manning."

"Why, Beauregard," Alex said in her best Southern drawl. "Fancy meeting you here."

"I told him we'd be here," Trey mumbled to her.

Her gaze went to Trey. "Why am I not surprised?"

The look he shot Alex told her to remain quiet. So she did. Besides, she didn't want to tell Trey who she also noticed skating up to join them.

"Miss Alex, you are a vision of loveliness," said Andrew as he took Alex's free arm.

"Thank you," Alex said, before tightening her grip on Trey. She prayed he wouldn't open his mouth.

"Leroux," Trey started.

The pressure on his arm increased.

Andrew nodded curtly. "Trey."

"Mr. Leroux," said Alex. "How nice to see you."

"Miss Lulabelle said you would be out of town for a month the last time she visited with Aunt Rose," said Trey.

"True. I was gone for four weeks," Andrew replied. "But I'm back now."

"It must be wonderful to travel," murmured Elizabeth.

"It is," said Beau.

"Have I ever told you about my trip to…" he asked as he led Elizabeth away from Alex, Trey, and Andrew.

Alex wanted to call them back or leave with them. She didn't want to see the confrontation she could feel brewing. If only there was a way to defuse this.

"Why are you still here, Leroux," Trey demanded.

"Paying my respects to your wife," he said.

She felt Trey drop back so he could plant himself between them. He stared at Andrew. "You're done."

After Andrew skated away, Alex glared up at Trey. "You have such a way with people."

"What would you have me do?" he grumbled. "I don't want that man near you."

She wanted to know what happened between them to make Trey behave this way, but there were certain things she knew not to ask.

"I can take care of myself." If they weren't in a public place, she'd show him instead of telling him.

"I know you can."

"Then why are you behaving like a chauvinist?"

Trey pondered her question for a minute. "Is that the same thing as a male chauvinist pig?"

"Ah, you remember that, do you?" She couldn't keep the smile from her lips. "Yes. It's an abbreviated version."

"What does it mean?"

Alex watched the floor roll by, looking for the bump that got her earlier. The sound of wooden wheels rolling against the hardwood floor filled the silence before she spoke. "Well, in my time women are more independent. Men can't tell us what to do."

Trey grinned. "I don't think many of us can now."

"I mean that a man can't dictate who a woman's friends are, where we go, if we work." She looked up to glare at him. "It is an archaic way of thinking. Any man that does is considered a chauvinist."

"And I am a chauvinist because I don't want you to get hurt? I don't understand."

"That's not what I meant. You know I can protect myself. I'm not dumb enough to get into a situation to allow myself to get hurt, yet your pride gets wounded because I don't fear Andrew as much as you do."

"I am not afraid of Andrew," he said too loudly.

"Did you say you were afraid of something?" asked Beau. He and Elizabeth had rejoined them a few seconds earlier.

"Only of you, boring my guest to tears," Trey said. "Let's get some refreshments."

Alex spotted Andrew heading toward the bleachers where his shoes were. She had trouble keeping him in view.

"What is wrong with you," Trey grumbled.

"Um, I'd like to rest for a moment. While you and Beau go get our drinks." She pointed away from where their items were. "Over there."

His brow arched. "And what is over there?"

"It's less crowded."

He spotted Andrew. "It's not crowded near our things either."

"Will you humor me?" she asked.

Two heartbeats later he grabbed Beau and headed to the refreshment stand. His terse voice floated back to her. "You better be rested when we get back."

She knew what he meant. Andrew better be gone when he came back. Alex smiled as Andrew walked up to them. "Mr. Leroux. It is so good to see you again. I must say I'm surprised that so many people like to skate."

He nodded. "Yes, ma'am." His gaze wandered over to Elizabeth.

"You remember my friend, don't you? Elizabeth Boudreaux?"

His smile lit his face. "Miss Boudreaux."

A slight blush crept up Beth's neck. "Mr. Leroux."

Alex wanted to jump for joy. Things started to go her way. All she had to do was keep Trey and Beau out of the picture for a moment.

Andrew must have read her thoughts, because he took his leave when he noticed Trey and Beau heading back to the women.

Alex could see Trey's anger and didn't want to face it. "Beau, I just realized that we haven't had our skate yet."

He looked at the two cups he held in his hands. "Trey, will you hold these for me?"

"Yes," grumbled Trey.

Alex beamed as she linked arms with Beau. They chatted pleasantly as they glided around the rink.

"I see that married life agrees with you," said Beau. "It definitely agrees with Trey."

"You think so?" She looked up at him.

"Oh yes, and I'm jealous." He smiled. "He never ventured too far from the plantation, but I could convince him to join me at the tavern once in a while. Now, he's too happy at home to think of leaving you for even a few hours. So now I have to find someone else to keep company with."

"Someone like Beth?" She reverted her eyes to the floor. She knew they were coming around to the heavily worn part in the floor and she refused to stumble again.

"Jealous? You could always come away with me," he teased.

"And have Trey chase me for the rest of my life? Don't think so." She veered away from the break. "Besides, you have too many female friends. I'd be lonely."

"You'd never be lonely," he said.

She looked up at him again. "Why?"

One corner of his mouth quirked up. "Too many servants."

"Brat." She gave him a big smile before letting go of his arm and heading back to Trey and Elizabeth.

He quirked one blond brow as he caught up with her. "Would you expect anything less?"

She turned to face him as she rolled away. Her eyes twinkled. "From you, no."

"Perhaps, I'll have to steal you away," he murmured to himself. A sigh escaped his lips as he followed her back to their friends.

~

*T*he warmth of his hands on her neck made her moan. She dropped her head forward to give him better access. They moved forward, caressing her throat. Her head rolled back. It felt good. She tried to open her eyes, but they were too heavy. The pressure on her throat increased. Alex's eyes flew open when she couldn't breathe anymore. Taking in large gulps of air, her gaze darted about. No one in sight.

She ran her fingers around the slim column of her throat, realizing she had dozed off in her chair on the porch while waiting for Trey to come in from the fields. Teaching the children had been taxing today, tiring her.

It was nothing more than a dream. A dream that seemed too real. She could still feel the pressure of those fingers on her throat when she went into the house to look at her reflection in the mirror in their room. Even though it was only a dream, she expected to find bruises.

A sigh of relief escaped when she found no marks. Then she grinned at herself. She was being silly. She had just stepped back out on the porch again when she saw the dust from someone's horse heading for the house. Who could be visiting? Beau was out of town. Elizabeth had only gone home four days ago.

Her father wouldn't let her come back for a visit so soon.

It didn't take long for her to realize the rider was male. Her eyes grew wide when she realized which male it was. The horse skidded to a stop in front of the pathway that lead up to the porch.

"Mr. Leroux! What brings you here?" She knew Trey wasn't going to like this.

"To talk to you, Miss Alexandra," he said breathlessly. "I came here to—"

"To what?" spat an angry voice.

Alex closed her eyes as she buried her hands in her skirt. This did not bode well.

"To warn you," said Andrew.

"Warn me?" scoffed Trey. "Why? To cover your tracks?"

Alex moved next to her husband and laid a hand on Trey's arm. "Please, don't do this."

"Do what? Tell him I know who's been trying to run me out of business? It won't work, Leroux." He turned his angry gaze from Alex to Andrew. "I'm onto your little game now."

Andrew's brow frowned in confusion. "My little game?"

"Yes, you know, the same one you pulled on me when we were younger?" questioned Trey. "I want you to stay away from my wife."

"What? Why?"

A red stain started to climb out from under the collar of Trey's shirt. He stomped past Alex toward the house.

"Mr. Leroux, I'm sorry. Maybe you should leave," Alex said.

"There is something you should know," he started.

The loud click of a rifle made Alex jump. She turned. Trey stood at the top of the stairs, rifle in hand. "I want you to leave. Now." The barrel started to swing up toward Andrew's chest.

Alex stepped toward Trey.

"Don't, Alexandra." He never took his eyes off Andrew. "Now get on your horse and ride."

"Are you crazy?" she demanded. Her answer was the repeat of the rifle. Small clumps of dirt hit her face when the bullet struck the dirt near Andrew's feet.

Andrew started. "Okay, Trey. I'm leaving, but you're going to wish you had listened to me." He swung up on his horse. Grabbing the reins, he sat back in the saddle. "You're going to regret this."

She watched as Andrew rode away. Her fingers were clinched in anger when she spun to glare at Trey. "You had to shoot at him? Are you crazy? This isn't the dark ages."

"You are my wife. I won't let anything happen to you."

"Look, Mr. Neanderthal. I can take care of myself," Alex snapped. "And put that damn gun away."

Trey uncocked the rifle before draping it over his arm. "I know how well you can protect yourself. I also know what a man like Andrew could do."

"What did he do to you?" she demanded.

CHAPTER 21

"That was a long time ago." His long fingers closed around the warm barrel.

"But it still bothers you." Alex knew she had to get him to talk about whatever stood between him and Andrew, one way or another. "Why won't you talk to me? Is it that painful?"

Trey's eyes locked with hers. He didn't want to bring up these old memories. Finally, he spoke. "Beau, Andrew, and I were best friends as children. Their family plantations bordered on either side of my dad's. We hunted together in our teens. I taught Andrew how to clean game. Andrew and I learned how to catch fish with just a spear from Beau." A sad smile played on his lips. "My expert horsemanship came from Andrew's training."

Alex gently pulled the rifle out of his hands and leaned the gun against the wall of the house. "It sounds like the three of you were very close."

"Until the summer of my thirteenth birthday," Trey said. "That's when Jacques Boudreaux's cousin came to visit."

"Jacques?" She entwined her fingers with his.

"My friend in France."

"Ah." Alex remembered. The other man Trey wanted to question about her. "You still think one of your friends hired me?"

"Not anymore." Trey had the grace to blush. "There were too many things that don't fit."

"Then you believe me?" she asked. Hope swelled in her chest.

"I don't care where you came from." He ran his thumbs over her knuckles. Gazing into her trusting blue eyes he wondered how could he not? "You're here now."

She looked away from him. Her voice came out very soft. "But do you believe me?"

Releasing one of her hands, he cupped her chin and tugged until she looked at him. "Yes."

Her smile dazzled him. Staring down at the face he loved so much he asked, "So where did I leave off?"

"What? Oh! Um, something about Boudreaux's cousin," she murmured.

"That's right. Boudreaux's pretty female cousin," he teased.

Her brow arched. "And of course it was love at first sight."

"It was the first time a girl caught my eye. Maybe her accent attracted me," he said. "I don't know. Andrew liked her too. We competed with each other to see who she would pick."

He stopped talking.

Alex tugged at their hands to prompt him. "So who won?"

"I did." Trey's eyes clouded for a moment. "Beau was on my side. He stacked the deck in my favor."

"And why does that bother you?"

"Because Andrew grew so jealous, Jacques's cousin feared for her life toward the end of her stay in America."

Alex's brow crinkled. "I'm not sure I follow you."

"She was supposed to meet me for a picnic, chaperoned of course, but she never came. I learned later that she went back to France. Jacques's parents said an emergency called her back, but Beau heard Andrew threatened her." Trey's hands caressed up and down her arms. "Of course, I didn't believe Beau. He's been known for his dramatics before."

"But everything changed when I came back after the war. My parents were gone. Killed. When I learned Andrew killed them, I went—"

"What?" Her brow crinkled. Her grandmother never mentioned him killing anyone. She always painted her great-great-grandfather as a hero. "How do you know this?"

Trey closed his eyes as he turned from her to lean against a porch support beam. "Believe me, I know."

"You must be wrong," she murmured.

"You don't know how much I wanted to be wrong, but I've seen the evidence." Trey turned back to face her. "I've held the proof in my hands.

"Yet, when I tried to bring Andrew to justice he just slid through my fingers. No one believed the boy who ran away from the war. They all thought I was crazy.

"I tried so hard to convince them, maybe too hard because I no longer fit in to this community. My friends were distant. My neighbors, hostile. The only one who still talked to me was Beau." Trey ran one hand through his hair. "And you know the worst part? At every turn, I found out Andrew tried to undermine me. If I wanted to buy a horse, Andrew offered more. A young girl caught my fancy; he outdid me in flowers and gifts. He was more romantic, or so I was told. I got sick of hearing his name and seeing his face."

"That's why you believe he's behind everything happening," said Alex. A hard knot formed in her belly. "You said you had proof?"

"I did. I gave the evidence to the sheriff. Somehow it disappeared. Andrew probably bought it back so I would never be able to prove his treachery," said Trey. "But I will prove it with my dying breath."

Alex swallowed hard as she aimlessly ran her fingers over the shirt covering his chest. Her great-great-grandfather couldn't be a killer. How would she be able to convince her husband that Andrew wouldn't do this?

Trey captured her hands against his chest with one of his own. With the other hand, he gently brushed his fingers along her jaw. "I want to change the subject to something that makes us both smile."

She blinked. "Like what?"

"Like that wonderfully soft bed in our bedroom," he teased. "We haven't been near it all day."

"Then we must remedy this immediately," said Alex, grateful for the change in topic. She needed time to figure out how to handle this new information.

Trey didn't give her a chance to move. He slipped one arm around her shoulders, the other under her knees, and then lifted her up.

"Trey, what are you doing?" she shrieked as he straightened with her in his arms. It embarrassed her when he did this in front of his workers. "I know how to walk."

He strode toward the house with her still in his arms. "True, but you would make it a leisurely stroll so no one would suspect what we're up to. I want them to know so they won't disturb us."

"Trey Dalton, you're incorrigible."

$$\sim$$

*T*wo days later, Alex smiled like a cat. Although she didn't get a chance to convince Trey of Andrew's innocence, they found better things to do than talk when they were alone. Married life agreed with her, or she agreed with married life. She wasn't sure which. Her hum filled the air as she gathered her notes for class from Trey's desk in his office. A shadow fell across the desk, making her jump back, dropping the papers.

"Do I make you nervous?" asked Beau.

"Only when I don't know you're here. You startled me." Alex picked up the papers she scattered a few moments before. "I'm surprised no one announced your arrival."

"I believe I saw Fleurette out around the side of the house."

"She must be working on the laundry." Alex looked up at him.

"Probably. I assume your husband is working in the fields?"

"Where would you expect him to be?" She arched one eyebrow. "At a cotillion?"

"You have such a unique brand of wit." Beau laughed. "I can see why Trey is so smitten with you."

"If you wish to talk to Trey I can send someone out to the fields for you." Tapping the papers on the desk, she straightened them up into a neat pile.

"No. That won't be necessary," said a deep baritone voice from the doorway.

Alex's face lit up at the sight of her husband. "Do you have eyes like a hawk? Beau's only been here five, maybe ten minutes."

"Just long enough to stable my horse and come into the house," quipped Beau.

"One of my hands saw the dust from his horse coming up the road."

She knew he worried they'd get another visit from Andrew. Alex walked toward the door where Trey stood. "I'll go make sure refreshments are on the way."

"Thank you, my dear," said Beau. "Trey and I have a few things to discuss anyway."

As she walked past Trey, Alex made a face that only he could see, showing how she felt about Beau's last remark.

Trey's hand snaked around her waist just as she passed. He whispered softly, "Male chauvinist pig?"

She laughed as she planted a kiss on his check. "Exactly."

While she went to prepare drinks and a snack, she wondered what Beau had to tell Trey. Normally, his news held nothing but fluff anyway. A rumor here, some gossip there. Beau reminded her of the fops she read about in romance books but wasn't sure if anyone used that word in the eighteen seventies.

Reentering the room with a heavily laden tray, she paused. The atmosphere of the room changed. Whatever Beau told Trey angered him. Silently, she placed the tray on the desk and handed each of the two men a tall glass of iced tea.

She looked up at her husband. Would he fill her in, or kick her out?

"Thank you, Alexandra," Trey said. He moved toward her. "Aunt Rose has taken ill. I have to go."

"Is she okay?"

"I don't know." Trey looked over at Beau. "The message only said she isn't getting better."

"I want to go with you," she said.

"That's probably a good idea." Beau spoke up. "I'm sure she would love to see you."

"No," snapped Trey. "We'll travel quicker without her."

"Are you saying that because I am a woman I'll slow you down?" Anger dripped from her words.

"We can travel faster without the carriage."

"Who says we have to take the carriage? I can ride a horse." Alex and Trey knew she was far from being an expert, but she could manage the ride to Rose's estate two hours away from Trey's plantation without incident.

"I said no."

Hands on her hips, she stood up to him. "Well, I'm going. Rose is my aunt too. If you try to stop me, I'll follow you."

"All right. All right." Trey rolled his eyes. "We don't have time to argue, but you will do everything I say. One peep, one complaint, and I'll tie you to your horse and send you home."

~

*A*lex rubbed the neck of the horse Jessie saddled for her. Now that she had time to think about it, she wondered if this was such a smart idea.

Fleurette came out and handed her a basket once she settled herself in the saddle. "Here's something to put some meat on Miss Rose's bones."

Alex opened the lid and sniffed hard as heavenly aromas escaped. "Oh. Fleurette. You outdid yourself."

She blushed. "Well, Miss Rose has alway' been nice to me. I made some chicken pie, some tea, and her favorite is in there."

Alex's eyes lit up. "Your brown Betty?"

Fleurette grinned. "Yes'm, I made enough for you, Mr. Trey, and Mr. Beau too."

"You mean enough for me," Alex quipped.

Fleurette laughed. "Yes'm. Whatever you say."

~

*A*lex slid from her saddle with a sigh. She couldn't set her feet on the ground fast enough.

Beau grinned at her from atop his horse. "The ride a bit hard on you, Miss Alexandra?"

There were times when she wanted to wipe that smug look off his face. She took the basket off the pummel of her horse and hooked it up over her elbow. "No."

Trey stepped up next to his wife, taking the reins from her. "Leave her be, Beau. Alex kept up with us and she didn't complain once."

A timid black woman cracked the door a little before peeking out. The moment she spotted Trey the door flew wide open. "Mr. Trey, thank the Lord. We's been worried about Miss Rose. She just ain't been herself."

"I know, Ruth. That's why I'm here." He handed the reins to a young stable hand who ran up from the carriage house. "What did the doctor say?"

"Miss Rose won' say. You know she don' trust doctors," said Ruth. "Even Mamie's remedy don' work. We don' know what to do."

"Come on." Trey took his wife's hand and gave it a gentle squeeze. "Let's go see for ourselves."

Alex felt her heart flutter against her chest. As they walked up the darkened flight of stairs and headed for the back of the house, she realized that although Trey made all kinds of noise about her not coming, secretly he was grateful she did.

"Why is it so dark in here?" asked Alex.

Ruth turned to look back at her oddly.

Okay, stupid question.

Before the woman could answer her, they arrived at Rose's room. Alex heard Aunt Rose's muffled reply to the soft knock Ruth gave the door. What happened to Aunt Rose? That weak reply couldn't be coming from the same woman who bullied her and Trey into marriage.

Ruth opened the door, and gestured Alex and Trey to enter. Once she did, the door closed silently behind her. Alex looked around. The heavy green curtains were drawn, blocking out any light. One small white candle burned on a pine table near the bed.

"Aunt Rose?"

The small huddled mass turned toward them.

The basket fell heedlessly to the floor. Alex ran to her side. "My God, Aunt Rose, what happened?" She rested her hand against Rose's forehead. "My God, Trey, she's hot as … as heck."

He knelt beside the bed, then touched his hand to Rose's head. His brow drew into a frown. "What's the doctor doing for you?"

The sight of her nephew galvanized Rose. "Trey Dalton, you're not supposed to be in my room while I'm indisposed. You march yourself downstairs right now. I'll be with you shortly." She struggled to sit up.

Alex pressed her back into the bed. "Trey, perhaps you should check on Beau while I help Aunt Rose become more presentable."

Trey nodded.

As he left the room, Alex helped Rose sit up. She started fluffing the pillows to make Rose more comfortable. "Trey and I heard of your illness. We thought it would be a good idea to come and visit."

"You needn't have bothered. I'll be fine in a few days."

"Aunt Rose, Trey and I wanted to come." Alex smoothed the blanket on Rose's bed. "We love you and were worried when we heard about your illness. Trey said you don't get sick very often. Besides, Fleurette fixed this basket just for you." She walked over and bent to pick up the basket she dropped earlier.

"Did she fix any brown Betty?"

She beamed. "As a matter of fact…" She produced the treat in question and sat it in Rose's lap.

"Do you mind if I open the curtains?" Alex already moved toward them. Without asking, she opened several windows in the room as well, to create a good back draft. A second later, fresh air poured into the room.

Alex found a chair near the bed. Once she sat down, she looked Rose over. Her skin had a jaundiced cast to it. Rose's face looked gaunt, and her eyes had sunk a little too deep in their sockets. She'd lost weight.

"What has the doctor said?"

"I can't keep nothing down, but he can't find nothing wrong." Rose dabbed her mouth with a cloth she had tucked up in her sleeve. "That quack thinks I have gastric fever."

"Really?" Alex played with the cuff of her left sleeve. An odd tidbit of information she learned in college filled her head. Gastric fever covered a wide variety of ailments, including poisoning. "When did this start?"

"I guess about the time I came home." Rose leaned back against her headboard.

"I noticed I was a little winded about a week after, but thought it was just the excitement wearing off. I didn't think it was anything to worry about." Rose blushed. "Until Achilles found me on the floor. I guess he realized it could be serious because he called the doctor out."

Alex shifted in her seat. "Aunt Rose, this might seem like a crazy question, but have you eaten or drank anything regularly since you came home?"

"Well, yes. Fleurette fixed me up a nice basket before I left your house. She put several bottles of the wine left over from your engagement party in the basket. I've had a few glasses here and there."

"I wondered if you still had an extra bottle?" Alex said. She needed to test that wine. "I thought it would make a wonderful gesture for me to have that wine at our three-month anniversary. Fleurette must have given you the last few bottles. I plan on having a terribly romantic dinner."

"Of course, chile. I'll have Ruth get one for you."

Alex helped Rose freshen up and don her day wrapper so she could receive visitors.

Later that evening, once she and Trey retired to the room Ruth had prepared for them, Alex sat in front of the mirror at the vanity, brushing her hair out. Wearing her hair up, and then attaching the hairpiece she wore everywhere now, made her spend a lot more time on her hair than she used to.

"I don't like the way Aunt Rose looks," said Trey. "She's never seemed so frail before."

"I think I know what's wrong with her." Alex watched him pace in the mirror.

"You do?"

"Yeah. She's been poisoned."

Trey stopped pacing and stared at her reflection in the mirror. "Are you sure?"

"Pretty sure. I've had some time to think about it. The doctor said she had gastric fever. In my time, we know what causes gastric fever. It's poison. Normally arsenic poisoning."

Trey sank to the bed. "Who in the world would want to poison Aunt Rose?"

CHAPTER 22

"Can you prove that Aunt Rose has been poisoned?" Trey asked.

"I think so. I'll need some ingredients, if I can remember all of them, and a quiet place to work."

"It might be a good idea if we kept this to ourselves until we're sure." Alex looked at his reflection in the mirror.

"Why?"

"I don't want to frighten anyone if I am wrong."

"That makes perfect sense." He kissed her neck. "You know what else makes perfect sense? You and me on that big brass bed."

Her eyes strayed to the bed before gazing back into his sexy green eyes. Her own eyes dilated at the thought of the two of them together. Trey's reacted in kind. Any thoughts about what she needed to test the wine bottle stashed in her bag fled as she watched her husband strip for her. Tomorrow, she'd worry about it tomorrow.

Everything was set up in an abandoned shack. Alex shook her head. It looked like a third grader's chemistry set, but it should do the job. Within a few hours she should be able to tell if someone had poisoned the wine.

After placing the last ingredient into the bowl, she worked with, Alex wiped a stray hair from her face. She couldn't wait until she could get back to Rose's house and take a nice long bath. The heat made her feel like she had a puddle at her feet. What she wouldn't do for a good stiff wind. Slowly, she swirled the bowl in her hands as she moved toward the door, hoping to catch a stray breeze. A light gust blew through the door, just what she needed. Alex closed her eyes in ecstasy.

"So this is what you do when I'm not around?"

Alex started. Her eyes flew open. Scanning the area, a familiar scent of hay and horses filled her senses. "Trey. Don't do that."

"What?" he asked.

"Sneak up on me. I hate it."

He grinned. "Do I make you nervous?"

"No." She glared at him. "Okay, maybe a little, until I know who it is at least. Anyway, I think I have our answer."

Trey walked into the shack with her.

"I've tested this wine three times. I keep finding poison." Placing the cork back in the bottle she lifted it up so they both could look through the glass. "If I had used my head I would have noticed the residue at the bottom. It looks like our poisoner dumped what they had left over into this bottle. It has the heaviest concentration."

Residue sat on the bottom of the bottle.

"What is it?" asked Trey.

"Arsenic."

"Damn." Trey walked back to the door. "This is my fault."

Her brow furrowed. "Why?"

"Because I told Fleurette to get rid of those bottles."

"I'm not sure I follow you."

"Andrew Leroux gave us those bottles." Trey ran his fingers through his hair. "I didn't want anything he gave us so I had Fleurette dispose of all but one bottle. Beau talked me into using one for our toast since that's why Andrew sent them to us."

"The same wine that made me sick," she murmured. "So the rest of our guests drank a different wine?"

Trey nodded.

"Why didn't you get sick?"

"I never drank mine." His gaze dropped to his shoes. "Not wanting to have anything to do with Andrew or his gift, I faked it."

"I can't believe this," said Alex. "Andrew wouldn't do this."

"Why won't you believe me?"

"Because I know my family history. My great-great-grandfather didn't try to murder anyone."

"Damn it, Alex, how do you know that your family didn't bury this bit of information so that Andrew's descendants would never know." Trey noticed a dopey grin on his wife's face. "What are you so happy about?"

"You called me Alex," she replied, throwing her arms around him.

"A slip of the tongue," he grumbled, loving the feel of her in his arms.

"It doesn't matter. You said it." Alex smiled. "As far as my family burying deep dark secrets, we're not that well-known. Besides, my grandmother would have enjoyed telling that tale. She used to tell people that her first toy came from Jessie James."

"Isn't he that outlaw in Missouri?"

"Yes. He also dies about twenty-five years before Grams is born," replied Alex. "Do you understand why I don't think a killer in the family would have been swept under the rug?"

"In fact, I just remembered something my grandma told me about Andrew. He was a hero of sorts. He saves some woman from a kidnapper. Grams showed me a clipping from the *Times-Picayune*."

Trey shook his head. "You must be as good at this tale spinning as your grandma."

She crossed her arms over her chest. She was not like her grandmother. "So what do you want to do about this information? Should we tell the authorities?"

"Aunt Rose was expecting her doctor. I suppose we should start with him."

~

*T*he loud crash that came from upstairs made Alex jump. "What was that?"

Ruth picked up the empty cookie dish from in front of Alex. "It's always like this when the doctor is visiting."

Alex stared at the ceiling. "And that makes those sounds okay?"

"Miss Rose is just expressing her opinion at what the doctor said. She can get quite expressive."

"I'd hate to be the one to bring her bad news. How long does the doctor normally stay?"

"Not very long." Ruth grinned. "Miss Rose should be kicking him out any minute now."

Alex got up and went to the kitchen door. Where was Trey? He told her to wait for him, but if he didn't hurry the doctor would leave before they got a chance to talk to him. She'd talk to the doctor herself if Trey didn't show up before the doctor got ready to leave.

Another loud crash filled the house. This time Rose's voice followed. "Get out of my house."

"Madam," said the doctor.

"I said out. Don't come back until you can give me a real answer."

"Rose, you are a very stubborn woman. If you hadn't helped pay for my education I wouldn't put up with your ranting."

"I want to know what is wrong with me. You don't have an answer."

Alex had heard enough. Up the stairs she marched.

"You're too ornery to keep anything for long, woman."

Alex quietly closed the door to Rose's bedroom behind her. "Okay. I've heard enough. Aunt Rose, stop being mean to the doctor. He's doing everything he can."

"Doctor, my husband and I would like to talk to you downstairs, if that is okay."

The doctor expelled his breath. "That will be fine, Mrs. Dalton." He turned toward his patient. "I'll be back, and not because you're such a good patient."

"Doctor," said Alex. Gesturing him out before Rose could retaliate.

She turned to face Rose before she closed the door she whispered, "We need to talk, Aunt Rose."

Alex followed the doctor down the stairs. Ruth waited at the bottom with a brandy snifter and tea.

"Ruth, if you ever get tired of that old biddy, you come see me." The doctor took the snifter with gratitude.

"Now, doctor, who would take care of Miss Rose proper?" Ruth laughed as she escorted them into the study.

Mahogany wood with rose accents dominated the room. Except for the grandfather clock the back wall was completely bare. The two walls on either side were covered with books.

A loose floorboard squeaked behind Alex, making her look back. There stood Trey, grinning at her sheepishly.

He slipped his arm around her waist when he joined her side. "Sorry," he whispered. "Beau cornered me."

The doctor nodded toward Trey. "Mr. Dalton, It's good to see you."

"Dr. McCoy."

Alex tried to keep her face straight. For a second, she wondered where Captain Kirk was. After setting down on a rose damask love seat, she busied herself by arranging her skirt.

Ruth served Alex and Trey some tea before leaving the room.

"How's my aunt?" asked Trey, as he sat next to Alex. He placed his untouched cup on the coffee table in front of the love seat.

"Rose has gastric fever." Dr. McCoy sat in a high-back leather chair.

Trey nodded. "I've heard. How long has she had it?"

"Several months. I have tried several different remedies, but so far nothing has worked."

Trey leaned forward. "Are you sure she took them?"

"Yes. I gave explicit instructions to Ruth."

"Ah." Trey sat back.

"Is gastric fever communicable?" asked Alex. Her finger gently slid around the edge of her teacup.

"If you're worried about catching it, no," said the doctor, sitting his brandy snifter on a small end table next to the chair. "There's no record of it."

A sharp jab to his ribs made Trey speak. "Have you checked for poison?"

"What?" The doctor stared at Trey.

"Poison? Is it something you checked for?"

"Who would poison Rose?"

"Then that's a no," remarked Alex, still sliding her finger around the rim.

Trey shot her an irritated look.

"We gave my aunt some leftover wine from our engagement party. My wife drank some of the same wine that night and it made her ill. Now Aunt Rose is sick."

The doctor nodded in understanding.

"Since they both had the wine and got sick, I feel it's something that needs to be checked."

"All right. But I will need a bottle of that wine to test," said the doctor.

"Not a problem." Trey smiled. "Ruth has put two bottles in a basket she has readied for you."

"Thank you," said the doctor. "I'll get in touch with you as soon as I find something."

~

*A*lexandra hadn't spoken to him since the doctor left. What had he done wrong now? "Alexandra?"

"Yes?"

Great. One-syllable words didn't bode well.

"Can I ask you one question?" Alex asked.

"Of course, sweetheart."

"Why didn't you tell him I already ran all the tests?"

Trey rubbed his forehead. "If I had told the doctor you found arsenic in the wine he would have scoffed. This way he'll come to his own conclusions."

"Fine."

"Alex."

The grandfather clock ticked loudly.

"Okay. It's not fine. It sucks."

"Sucks?"

"Yea, you know the pits, rotten, not nice, um, let me think."

"I get the idea," said Trey. "Alex, Dr. McCoy is old-fashioned."

The left side of her lip quirked up.

"Okay. He is a male chauvinist pig, as you call us. He wouldn't believe the word of a woman. He knows I know nothing about how to detect poisons in food or drink. This will work better."

"You called me Alex again."

"I did, didn't I." He took a step closer to her. "I've decided that it does suit you."

Alex placed her hands on her hips. "Really."

Really," he mimicked as he wrapped his arms around her. "I'll tell you another thing that suits you. My lips." He kissed her forehead. "My hands." He rubbed his hands up and down her back. "My body."

Neither saw the shadow slink away from the window.

❧

wo weeks later, Alex waved at Trey across the street. He surprised her by bringing her into town and allowing her several hours to herself.

She just finished having lunch with Elizabeth. They caught up on the latest gossip, and just enjoyed each other's company, which included the fact that Aunt Rose was poisoned but the doctor caught it in time and she was doing much better.

Stepping onto the dirt road, Alex smiled. Her mind already working on how she would repay Trey. She didn't hear the sound of wheels turning.

A loud whinny pierced the air.

Alex's head snapped around. Barreling toward her was a runaway carriage.

CHAPTER 23

*T*rey watched in horror as the horse stampeded past, heading straight for Alex. She would never get out of the way in time, and he couldn't reach her before the runaway carriage ran her over. A flash of color caught the corner of his eye just before the carriage thundered by. Her name tore from his lips.

Dust hung in the air, clinging to his clothes, and burning his eyes, as he worked his way across the street. His mind wouldn't move, his heart refused to beat. This couldn't be happening. He didn't want to see what happened to Alex. It would break his heart.

"Andrew, I can't breathe," someone rasped.

"I'm so sorry, Miss Alexandra."

"Alex?"

"Trey?" Alex scrambled to her feet. In seconds, she found herself enveloped in Trey's embrace, his kisses raining on her face.

"Oh, thank God, thank God. I thought I'd lost you."

"Trey, I'm fine." She rested her head against his chest. "Really."

"What happened?" he asked, stroking her hair.

A crowd started to gather around them.

"I'm not sure, but if it hadn't been for Andrew I'd be dog chow."

"Andrew?"

"Yeah. He pushed me out of the way." She wiped her face, trying to remove the dirt she kept tasting.

Trey looked up at Andrew, who stood a few feet away. "Why did you do this?"

Andrew looked at him oddly. "Because I didn't want to see her killed."

Alex knew what Trey thought. "This neither the time nor the place, Trey."

"Stay out of this, Alex."

Alex heard several sharp intakes. Her name couldn't be that outrageous. "Please think about this. Those horses were running at a good clip. There is no way he could have saved me if he was responsible for this."

"Sweetheart, he could have hired someone." Trey never took his eyes off Andrew. "He could have done all this just to throw me off because he knows we're getting close."

Alex looked at the ground for a minute. Man, talk about paranoid. When her head came up, she wished she had been paying attention.

Trey launched himself at Andrew. Punching him hard in the stomach. "If you so much as think about my wife, I'll find out about it. I don't want you near her." He punched him in the face. "Do you understand?"

"What the hell is wrong with you?" shouted Alex. She heard some more sharp intakes of breath. She ignored the people around them as she grabbed one of Trey's arms.

"No, Miss Alexandra," interrupted Andrew, wiping blood from the corner of his mouth as he stood up. "Trey and I have something to work out. It is long overdue."

She placed her hand on her hips. "Not in the middle of the street like two thugs."

"You're right. We should handle this like gentlemen. How about it, Trey?"

Trey slugged him again. "I'm not letting you out of my sight. You want to have this out, then let's do it, here, now."

Andrew shrugged out of his coat. "All right. If that's the way you want to do this." He held his fists up in front of his face. "I want to know what I did that was so terrible anyway, to cause you to hate me so."

Trey's eyes narrowed to slits. "You know why."

"Humor me." Andrew circled around Trey.

Trey fought the inner trembling that shook his body to the core. How could this man not know? Was he that callused? He moved with Andrew. "Son of a bitch!"

He threw another punch, which connected with the side of Andrew's head.

"Trey, stop this now," demanded Alex.

"You killed my parents and don't even remember?" asked Trey.

The whole congregation sucked in their breath. Alex thought it was like a bad old movie.

"I did what?" Andrew dropped his hands.

Trey punched him in the nose. "My parents. You killed them."

"What are you talking about?" Andrew continued to fight. He swung, hitting Trey in the eye.

Elizabeth stepped out into the road and took Alex's hand. Gently she pulled her back to the edge of the crowd.

"Trey," said Andrew. "I didn't kill your parents."

"I have seen the evidence."

"What evidence?" Andrew dodged a blow from Trey.

"The head of your cane," said Trey as he tried to plant another blow.

Alex looked down at the cane at her feet. She bent at the knees and stooped down to pick it up. Turning it over slowly. This was the same head she found near the burnt barn. Was Trey right?

"My cane?" Andrew landed another punch. This time to Trey's midsection, knocking the air out of him. "The head of that stupid thing is not special made. You can buy two or three of them yourself if you were to go to New Orleans."

Trey's brow furrowed. "It's not your family crest?"

"No." Andrew stopped for a few seconds. "I just buy them from the same store that my father did. It's the only pattern they sell. If it weren't for that piece of shrapnel in my foot, I wouldn't even need the blasted thing, but there are some days I can't put any weight on the foot, thus the cane."

"That cane was found near my parent's bodies," snapped Trey. He swung and connected with Andrew's jaw.

"Then Alex...Alexandra, found another one near the barn that you burned down on my land a couple months ago. Shall I go on?"

"No." Andrew paused. He dropped his hands. "Come on. Finish me off. I'm sure it will make you feel better."

Trey got a feral gleam in his eyes. Alex prayed he wouldn't make a fool of himself. She thought he would hit Andrew again, but he also lowered his arms. A sigh of relief escaped her.

"Do not come near my home, or my wife. If you do, I will kill you," said Trey, as he placed a protective arm around Alex. With quiet dignity he escorted his wife away.

Andrew watched them leave. Anger etched on his face.

As Trey and Alex walked toward their carriage Alex asked, "Why didn't you tell me about the cane? I asked you about the evidence and you just kept it to yourself. Why?"

"Because I know how much you want to believe that Andrew is innocent. He's not, Alexandra." Trey shook his hand out before flexing his fingers. His knuckles were swollen and starting to turn purple already.

"So it would seem," she replied. Alex accepted Trey's bruised hand up into the carriage.

"The cane disappeared. If I had said anything you would have demanded to see it. Then when I couldn't produce it I'm sure you would have defended him and said I was accusing him unfairly."

"True," admitted Alex. She brushed her hand across her skirt. Her hand trembled against the linen fabric.

"Are you all right?" asked Trey.

"Huh? Oh yeah. I'm fine. Just a little shook up. It's a little disconcerting to have a team of horses running down your throat," said Alex. "I know better than to step out into traffic, I always look both ways. I don't know how I missed them."

"They just suddenly appeared, Alex, as fast as they moved, you wouldn't have spotted them until you were almost halfway across the street."

"If Andrew hadn't been there"—Alex locked eyes with Trey—"I would have been killed."

Trey broke her gaze. He didn't want to think about that right now. He was just grateful she was alive and well. Something he planned to show her the moment they got home.

～

*J*essie stepped out of the new barn as they alighted from the carriage. "Mr. Trey, somein' happened."

He stopped in his tracks. "Aunt Rose?"

"No sir," said Jessie, rubbing one wrist nervously. "It's Blue Thunder."

"My horse?"

Jessie nodded.

Trey strode past him, heading toward the opened doors of the barn. "What is wrong with my horse?"

"He's dead, sir."

"Dead?" Trey started to run toward the barn.

Alex rushed to keep up. The stench of blood assailed her when she entered the enclosure. She swallowed hard, praying her stomach wouldn't revolt. Just thinking of what she might see already had it rolling. Peeking around Trey's back she gulped.

"Oh God." The sight she viewed of a few seconds would be stamped in her mind forever. Someone beheaded the horse. It reminded her of the scene in the Godfather. Blood covered the stall, the hay, and the saddle she saved from the fire. She noticed a slight glimmer on the dirt floor of the barn.

No one paid any attention to her so she walked over and stooped down. It turned out to be a piece of silver. Brushing hay away, she found another cane, this one without a casing, revealing a bloodied sword beneath. Alex closed her eyes. She knew how Trey would react the moment he saw it, but before she had a chance to hide it Trey turned around looking for her.

A glint of light reflected off the blade and into Trey's eyes. "What is that?"

Alex stared down at the sword. "The murder weapon."

Trey reached her in two steps. A growl escaped his lips as he tore it out of her hands. His anger allowed him to bury the sword deep in the dirt under her feet. "I'm going to kill him."

Without another word he spun on his heels and strode toward the house.

Alex stared at his retreating back. "Jessie?"

"I think he's serious, Miss Alexandra."

Alex knew she had to stop him. "Jessie, he can't leave this plantation in that mood. If we have to tie him up and throw him in the root cellar."

"Are you saying we needs to chase him down?"

"I have one idea that might work better, but I'll need everyone out of the house, and no visitors until you hear from me. I'll have to pull out all the big guns."

"Guns?"

"A figure of speech, Jessie. It means I'll use any means to stop him from going after Andrew." She started walking toward the house.

"Oh." A big grin spread across Jessie's face. "Oh."

He headed toward the back of the house to fulfill Miss Alexandra's request.

~

*A*lex found Trey on the porch, cleaning his rifle. "Trey."

"No. Nothing you could do or say will stop me," said Trey. He didn't look up from working on the rifle.

"Nothing?" she asked quietly.

Trey looked up. "Noth—"

Her dress slipped off one shoulder. She undid most of the buttons while she walked toward him.

He stood up to shield her from prying eyes. "Get in the house."

"Only if you will come with me." She grabbed his hand and pulled it toward her.

"Alexandra, what are you doing?" The spark of desire appeared in his eyes.

"Seducing my husband."

He pulled his hand free. "He killed my prize horse."

"And he saved my life." Alex pulled one sleeve down, then the other. "I want to celebrate that, with you, now."

"Here?" he asked, looking around.

"On the porch, why not?" She saw the spark become a fire. Ah, she just might have hit on one of his sexual fantasies. A quick push and a rustle of fabric sent her skirt to the floor.

"Someone could see us."

She smiled at him as she worked the strings of her corset loose. "No one will catch us. I've made sure of that."

"Is this the same modest woman who squeals when I carry her into the house because I want to make love?" Trey turned her around to help loosen the strings.

A faint blush filled her cheeks.

"Why are you doing this?" He nibbled on one of the shoulders she bared for him.

She leaned her head against him to give him better access to her shoulder. "Because I love you."

"Show me how much." He gently cupped her chin and turned his face toward him.

CHAPTER 24

$\mathcal{A}$lex turned in his arms and pressed herself against him as their kiss deepened. Her body trembled, half in fear, half in excitement. This was not something she would normally do, but for this man she was willing to do anything, and she actually enjoyed being a bit of an exhibitionist.

"Let's go inside." Evidence of Trey's desire pressed against her belly.

She stood her ground. "Here. Now."

A sultry smile played across her lips as his nostrils flared. His eyes dilated in a sexual haze. Power surged through her veins, knowing she caused this reaction.

Her hand slid up his chest, drawing little circles on the shirt that covered his nipples, before moving to the buttons. One by one she undid them. Once the final button came undone, Alex pushed the shirt off his chest. Her lips worked their way across the wide expanse, giving him a little nip here and there. When her tongue circled his naval she heard him groan.

"Having a problem, dear?" She straightened and looked up at him. Her eyes stared into his as she worked at loosening his trousers.

"What do you think?" Trey grabbed one of her hands and pressed it against his hardened member through the rough linen of his trousers.

"I think," she said as she slipped her second hand inside of his pants and ran a finger against his velvet tip, "you are enjoying this a lot more than you let on."

"Then you know I can't take much more of this." He shuddered against her gentle caress. "I want to feel myself inside you."

"All in good time, my love." She eased his pants down his legs, stopping to lick the length of him along the way.

"Alexandra."

"I am making love to you, Trey. I'm calling the shots here. Don't try to fight it. If you do, I'll just make it worse." Pushing against his chest, she forced him to sit in one of the rocking chairs on the porch.

Heat started to pool in her loins as she knelt in front of him. Dipping her head, she took his length into her mouth. Trey almost jumped up out of the chair.

"Now, Alex," he said through gritted teeth.

She shook her head no. This was something she had wanted to do for a while, just didn't know how to ask him if he wanted her to. His thigh muscles contracted beneath her hands, showing her what he enjoyed more. When he started to rise out of the chair she stopped.

Trey leaned down and captured her lips.

She felt him draw her up toward him. As she straightened up again, she slipped her chemise off her shoulders. Her pantaloons came off next, and then she straddled his lap.

Trey broke the kiss when he felt her body rubbing against his. "You are a wanton thing, wife. Thank God you're mine."

She laughed as she leaned back.

Her husband gazed hungrily at her exposed breasts. He took one into his mouth before Alex had a chance to stop him. She squirmed in his lap as he suckled her hard. The moist heat sent spirals of desire through her.

In one swift motion Trey moved her up and then down, onto his erection. They both sighed as he filled her. Alex found Trey's hands on her hips, setting the pace. Losing control at this point didn't upset her.

His mouth had found her other breast. One of his hands worked magic between them as she slid up and down on his shaft. She couldn't control anything if she wanted.

Her release exploded around her quickly. A low keening wail escaped her lips as she climaxed.

Her husband gave her a wicked smile.

She returned that smile as she contracted her muscles around him. "Your turn."

His smile widened. "It is, isn't it?" With his hands on her hips, Trey set the pace again.

The friction from his movement in and out made Alex's muscles contract more. She bit her lip. This felt too good.

Wet kisses were spread all over her body. The gentle tugging of Trey's lips on her left nipple brought her to the edge again. She arched back as she started to climax once more. Her body took on a life of its own as it moved against Trey's. His breath became harsher, as she rode him. Her muscles tightened against him. Faster, and faster, they moved. Just as she felt the rush again, she heard Trey's shout and felt his sharp movement as he went over the edge with her.

"Wow." She gulped in air as her heart hammered in her chest.

A deep laugh rumbled in Trey's chest. "Is that all you have to say after that?"

"And what would you like to hear? That was the best I ever had?" Alex rested her forehead against his shoulder. "You know every time is the best I ever have. Although I have to admit I like being in control."

"What woman wouldn't?" He kissed her ear.

She leaned back to glare at him. "Hey."

"So, just how long is everyone supposed to stay away from the house?" Trey swept her up in his arms and headed inside.

She linked her arms around his neck. "Until I send for them."

"Good, because you have only whetted my appetite. I want to feast, for a long time, and for as much as you can stand."

"Then we'll have to see who begs for mercy first," said Alex as she squirmed in his arms until she could wrap her legs around his waist.

"Keep that up, woman, and we might not make it to our room."

"Who says we have to make it to our room?"

Trey groaned as they sank to the floor.

It took a long time, and several tries before they did make it to their bed.

~

*B*eau noticed that Trey and Alexandra wore the same cat-like smile as he drank coffee with them the next morning. "So, have a good evening?"

"Very much." Trey linked fingers with Alexandra.

Beau's brow furrowed. He saw the blood all over the stall. Something definitely happened, yet Trey acted like the only thing he cared about was having sex with his wife. He wanted to get his friend alone, but these two seemed joined at the hip.

"Miss Alexandra, you seem to glow this morning," he commented.

"Yes, well, thank you." Her eyes cut demurely to Trey.

Beau was bursting with questions. He prayed Trey could sense it. Taking another sip of coffee, Beau tried to figure out how to handle the loving couple before him. He never expected Trey to fall for this woman so hard. "I'm surprised to see you here so late, Trey. I thought you'd be in the field by now."

"Normally I am, but Alexandra and I decided to celebrate, so I have taken the day off."

"Celebrate what?"

A shadow crossed Trey's face before he answered. "I almost lost my wife yesterday. A runaway team came close to trampling her to death."

"Are you all right?"

"A little shook up, but fine." Alexandra smiled at him. "Thank goodness Mr. Leroux was there to push me out of the way."

"Andrew was there?"

"He threw himself at Alexandra as the carriage bore down on her." Trey nodded yes. "Knocked her out of the way. Then he tried to knock some sense into me. I refused to believe him capable of any kindness until Alexandra convinced me."

Beau took another sip of his cooling coffee. The scent of rich chicory rose from the cup. He liked his hotter than the cup he held now.

"It makes me wonder if I've been wrong all these years." Trey took one of his wife's hands and kissed her palm.

"But I thought, well, never mind." He watched them a few more minutes, realizing that they didn't need him around right now. Hell, they probably didn't even know he was in the same room they were. He made a big show of stretching. "I do need to go."

"You do?" Trey stood up with him.

"Yes." Beau winked.

Trey walked him to the door.

"I'll be going out of town for a while. I'll contact you as soon as I get back." Beau took the reins from the young boy who brought him his horse, then swung up on the horse. "Have fun with your wife, Trey." With a wave he was gone.

❧

*A*lex scuffed her feet along the bank of the bayou. Dust clouds rose around her as children ran about. She decided to take the children on a makeshift field trip to spur their interest in science. All she'd gotten them interested in was Amos dumping frogs down the back of Daisy's dress. After Daisy knocked Amos down, the boy lost interest in any more frogs.

"It's time to head back."

Several children moaned in response.

"We still have arithmetic, and our ABCs to work on."

She stayed a few feet behind, making sure no one straggled, and giving herself time to think. It didn't take long before the children had gotten so far ahead, she could only hear their giggles and laughter.

Since her near fatal accident three days ago, Trey wanted her to take a break from teaching the children. It took a lot of arguing to convince him she felt fine. His attitude had gone through a three hundred sixty-degree turn too since then. Trey started to believe that Andrew might not be the one trying to drive his business into the ground. Of course, it made her wonder who would.

Light shimmered off the brackish water. Spanish moss hung from trees towering over the bayou. A musky scent hung in the air. Before her little trip through time Alex never paid much attention to the beauty of this area. Now she felt like it enveloped her, drawing her into the spell she fought to ignore before. "Guess that's what happens when you fall in love."

She smiled to herself as she reached down to pick a wildflower blooming close to the water. What her grandmother would give to see her granddaughter in love. She plucked one of the velvet petals off. "He loves me."

The second petal fluttered to the grass. "He loves me not."

Half the petals had been plucked when she heard a slight sound behind her. Alex turned quickly, wondering which child had snuck in behind her. Nothing there, but the Spanish moss swaying gently in the trees. She shrugged to herself as she continued to follow the path along the water's edge.

About five minutes later she heard a sound again. "Amos, is that you?"

A sharp blow to the head knocked her to her knees. The second knocked her out.

"Nope," said her attacker. "And you'll probably never see him again, missy."

Picking up her limp body, he threw it over the saddle of the horse he tethered nearby.

❧

Trey paced the floor of the sitting room. Dinner had come and gone but no sign of Alex. The children had come back hours ago, saying that she had been walking so slow they decided not to wait for her.

Deep in his bones, he knew something was wrong. His wife would never stay away like this unless she was hurt. He had waited long enough. Striding into the kitchen, Trey spoke to Jessie, who ate with his daughter. "Gather the men. I want to search for her."

Jessie nodded as he got up. Within minutes, he had most of the hands rounded up and standing near the back door. Trey gave his orders before leading the men off. They had to find Alex.

Their search turned out to be futile. They knew she had been near the bayou by her prints, but that was where they ended, as if she just disappeared.

Trey trudged up the stairs to his home. He found Beau and Fleurette waiting for him. Fleurette looked frightened.

"What?"

"A package arrived for you while you were gone, Mr. Trey. It's in the sitting room."

Trey nodded. He glanced at his friend. "Alexandra is missing."

"That's what Fleurette told me. Did you find her?"

Trey shook his head. He walked into the room to find a large wrapped painting leaning against the fireplace. "Fleurette!"

"Yes, sir?" she asked, wringing her hands inside the folds of her dress.

"When did this arrive?"

"About an hour ago," she replied.

He rubbed his forehead. Who sent this? Trey ripped the packaging off. The part of the painting he saw was a bared, slim shoulder, a gloved hand, and a patch of dark green. "What the hell?"

The rest of the wrapping came off in seconds. Trey turned white as he stared at a painting of Alexandra, seated on a settee. Andrew stood behind her chair. He raked his fingers across Andrew's image in anger. The semi-dried oils smeared, distorting Andrew's face.

He threw the painting into the fireplace. He stalked into his office and picked up his gun. Metal scraped as he placed two shells into the chambers of his shotgun and dropped four extra into his pockets. Three strides got him out of the room and into the hall that lead to the door.

Jessie stood just inside the door.

"Get a horse saddled." Trey swallowed hard. This man had caused him nothing but grief. It was time to end that grief.

Beau stepped up to him, placing his hand on Trey's shoulder. "Trey, maybe you should think about this."

The heat of his friend's hand penetrated his shirt. "I have thought about this for too long. It's time for some action."

"I'll come with you."

"No." Trey turned cold eyes on his friend. "This is something I have to do myself."

Beau searched his eyes, then nodded. "Be safe, my friend."

Trey marched down the steps, swung up on his horse, and charged down the road. He didn't think on the trek to Leroux's. Andrew better be alone this evening, or whoever might be with him could be hurt too. Right now, he didn't care.

One foot kicked against Andrew's door, sending it crashing down. "Where is she, you son of a bitch?"

"Trey?" Andrew shot up out of the chair he sat in. The papers in his lap slid to the floor, pinging as they hit. "What are you talking about?"

"Alexandra. What have you done with my wife?"

"We need to talk."

"Like hell." Metal scraped metal as Trey cocked his rifle, then pointed it at Andrew's heart. "Where is she, Andrew?"

"I don't have your wife, Trey." Beads of perspiration appeared on his upper lip. "Think about this. If I had your wife, would I be here right now?"

"Explain the picture."

Andrew's brow creased. "What picture?"

Trey gripped his rifle hard. The metal warmed in his hands. He closed his eyes, trying to control the anger he felt overpowering him. "The painting you sent."

Andrew eyed the rifle warily. "Could you please elaborate?"

"The painting of you and my wife." The sound of wood hitting bone dominated when Trey whacked Andrew with the butt of his rifle. Andrew fell to the floor.

Andrew stared up at him. "Trey, you've got to believe me. I didn't send you a painting of any sort."

Trey lifted the rifle up again. "You lie."

"Are you going to hit me every time I say something you don't like?" Andrew glared at him. "If so, go ahead and shoot me."

Silence.

"Then put that damn rifle down and let's settle this like men." Andrew scrambled to his feet when Trey dropped the gun. Before he stood up completely, he was cold-cocked in the face.

"I am sick of you," Trey growled. "You stalked Janette until she left America in fear."

"Janette? Jacques Boudreaux's cousin? Are you kidding? I was afraid of her after she beat the crap out of Beau and me that summer. I wouldn't go near her."

Trey swung and connected with Andrew's ear.

"Ow." Andrew blocked another swing. "That girl might have been sweet on you, but she was a bully. You know that she grew up as the youngest of ten. The other nine were brothers. She learned young how to get her way with her brothers."

This wasn't the same image that Beau painted of her. He made her sound like a frail flower, not the type of girl who could control nine brothers. "Then why did she leave suddenly?"

Andrew grinned. "She put three frogs in Father Richard's milk at a formal dinner they threw for the good Father. He said that the, and I quote 'little heathen should be sent packing on the next boat.' The Boudreaux's followed the father's advice."

Trey stopped moving for a few moments.

"Exactly what did you hear?"

"That you were so jealous you started to follow her everywhere. She started to fear for her life so much she fled back to France."

"Who told you that?"

"Beau," Trey said. "What about my parents?"

Andrew walked to a closet. He pulled out a folder full of receipts. "As I said we need to talk."

CHAPTER 25

*A*lex's head hurt. Pain shot through it as she rubbed her forehead while she looked around. Where was she? How did she get there? Nothing looked familiar. Her mind didn't seem to be working. She had no clue about what happened to her.

A small lamp burned on a table close to the bed where she found herself lying. Its pitiful illumination didn't help at all. Rubbing the back of her head, she found a small knot, and then she remembered. Someone had bashed her in the back of the head, but why?

Once she felt sure enough to be on her feet, Alex stood up and started to examine the room she was in. As far as she could see there were no windows unless they were blacked out. Her hands slid along the rough wood wall. She flinched at the splinters she picked up. There were no smooth sections on the wall, which meant no windows. So she was probably in a cellar. Her eyes widened. Most people didn't have cellars in New Orleans; there was the small problem with them being below sea level. She wondered if the room flooded on a regular basis. She could be in trouble if it did.

"How much time has passed," she wondered, as she picked up the candle and wandered around the small room. No extra doors. She rubbed her hands along the walls looking for a lever or something that would reveal a hidden door or passage. Nothing. "Okay, there has to be a way out."

The door that kept her from freedom swung open. "Good morning, Mrs. Dalton."

"Morning?" she asked. "How long have I been here?"

"About fourteen hours. You took quite a blow to the head. We're sorry about that, but kidnapping can be a little messy at times."

"Why was I kidnapped?"

"Now, Mrs. Dalton, don't ask too many questions if you want to see your husband again." The tray he placed on the table made a hollow metal sound.

What did he think she was, a helpless female? Perhaps that wouldn't be such a bad idea. It might give her the edge she'd need to escape.

"Here's some breakfast. The one good thing is that we have an excellent cook. Please enjoy."

She eyed the tray suspiciously.

"I can promise you that the food is not poisoned. Our boss doesn't want anything to happen to you."

So someone else called all the shots. She perched herself on the bed and lifted the cover off the plate. Rich aromas filled the cramped room. "It smells heavenly."

The young man smiled at her.

Alex took a small bite of the eggs, then closed her eyes. It had been a long time since she ate. There was a slight hint of ham in the flavor, and an herb she didn't recognize.

She studied the young man before her as she ate. He couldn't be over twenty. His worn clothing showed quality. Another post Civil War gentry forced to work for a living. As least he had manners.

Those eggs disappeared fast; in fact, she ate everything in front of her, with the exception of the grits. She never acquired a taste for them.

He picked up the tray and turned to leave.

"Um."

"Yes, ma'am?"

"Is it possible to get a little more light down here? It's awfully dark, and I don't like the dark much."

"I'll see what I can do."

"Thank you," she said. "Oh, and maybe some reading material? Something to keep me occupied."

"Anything else?" He gave her a lopsided smile.

"No." She placed her hands demurely in her lap.

The door closed, and Alex heard a bolt slide home before the man's steps started to retreat, then his heavy tread on wood as he went upstairs. A few minutes later she heard the same heavy tread on the floor above her.

Time passed slowly. She counted all the timbers in the room and the print in the threadbare rug on the floor.

Alex bolted up on the bed she lay on at the sound of boots overhead again. She must have drifted off. The sound faded but grew again as they clomped down the steps to her door. The bolt squeaked as someone slid it back.

The same young man walked into the room carrying another tray. "Lunch." He sat the tray on the table. "I have also gotten another lamp for you, and something to read."

Her lunch was more of a feast, chicken, mashed potatoes, gravy, biscuits, green beans, corn bread, and for dessert, wild blackberry cobbler. Her guard watched as she ate. "You don't have to stand here and wait. I could bang on the door, or something."

"Sorry. Orders are to wait till you're done and take the tray away."

She nodded. She picked up the spoon, the only utensil they gave her. "Afraid I'll dig my way out?"

He grinned. "I have been told you're very resourceful, and not to trust you."

She laughed. So who ever was behind this knew a lot about her. That narrowed the suspects considerably. "What is your name? I'm getting tired of thinking of you as just my jailor."

"Junior will work."

"Junior." Alex ate as much as she could, before pushing her plate away. "Thank you, Jr."

He nodded. After removing the extra lamp and reading material she requested from the tray, Junior picked it up and headed out once more.

She stretched before picking up the literature he left for her. A Sears and Roebuck catalog, a copy of *The American Woman's Home* by Catharine Beecher, and a *New Orleans Picayune* newspaper. Placing the table at the foot of the bed, Alex plopped down and started to peruse the catalog first.

Inside she found all the basics a person would need for their home, for pennies. The newspaper made her grin. They didn't give her the entire paper, only the items that might pertain to a woman. A giggle escaped when she saw the obituaries. Why would they think she'd have any interest in that, unless they were trying to tell her something?

Dread pooled in her stomach, turning her giggle into a laugh. She tried to get angry over the thought, but all that did was make her laugh harder. She hated when this happened. Nerves made her laugh uncontrollably and there was nothing she could do to stop it.

Her laughter floated up to the floor above.

"I wonder what she found so funny?" said Junior.

"She won't be laughing soon," replied another man, the one that knocked Alex out. "The boss will be coming, and I don't think she's going to like what he has in store for her."

&

*T*rey paced the floor of the sitting room. It had been twenty-four hours since Alex's kidnapping. The ransom note arrived just before dawn that morning. They wanted Trey to bring the deed to his plantation to some abandoned slave quarters by noon today if he ever wanted to see his wife alive again.

He tried to rub the sleepiness from his eyes. Damn, his life flipped upside down in the last twenty-four hours. And where the hell was Andrew? There was only a half hour left before the meeting time.

He and Andrew worked out their differences. One black eye, a swollen jaw, and three sore ribs he sported were proof. A cloud of dust caught his eye. "Finally."

Trey threw the front door open and strode down the steps before Andrew brought his horse to a stop. "Well, what did you find out?"

"I'm not sure. There's a trail all right, and it leads to some abandoned slave quarters on my aunt's land. But there has been no sign of life there. It could be a trap."

Trey still had a hard time believing that Andrew was one of the Pinkerton men. That he had been out West chasing down a notorious spy named Beaumont, who was still trying to restart the war when his parents were killed. And the only reason he was visiting his aunt now was because he had tracked the spy to their hometown.

"I don't care. This is my wife we're talking about. I'll do anything to get her back."

"I know, and that's what they're banking on too. I want to get your wife back without getting either of you killed."

"What are you suggesting?" Trey leaned his hands against the porch railing.

"Someone go in your place."

"No," said Trey. "What if they find out?"

"What if it is just a ruse to put a bullet in your head?" Andrew slid from his horse. "Whoever kidnapped Miss Alexandra is probably the same one who has been sabotaging you. He wants to see you destroyed."

"I will make the exchange."

"It's not a wise choice," said Andrew.

"I don't care. This is my wife's life we're talking about. I won't do anything to jeopardize that."

"Then you better pray hard that nothing goes wrong."

～

The pounding of feet over her head made Alex stare up at the ceiling. "They must be having some kind of meeting."

She could hear them dragging a table across the floor, revealing a hole one of the legs had covered. Light from above streamed into the hole. Alex watched the dust mites' dance in the beam. More feet trampled in, followed by silence. Then she heard the sound of a new set of feet walk into the room. As the person moved toward the table the beam of light was blotted out for a few moments.

She moved to where she could get a view from the hole without being seen and settled down to listen to the conversation.

"How is she, Jake?"

"Fine, Mr. Beaumont. Just like you ordered."

She recognized Junior's voice. So Junior was a Jake.

"Good. Is everything ready?"

"Yes, sir," said another voice. "We have two dozen men waiting for Dalton to make the exchange. The moment he gets close enough he'll be captured and brought here."

"Good. I can't wait to see his face when he realizes who has been the one behind the destruction of his life."

That voice sounded familiar. Alex tried to get a look at the man talking, but the table blocked her view. The other man moved into view for her. It was the guy from the stream when she first got here. He handed a telegram to the leader.

"The preacher will be here in two days. He's sorry for the delay, but Pinkerton's men—"

A hand slammed down on the table making Alex jump.

"I don't care about Pinkerton's men."

"Yes, sir." The man from the pond backed up.

The man calmed instantly. "Now, how are the plans going for the wedding?"

Wedding?

"I sent a telegram back to the preacher, telling him he will be performing a wedding, then a funeral."

"Excellent. Poor Trey Dalton. First, he'll see his wife marry another man. Then he'll have a fatal accident."

A wicked laugh filled the room, making Alex shudder. She had to see who this man was. She also realized that time was of the essence. Somehow, she had to escape and warn Trey.

The man from the pond spoke. "It is noon now. Dalton should be at the meeting place. He'll be here within the hour. Where do you want us to put him?"

"Why, in with his little wife. I'll give them a few hours together before we separate them forever."

Alex heard that wicked laugh again.

"Everything is finally coming together. All the hard work I have done will finally pay off," the leader said. "Keep the spies on the Dalton plantation. I want to know if they'll try to rescue Dalton and his wife."

Alex blanched. Spies? Were there spies watching them the day she seduced Trey on the porch? Finally, the man stood up and moved from the table to give Alex a clear view of his face.

"Within thirty-six hours I will finally have everything I deserve. Once I do, we'll rejoice."

Alex's heart stopped at the sight of the man who'd caused all their trouble. She swallowed hard as she stared at the face of Beaumont Manning.

CHAPTER 26

*T*rey glanced around at the abandoned shack. He didn't like feeling the hairs on the back of his neck stand up. Andrew was right. This was a setup. He tried to walk backward, away from the impending doom he sensed, but when he backed into something solid he realized it was too late.

He spun, pushing his leg out and swept the assailant off his feet. Unfortunately, there were three more behind the man he felled. Using the training he learned from Alex he did take out two more. Maybe he would escape after all.

A whisper of movement behind him alerted him to new danger seconds before his world went black.

*T*he soft whisper of his name from his wife's lips was the sweetest thing he heard. Trey knew he must be dreaming, a dream he didn't want to wake up from.

"Trey. Please, Trey, open your eyes."

He felt her fingers gently brush his hair back from his face. A dank, dusty odor filled his nose. "Make sure Fleurette washes these sheets today," he mumbled. "They stink."

"They stink because you're inhaling dirt."

He blinked. Licking his lips, he tasted the dirt caked on them. "Since when did we have a dirt floor?"

Trey rolled over. He felt the heat of Alex's hand on his chest.

"Since we've both been locked up in this cellar."

Trey sat up quickly at that. The movement caused his head to pound. "Ow."

Alex swam in front of him for a few seconds while his eyes readjusted themselves. Her smile melted his heart.

"You have a very nasty bump on your head. I was afraid you wouldn't wake up." Kneeling beside him, she gently touched his face.

Trey opened his arms, and she practically knocked him down on the floor again as she flew into them. They remained locked in the embrace for a while.

He kissed the top of her head as he hugged to tighter. "Are you all right?"

She nodded as her fingers grasped his dirtied shirt. "Besides a bump to match yours, I'm fine. They've pretty much left me alone. My guard only comes around at mealtime. Other than that, I'd say there are no other guards."

"What happened?" Alex leaned back far enough to look at her husband's face. "How did you get here?"

"Your kidnapper sent a note asking for the deed to the plantation." Trey felt in each of his pockets, finding the deed still tucked inside the pocket of the vest he wore. "So I guess Andrew was right."

"Andrew? You're losing me."

"Yes. It's a long story."

"Trey, we're not going anywhere right now."

"You're right." He looked around at their prison and smiled ruefully. "Let's get a little more comfortable first."

They stood up and moved to the single bed. Propping his back against the wall, Trey took Alex into his arms once more. "I guess I'll start when the painting arrived."

She rested her head against his chest. The heat of his body and the beat of his heart relaxed her. "What painting?"

"Shush. Once we realized you were missing, we went out looking for you. We had just come back from searching when Fleurette told me a package arrived. It turned out to be a painting of you and Andrew."

Alex shifted so she could look at him, making the small bed creak. "Was I wearing a dark green dress?"

"Yes."

"That's the painting." She touched his arm. "The one that brought me here."

Trey searched her eyes. "That's what I thought, but you never mentioned Andrew in it."

"He wasn't. Between now and my future he is removed. I guess someone painted over him," she said. "I have to assume you went to Andrew's place ready to kill."

He nodded. "Had my rifle in my hands. Andrew didn't expect me, that's for sure. I threatened his life, trying to find out where you were. Something inside me cracked when he swore he didn't know. I hit him with the rifle. The anger that controlled me wanted me to tear him apart limb from limb. It made me ask questions I had buried for such a long time."

Trey leaned the back of his head against the plank wall. "He made me see how wrong I was. Jeanette was a real hellion. I knew that but buried it deep inside. She flirted with all of us. Well, everyone but Beau. For some reason she didn't like him. She enjoyed having us compete for her attention. I found out from Andrew that she was sent home for indiscretions instead of fear like Beau told me. Once I started thinking about it I realized Andrew was telling the truth. The whispered rumors I heard years ago weren't about how she fled, but what she got caught doing. My anger made me block that part out."

"About Beau—"

"No. Let me finish. I need to get this off my chest." Trey laced his fingers with Alex's. "Beau has been feeding me nothing but lies all my life. I found out Andrew couldn't have killed my parents. He wasn't here. He's a bounty hunter. While I was working overseas, he was earning the right to work for Pinkerton. The only reason he's here is because he's chasing a spy named Beaumont."

"Beaumont is here. I've seen him," said Alex. She rested her head on Trey's shoulder while staring up at the wooden ceiling. "His real name is Beau Manning."

Trey grabbed her shoulders. "Are you sure?"

"The men who are holding me—us—captive, work for that man. He came here earlier today. They kept calling the man Beaumont. I got a good look at his face. It was Beau," she said. "He plans on killing you, Trey."

"I'm not going to give him a chance."

"Then we've got to get out of here." Alex stood up and started to remove her dress.

Trey gave her a leer. "Sweetheart, don't you think we should start working on our escape first?"

"Don't be an ass. I can't think about escaping with this damn corset on. It will impede me too much."

Trey stood up to tower over her. "There is no way you are going out in public without your corset."

Hands on her hips, Alex glared up at him. "Have you ever worn one?"

Trey looked indignant. "Of course not."

"Then you don't know how they make a woman short of breath all of the time. I can't run in it. If I'm lucky, I'll probably get about five hundred feet before falling into a faint. Then you'd have to drag me the rest of the way. How far do you think we'll get?"

He ran his fingers through his hair. "You are the most exasperating woman!"

She arched one brow. "But I'm right."

"All right, but I'm not happy about it."

"You wouldn't be Trey Dalton if you didn't object. I like your staunch ways, most of the time." She turned her back to him. "How about helping a girl out?"

He shook his head as he loosened the strings on the corset. "How do you plan on getting into your dress without it?"

She gave him a quick peck on the cheek as she tore the corset in half. "I'll button the dress as far as I can and leave the rest undone."

"What?"

Footsteps sounded above them. Trey hastily helped her rebutton her dress.

Alex stepped into his warm embrace, hiding the torn corset behind their backs. She started to roll it like a parchment.

The door opened slowly. Jr. had a tray filled with their lunch, but he also carried a pistol. "Good evening, Mr. and Mrs. Dalton. I have your meal."

He placed the tray on the small table.

"Thank you, Junior." She shoved the rolled corset into Trey's waistband.

Trey looked at her. He pushed the corset deeper into his pants and pulled his shirt and vest over it. "Junior?"

Alex gestured to the table. "Well that's the name he gave me so I wouldn't have to call him my jailer."

Trey held out the one chair in the room for her to sit on.

"Mr. Dalton, your shirt is undone," said Junior.

Trey straightened, patting his back, and he nodded. As he pushed his shirt back into the waistband, he thanked Junior.

Alex watched him wide-eyed the entire time. Praying Junior wouldn't search Trey, thinking he was hiding something. Too many questions would be raised about her corset.

He sat on the bed. Their meal consisted of breaded pork chops, mash potatoes and gravy, corn, and rice pudding. While they ate quietly, he remained aware of the pistol trained on them. "Must he stand there like that?"

"Oh, Junior always waits while I eat, although I must say the gun is new."

Trey grunted as he finished his meal.

Junior waited for Alex to finish, then retracted the tray and himself from the room.

The moment his boots pounded overhead Alex grabbed Trey's arm and pulled him to his feet. She grabbed her corset and opened it up, pulling the stays out one by one.

"What are you doing?"

"Hoping I can pull the bolt back with these things. There's a small hole right above the lock. I'm hoping we'll be able to angle one of these things though the hole so we can pull the bolt back from in here."

"And if we can't."

Alex looked at him, her eyes huge. "I don't want to think of the alternative."

"What exactly did Beau say?"

She turned her back to him and peered out the hole in the door. "You don't want to know."

"Yes, I do. Tell me." Trey walked up behind her. Gently, he placed his hands on her shoulder and turned her around.

Alex released a shaky sigh. She puffed some air out of her mouth as she tried to figure an easy way to explain this. "Beau plans on tying you to a tree while some man called the preacher marries me to him. Then, he's going to kill you."

"My God."

"He wants everything you have, sweetheart. I don't know why, but he really hates you."

Trey wrapped his arms around his wife. "You know, I like the softness of your waist instead of that rigid corset."

"How do you think I feel? I lost about twenty pounds just by taking that thing off."

He looked around at the room. The only way out was the bolted door. "So. How are we going to escape?"

"Well, they played cards and got pretty drunk last night. I'm hoping there will be a repeat performance tonight. It depends on how much they see you as a threat."

Evening descended. Crickets and bullfrogs filled the air with their cries. Alex stared at the ceiling, almost willing the men to come back and drink themselves into oblivion.

"I don't think—"

"Shh," she said. A faint tread of boots ascended a flight of stairs.

A door opened on squeaky hinges before slamming shut.

"Jake," someone called.

A hasty pounding of boots stopped over their heads. "Sir?"

"Are the prisoners secure?"

"Yes, sir."

"Good. Mr. Beaumont wants you to check the outside perimeter of the house. Dalton can be tricky."

"Yes, sir."

They heard Jake's boot steps get softer as he headed out the door.

"Trey? Miss Alexandra? Where are you?"

They looked at each other.

"Andrew?" questioned Trey. "We're in the cellar."

They went to the door and heard the bolt slide back.

Andrew grinned at them as the door swung open. "Enjoying your stay?"

"Not particularly," said Alex.

"Good. In about fifteen minutes, we're going to cause a diversion to give you a chance to get away. There are about two dozen men watching this place, most are guarding the perimeter. "Stay here until you hear gunfire. Give your guard about five minutes to get out of the house and slip out. Go left and within five hundred yards you'll be under the cover of the woods along the edge of the bayou. Head north for about a half a mile along the water's edge. One of my men will be waiting for you with a pirogue. He'll get you home."

"Thank you."

Andrew nodded before closing the door and heading back up.

Jake reentered the house just as they heard Andrew reach the room over their heads. "Everything is clear, sir."

"We've heard there will be an attempt to break them out tonight. We have called most of the guards away from the house to double the patrol of our borders. If they break through you are the only one who can stop them. Don't fail us."

"No, sir."

Andrew headed out the door without another word.

Ten minutes later, Alex felt like she sat on pins and needles. "I wish this would start. I hate this waiting."

Her husband patted her hand.

They continued to listen. Every sound made Alex jump.

A sharp crack forced a squeak out of her. "Was that it?"

Trey nodded.

They both stared at the ceiling, hoping the gunfire would draw Jake outside quickly. About two minutes later, they heard him run across the floor, and bound out into the night.

They eased the door open and peeked around.

"So far, so good."

Trey took Alex's hand and guided her up the stairs. Again, they paused, making sure no one else was in the house to stop their escape. The doorway to the porch beckoned. Just before they slipped out, Trey checked to be sure no one was nearby. They slipped down the porch stairs and started to run to the copse of trees Andrew directed them to. Just as they reached the first few trees someone dropped down in front of them.

Although Alex couldn't see the man's face she did see the gun.

"Going somewhere?"

"As a matter of fact, yes." Alex kicked the gun out of his hand, then kicked him in the face, knocking him out cold.

Four more surrounded them.

Alex and Trey stood back to back when one more joined the other four. "Do you remember what I taught you?"

"Yes."

"Then on the count of three. One, two, three." They kicked chest high simultaneously, knocking down two. Alex whirled and took out two more. That left the one assailant.

Trey took him out with one quick chop to the neck.

They started to run again.

A loud repeat of a pistol stopped Trey in his tracks. Warmth spread through his body. He gave his wife an odd little smile as he sunk to his knees.

CHAPTER 27

*H*er scream pierced the night, causing the birds nesting in the trees to squawk and flap away. In her anger, Alex charged the man with the gun without thinking. Two well-placed kicks knocked him down. "If he dies, I will hunt you down, and kill you myself."

The moss hanging on the trees blocked any light she might have gotten from the moon. The pounding of her heart almost overpowered the sound of a croaking bullfrog and the buzz of mosquitoes. Taking several deep breaths, she forced herself to relax. The scents of the bayou filled her, slowing her racing heart.

Soft rustling filled her ears. She jumped into a defensive mode as four unknown men walked into the clearing.

"Miss Alexandra?" Andrew's brow crinkled as he looked at her stance.

"Mr. Leroux?" She relaxed, brushing her trembling hands against her cotton skirt. "I thought we were under attack again."

"You don't have to worry about that anymore. We've arrested the whole lot of them," he said. "And please call me Andrew. I think we've progressed beyond the formalness of society."

Alex smiled at him. "Thank you, Andrew."

"Remember me? The wounded one?"

"Trey." She knelt down beside him in the soft dirt. Her hand touched the side of his face. "I was never so scared." Then she punched him in the right shoulder. "If you ever do that again…"

"Ow! Sweetheart that is the shoulder the bullet entered."

As if she suddenly realized he was hurt, Alex started to fawn all over him, peeling his shirt away from where the bullet entered. She examined it thoroughly, realizing that five months ago she would have run away in horror. Now the metallic stench of blood didn't even faze her. Sitting back on her heels, she blinked.

She could live in this time, as long as she had Trey. She loved him. In fact, her world without him held nothing for her at all now. A smile spread across her lips. As much as she wanted to blurt it out she knew she had to wait.

She ripped her petticoat, placing a wad of cloth against the wound, then wrapped a longer strip around his shoulder. "It's a clean wound, but I can't tell if the bullet is still in there."

Andrew crouched down beside her. "I'll have a doctor look at it before we leave."

"All right, but I want to be present." She remembered the horror stories about the doctors from this era.

He escorted them to a small camp nearby.

A half hour later, with a freshly bandaged shoulder, Trey helped his wife onto the small pirogue that would bring them back to the plantation.

Andrew joined them as another man launched the boat into the bayou and proceeded to steer using a poll. "We need to talk about who did this."

"It was Beau," said Alex. "He's the one responsible for the sabotaging of Trey's plantation too."

"He's Beaumont," added Trey.

Andrew sat up, rocking the small pirogue. "Are you sure?"

"Positive."

Water lapped against the side of the boat, threatening to spill in.

"I'll bet money Beau will be at the house when we get back. How are we going to handle that?" asked Alex. "He has to be caught."

"He will be caught, with your help."

"How do we fit in?" Trey placed a protected arm around Alex.

"First, he doesn't know about me. Let's keep it that way for as long as possible. And until we have set a trap, don't make him suspicious. He can't figure out you know the truth," Andrew said. "We don't really have any proof that he is Beaumont."

"But I saw and heard him while he was using that name," said Alex.

Trey rested a hand on her arm. "The court will take a man's word faster than a woman's."

That pissed her off. "That is such a—"

"Alex don't stand…" The boat flipped as she stood. "…up."

The four of them came up sputtering.

Dripping with the pungent bayou water, Andrew asked, "Is she always this headstrong?"

Trey grinned. "Yes."

The fourth man, who steered the pirogue, righted it and climbed on board. He offered a hand to Alex first. Once she seated herself, he helped Trey, then Andrew.

"Didn't anyone ever tell you to never stand in a boat?"

She glared at Andrew, who had asked the question. "I don't normally travel by boat."

"My wife doesn't care for some aspects of our society." Trey wrapped a soggy arm around her.

"Let's get back to how we're going to trap Beau." Alex didn't want to explain that comment. "I think we should confront him."

"He'll run. We have to handle this properly. Beau Manning is very cunning, or we would have caught him a long time ago." Andrew rubbed his hand along his jaw. "I'd like to use Alexandra as bait."

"No."

"Trey, your fears are unfounded. Your wife will be well protected. I believe she will be able to get Beau to talk. All she has to do is to get him to reveal that he is indeed Beaumont and we'll grab him."

"I don't like it."

Alex turned toward Trey. All three men grabbed the side of the pirogue quickly with her movement. "Very funny. He's right, Trey. Beau did want to marry me."

"What?"

"Long story," she said to Andrew. "Beau planned on killing Trey and marrying me. He doesn't know I saw him. Perhaps I could use that to my advantage. Beau might want to gloat; the right placed words could get him to reveal what we need to know."

"You won't be able to do anything for a few days," said Andrew as they pulled up to the shoreline of Trey's property. "You have a houseful."

"A houseful?"

"The moment people heard you were taken they started arriving."

"Then we have to pretend we know nothing about Beau until we can get everyone to leave." The man steering the boat helped her out then Trey and Andrew. "When should we trap him?"

"We're going to have to see how Beau behaves when he sees you. It will make it easier to make a plan that will trap him." Andrew shook hands with Trey and gave Alex a hug. "I'll be in touch. Just remember don't let him know we're onto him."

"There are three rules." Trey spoke to Alex as they headed to the house. "You will follow Andrew's word to the letter. I will be nearby when you talk to him, and he cannot touch you."

❧

*A*lex stared at the well-lit house with apprehension. "I'm not sure I can do this."

They spied Beau's horse earlier.

"You have to," said Trey as he slipped his arm around her waist for a quick hug. "Because we've been seen." He nodded toward the back porch. People started to pour out of the house.

Aunt Rose came down the stairs a lot faster than Trey expected her to. "It seems Aunt Rose is a little spryer than she let on."

"There's a lot that our aunt doesn't let on," she returned. She sucked in her breath at the sight of Beau, who just stepped out on the porch.

"I love you." Trey took her hand and tucked it into the crook of his arm.

She looked up at him with love filled eyes. Before she could utter a word, Alex found herself enveloped in Rose's warm embrace.

"Oh, my chile, I was so worried about you. And here you are acting like you're coming back from an evening stroll. Are you all right? Did they hurt you?"

"No, Aunt Rose, they didn't hurt me." Alex smiled. "In fact, they were quite nice, as far as kidnappers go."

Rose snapped open her fan. "Humph."

"Miss Alexandra. I see you came through your ordeal unscathed," said Beau as he joined the small group.

"Unscathed?" Alex fought to keep the fear she felt out of her eyes. "Not really. Lucky, yes."

She tugged on Trey's arm to get him moving again.

"Very lucky," commented Aunt Rose. "My heart fluttered when I saw Jessie standing on my porch looking like he hadn't slept in three days. After he told me that you had disappeared, and they didn't know what had happened to Trey, why, I just couldn't breathe."

"We're fine now, Aunt Rose." Trey patted her arm.

"Thank goodness." She nodded as she wiped her eyes. "I don't think my heart could take another scare like that."

"How did you escape?" asked Beau.

They had just reached the porch steps. Alex blinked while she tried to come up with something realistic. Trey butted in before she could open her mouth.

"It was the strangest thing, really. Alexandra and I were locked up in the root cellar of the old abandoned Beauchamp plantation home. We heard gunfire nearby. Whoever was guarding us ran out of the building. I assume he went to find out who was shooting."

"My wife here came up with a very ingenious way to get out." He hugged Alex tight. "We found no one around to stop us. Headed for the nearest trees and here we are."

Rose's fan moved furiously. "What was the ingenious way?"

Alex ascended the stairs and claimed her favorite rocker. She blushed prettily. "My stays."

Beau gave her a confused look.

Aunt Rose's fan stopped. She looked at her wide-eyed. "You mean...?"

Alex nodded.

"Oh my!" That fan started moving rapidly again.

"Her stays?" Beau turned toward Trey.

Trey held out his palm. In it were three of the bone stays from Alex's corset. He broke them to make it look like they had been under a lot of pressure. "Her stays from her corset. I used them to slide the lock open."

Beau laughed.

Trey looked up at his wife. "Sweetheart, are you feeling all right? Your color is fading."

"I'm fine." She arched a brow at him. "I guess all the excitement is catching up with me."

"I'm just worried about you fainting again."

"I'll be all right. I just need my fan." She shot him a piercing look. What was Trey trying to tell her? Alex stood up and swayed just a little. Trey was beside her in an instant. "Oh my. I guess I got up a little too quickly."

"Perhaps you should sit back down," said Beau.

"Yes. That sounds like..." Alex had never faked a spell before. She cleared her mind and relaxed her body so that she could slide boneless to the floor.

CHAPTER 28

*A*lex opened one eye cautiously. "Is he gone?"

"Aunt Rose took care of that." Trey smiled at his wife, reclining on the settee in the sitting room. He gently ran his knuckles along her jaw. "She sent him to the doctor's house."

She sat up a little straighter. "So now what?"

"We wait for Andrew. I sent word that Beau has left so I expect him soon."

She rested her hand against his chest, feeling the fast beat of his heart. "Aren't you afraid that Beau will come back?"

"He'll probably go straight to the Beauchamp plantation to find out what went wrong."

"Where is the rest of the household?" Alex set her feet on the floor and stood up, noticing no one was around. "They're too curious to go meekly."

"I told them you needed some time to rest and they should get some themselves."

Alex nodded. Everyone listened to Trey. "I could use a strong drink."

Trey went for the brandy snifter.

"Huh-uh. Whiskey."

He looked at his wife with raised brows. "I have never seen you drink whiskey."

"You didn't know I could roller skate either."

The crystal decanter dinged against the glass he filled before handing it to her.

Alex took a quick sip to see how strong it was before downing the whole content. As the warmth spread through her body, she plopped back down on the settee they laid her on. "That's good stuff."

"This has been one hell of a day." Trey took the glass from her hand and poured himself a small drought.

"Yes, it has," Alex leaned against the white marble fireplace. "He's very good, you know."

"What do you mean?" He placed the glass on the secretary near him.

"If I didn't know the truth, I would believe he was actually happy to see us home safe and sound."

A sharp knock on the door grabbed their attention. Trey opened it to allow Andrew into the room.

Alex's mouth quirked up.

"What?" asked Trey, after he closed the door.

"You. Two days ago, you wanted to kill him. Now look at you."

"Two days ago, he did try to kill me, Miss Alexandra," said Andrew. "But his love for you made him see the light."

Trey poured another glass of whiskey and offered it to Andrew.

"Hah," Alex quipped. "It probably was a blow or two to the head that made him see any lights."

Trey laughed. "You're right. But it did make me see what you tried so hard to make me believe. I'm not as blind as you think I am."

Andrew sat in one of the high-back chairs. "Well, now that you are a wiser man. Let's catch the real criminal and put him away for good."

～

*A*lex sat on the settee with her dress fluffed out around her. Trying to trick Beau into revealing his plans would not be easy.

Even if Trey, Andrew, and half of the plantation workers were hiding in the next room.

She swallowed the knot she felt in her throat when Fleurette announced she had a visitor. Andrew was right. Beau was very predictable. He walked into the room with all the grace and ease of a true Southern gentleman.

"Why, Mr. Beau, what a pleasant surprise." Alex stood up to greet him. "I must apologize for my behavior last night." She placed her hand over her heart. "I don't know what came over me."

"It's all right, Miss Alexandra." He smiled at her. "With all the excitement you went through the last few days, I'm proud you made it as far as you did."

"Why, thank you, Mr. Beau." Alex opened her fan. The soft breeze caused a few tendrils of her hair to move. "That is very kind. You don't know how frightened I was. If it hadn't been for Trey, why, I'd probably still be in that awful place. But here I am, talking your ear off, when you probably came to see Trey." She stood and walked toward the door.

"Actually, I came to see how you were doing, Miss Alexandra. I was worried about you."

"How very kind you are." Her fan fluttered in her grasp. She uttered a soft sob. "I had never been so frightened. Not knowing what would happen to me or if I'd ever come home again."

Beau cupped her elbow and guided her back to her chair. "Perhaps you'd like something to calm your nerves."

"Yes, please." She accepted the snifter of brandy he poured for her.

"Did Trey learn who kidnapped you?" Beau asked as he sat down in a chair near the settee she sat on.

Alex gazed down at her hands. She couldn't lie if she looked at him. "No. My kidnapper was too smart for Trey. Although he believes Andrew Leroux is behind everything, he can't prove it, so won't move against him."

"Andrew can be a dangerous man. Perhaps, you should go visit relatives until this is finished."

"Oh, I couldn't leave here right now." She looked up at Beau with frightened eyes. "You don't think he'll try it again, do you? I don't think I could go through that again."

"Don't fret so, Miss Alexandra." He patted her hand. "Trey will keep that from happening."

"He didn't stop it the first time."

"He wasn't prepared." Beau's nostrils flared. "This time he is."

"Why would someone kidnap me?" Her eyes filled with unshed tears.

"You are a very beautiful woman."

"Flatterer." Alex wanted to snort. Instead, she fanned herself and batted her eyes. "I'm sure there's a lot of people who would disagree with you."

"Then they are blind, Miss Alexandra." He gave her a dazzling smile.

~

"*W*hy is she being so nice to him?" whispered Trey.

Andrew glanced over at Trey for a second before going back to his vigil at the peephole they placed to spy on Beau and Alexandra. "What would you expect? Her to hog-tie him and beat a confession out of him?"

"That's what I'd do," mumbled Trey. "I don't like this. They've been talking for at least ten minutes and he hasn't said a thing. He's not going to rise to the bait."

"We don't know that for sure." Although Andrew silently agreed with Trey, he knew they had to give Miss Alexandra enough time to try everything to get Beau to confess.

~

*S*he felt the conversation start to wind down. Beau would slip away if she didn't get him to confess. Her fan moved methodically. Somehow, she had to get him to talk, but how? Alex rubbed her brow.

"Well. Miss Alexandra. I'll be taking my leave now."

She stood at the same time. "Oh, must you?"

Her skirt wrapped itself around her ankles, pitching her forward into Beau's arms. The brandy she never drank soaked his shirt. "Oh no." She tried patting it with the hanky she kept up her sleeve. "I am so sorry, Mr. Beau."

His first reaction was fury, which he quickly disguised. He gave a strained laugh. "It's all right, Miss Alexandra. I'll just go home and—"

"No! I mean, please let me make this up to you. I can have Fleurette clean it in no time."

"Why are you so nervous, Miss Alexandra? Is something wrong?"

Alex could feel her heart beating too fast. She had to turn this around fast. "Nothing is wrong." She glanced toward the door. "It's just Trey has changed since all this started. He is jealous of everyone."

"Even me?"

"Especially you." Alex blushed.

"Why, Miss Alexandra."

She placed a hand on her face, feeling the heat rise. "Well you are a very handsome man."

"Thank you."

The heat of his gaze bothered her. Not knowing what he thought made matters worse. When he took a step toward her, she took one back.

"Do I frighten you?"

"No." When he stepped closer again she forced herself to stay put. His cool fingers brushed a stray hair behind her ear. She giggled nervously.

Beau grew bolder, caressing the right side of her neck with his fingers. "How did Trey get so lucky?"

Her eyes widened as she tried not to react to the intimate caress.

"He has always had luck like this. You know he doesn't deserve you. Yet, he always ends up on top." He walked around her. "When we were children he was always the best child. If we raced, either by foot or by horse, he always won. He'd catch the biggest fish when we went fishing. The girls liked him more."

"But you..."

"There was never room for me. Even my own parents wanted to know why I couldn't be more like Trey. It drove me crazy."

Alex just stood there, feeling his fingers slide across her collarbone to the other shoulder as he continued to circle her.

"I was supposed to be the one who did everything best, not Trey." He gripped her left shoulder. "No one cared, though."

"Beau, you're hurting me."

He loosened his grip. Standing behind her, he whispered in her ear. "So I took matters into my own hands."

"How?" They wouldn't hear his confession if he whispered it to her.

"Why by making sure Trey's life wasn't perfect." He spoke in a normal voice.

"I don't understand." Her brow crinkled. She turned her head toward Beau, finding his face only inches from hers.

"I made sure things would happen, like frightening a young girl he liked, or getting someone to outbid Trey for land, supplies, or animals." Beau moved until he stood in front of her again. "But he just laughed. It didn't bother him. I went out of my way to make him miserable and he just ignored it. Then the war started.

"I thought I'd finally get my chance to shine. Everyone would take notice. But no," he said, his voice harsh.

Alex flinched.

"Just before war broke out Trey was sent to France to earn his keep with relatives. Boudreaux and Leroux went west about the same time. They had investments in the railroad and wanted to make sure their investments were protected. I am the only one who went to war."

"So you were the only hero."

"Ha." He started to circle her again when she showed she was on his side. "One would think, but no. Within six months, I ended up in a Yankee prison."

"How did that happen, Beau?"

"I was sent to find out what happened to two members of our regiment." He paused in his circling of her. "We had lost track of them two days before."

"What was so important about these two men?"

"One was our captain, the other was a surgeon who had just joined us." Beau rubbed the back of his neck. "Some Yanks were tracking us. Our captain and the doctor were supposed to lure those filthy Yanks away from us. When they didn't return after four days, what was left of the regiment decided to go look for them."

"And you got caught."

"We walked right into a camp of Yanks without realizing it." His eyes bored into her. "I was able to escape a couple months later. Went west for a couple years. Once the war was over, I returned home." He moved to stand beside her. "I expected a warm homecoming. No one could have really known what happened to me, but they did." Beau growled. "My parents disowned me. Our friends laughed at me. Trey's parents pitied me."

Alex wondered why Trey had never heard this.

"I hated their pity."

A cold finger of dread slid down Alex's spine. "You killed them, didn't you?"

"Killed is such an uncreative word. They deserved to die for the way they treated me. Their son abandoned me, my family abandoned me, and all the Dalton's could do was pity me!" He stepped behind her and gripped her throat. "I don't want anyone's pity."

She tried to pry his fingers loose. "Beau, you're hurting me again."

"I'm sorry, Miss Alexandra." His grip loosened immediately. "Sometimes my emotions get the better of me."

"You must have had an ingenious plan." She swallowed against his softer grip. Beau Manning was wacko. "No one ever suspected you. How did you do it?"

"I brought them a gift from Trey, laced with arsenic." A cold smile spread across his face. "The poison seeped into their systems slowly. My visits to their home made sure they continued to take the poison. But it took too long, and I got tired of waiting. So I had to make sure they died quicker."

"How?"

"By slitting their throats, placing them in a carriage and sending that carriage deep into the bayou. They made a great meal for several big gators."

Color drained from her face.

His fingers gripped her chin. "But you don't have to worry about that fate, Miss Alexandra. You will become my loving wife once Trey is dead."

Fingers of fear gripped her heart. "How does Andrew fit into all of this?"

"He was just a good scapegoat. He became too close a friend with Trey. I was supposed to be Trey's only close friend, not that simpleton." Beau grabbed her slender wrist. "I want you to call in Fleurette and send word to Trey out in the fields. Tell him that you're too afraid to stay here, and that you're going back to California."

He dragged her over to the small secretary and pushed her into a chair. Snatching a pen from the inkwell, he pressed it into her hand. "Write."

"Who taught you to write?" Beau looked at the letter. She couldn't help that she never learned to use an inkwell. Keeping one hand on her wrist, he wrote a quick note for her to hand to Fleurette.

She jumped when Beau shouted for her to call Fleurette. No one else was supposed to get involved in this. Beau could kill her the moment she walked in the door if Fleurette hesitated for just a second.

Beau twisted her hand up behind her when the door opened.

Alex started when she saw a small gray head pop in the doorway. "Jessie?"

"I'm sorry, Miss Alexandra, Fleurette is out tending the garden. She asked me to stay here in case you needed me." He looked from Alex to Beau. If he noticed anything odd he didn't express it.

"Could you please deliver this message to Mr. Dalton for me?" She held the note out for Jessie.

"Yes, ma'am." He turned to head out the door.

"And Jessie?"

He turned back to her. "Yes, ma'am?"

Beau tightened his grip, making her wrist throb. "I need to pack a trunk or two."

"Yes, ma'am."

"That was very smart," Beau murmured in her ear. "I thought you were going to warn him somehow."

"We must make the note believable, right?"

Beau moved her over to the settee. "True."

A loud commotion could be heard in the hallway. Alex prayed it wouldn't push Beau off the deep end. She had barely started to sit down when the door burst open. In the doorway stood Elizabeth Boudreaux.

"Alexandra! Are you all right? I came as soon as I heard."

Alex buried her face in her hands. This was something no one bargained for.

CHAPTER 29

*E*lizabeth entered regally, her head held high. Her skirts whispered across the floor as she rushed to Alexandra's side. "Oh, my poor dear. The moment I heard about your horrible ordeal, I rushed right over."

"Your timing is impeccable," mumbled Alex. She looked up at her friend, who didn't know that her life was now in jeopardy too. "No one informed me you were coming."

"I didn't have time to send a message. Papa barely gave me permission to come. Any delay would have changed his mind." Elizabeth sank down beside her.

Alex clasped hands with Elizabeth. "I love your company, Beth, but I really wish you had given me some warning."

"Is there a problem?" Elizabeth's brow crinkled with a touch of worry.

"Um." Her eyes slid to Beau who had moved into the corner. "No, it's just that everyone is out in the field right now. I don't have anyone to ready a room for you."

"Oh, that's all right. Perhaps Mr. Beau would be cavalier enough to move my trunk in." She batted her lashes at him.

Beau smiled. "Of course, if you ladies would accompany me out to the carriage."

They rose in unison and followed Beau outside to Elizabeth's buckboard. Heat rose off the ground. The horses snuffed and snorted as he hefted the trunk and deposited it, with a grunt, in the front hallway. "Jessie can carry it up to the room once Fleurette has a chance to prepare it. In the meantime, why don't both of you ladies accompany me for a ride?"

"Oh, what fun," exclaimed Elizabeth.

Beau gave Alex a knowing smile. He walked to the buckboard and gestured for them to join him. "Miss Alexandra, why don't you sit on my left, Miss Elizabeth, on my right."

Alex silently climbed up beside him.

"It is a beautiful day, is it not?" asked Elizabeth.

"Yes, it is," replied Beau. "How could it not be when I have two of the most beautiful women in the town with me."

He clicked at the horses as he shook out the reins.

Alex stared back at the house, knowing that all their plans just went up in smoke.

~

"Shit." Trey emphasized his anger by kicking the wall and putting his foot through it. The crunch of wood drifted down the hallway.

"Very good," said Andrew. "Your level head will be a great asset in rescuing your wife."

"Don't be sarcastic." Trey ran his fingers through his hair. "How the hell did this happen?"

Andrew grabbed his hat and duster and headed for the door.

"Where are you going?"

"After them." He grinned at Trey. "My men are all over. They'll spot Beau quickly. We need to keep up with him, or the women could be hurt."

"I hope we find him quickly." Trey wasted little time in catching up with Andrew.

"Me too. My friend. Me too."

◇

*A*lex watched the bayou whip by as they traveled down one of the dirt roads. Dust covered her clothes, and her hair. Every time she breathed, she sucked some into her body. She could feel it in her mouth. When she bit down, she tasted grit.

She wondered where Beau was taking them but didn't dare ask. So far, Elizabeth had no clue as to what was really going on. Hopefully, she'd be able to talk Beau into letting Beth go before she caught on.

The woman in question had chattered endlessly since they left the plantation an hour ago. A stray piece of hair blew into her face. She tucked it behind her ear.

"You've been quiet, Alexandra," said Elizabeth.

"I know." She smiled at her friend. "I have been through a lot this week. Sorry, I didn't mean to be rude."

"You're not being rude." Elizabeth leaned across Beau to touch Alex's arm.

Alex looked at her friend. The smile that started to spread across her face died. The spark of fear in Elizabeth's eyes caught her attention. Somehow, Elizabeth knew. "I guess the kidnapping affected me more than I want to realize."

"I can imagine. It's something no woman wants to go through. Just the thought frightens me to death. Do you know who did it?"

"No." Alex shot her a warning look. "They kept me in a cellar."

"Oh. Then you must have been kept at the Beauchamp place."

Beau looked at her. "What makes you say that?"

She paused for only a second, and then snorted. "It's the only cellar around. Almost all the houses around here are right off the bayou. Anyone crazy enough to build a cellar normally found it full of water. The Beauchamps picked the highest point of their property and then added dirt just so they could be the only ones for miles to have a cellar.

It seems that Mrs. Beauchamp went to visit her sister in Kentucky and had to have one."

"You always seem to have that juicy tidbit that no one else has." Alex smiled. "How is that?"

Elizabeth opened her fan. It slowly moved up and down, causing loose tendrils of hair to float around her face. "I don't know what you're talking about."

"Yes, you do." Alex laughed. "Somehow, you always know the newest gossip just before anyone else does. It's almost like you make it up as you go along except it's always turns out true."

"Alexandra Dalton! Really!" said Beth. She fanned herself vigorously for a second before she spoke again. "Which reminds me. Did I tell you that a whole bunch of them Pinkerton men came into town? They're a fine sight."

"The Pinkerton Agency?" She paled a little. "Why are they here?"

"Don't know. Hear tell they're looking for a spy."

"Really?" Alex gaze slid from Beth to Beau. "How exciting. Who is the spy?"

Beth tapped her fan on her left cheek. "I heard the name, but I don't remember. Not a name I'd recognize. Wouldn't it be absolutely famous to have a spy in our mist?"

"As if he'd seek out our friendship." Alex tried to sound noncommittal.

"But would it not be fun? Imagine, the two of us involved with a wanted criminal."

"Are you crazy? We could be killed."

"Oh no." Beth turned in the seat toward Alex a little. "Most spies are gentlemen."

"What book did you get that one out of?"

"A pulp." A slight blush filled Beth's cheeks. "Please don't tell Father. He'd be so mad."

Alex arched a brow. She thought the dime novel normally featured a cowboy. Knowing that her friend read them made her like the woman a little more. Her gaze moved across the area they rode through. She noticed a small farmhouse in the distance. "Who lives there?"

"No one now. The LeBlancs built that for their son and his bride before the war but he didn't return. The bride-to-be moved west about a year ago."

Beau pulled the coach up to the front porch.

"We're stopping?" asked Elizabeth.

"Yes," he said.

"But Father—" Beth stared hard at the gun that appeared in Beau's hand.

"Now, ladies. You need to cooperate with me. Inside, now."

The two women's eyes locked for a second before lifting their skirts enough to climb down from the carriage without landing on their faces.

Alex wanted to reason with him. "Beau, why are you bringing Miss Elizabeth in this? She has nothing to do with this."

"Oh, but she does." He gestured for them to enter the abandoned house. "Leroux is sweet on her."

"He is?" asked Elizabeth. A slow blush filled her cheeks again.

Once inside, Alex placed herself between Beau and Elizabeth. "What does Mr. Leroux have to do with this?"

Beau smiled as he closed the door. "Because Andrew Leroux works for the Pinkerton Agency."

Alex's eyes widened.

"Don't look so surprised." He slammed the bar to block the door into place. "Did you think I was stupid?"

She flinched at the sound. "Of course not."

"It was easy to figure out," Beau said. "He showed up too many times in too many places for it to be a coincidence. That's why I came back to Jennings. I knew Andrew would follow and I could kill two birds with one stone."

Beth tapped her on the shoulder.

"Not now," she whispered to her friend.

"And you two ladies will draw them in for me." Beau leaned against the wall, keeping the gun aimed in their direction. "You don't know how surprised I was to find a pretty woman in Trey's home. I knew I'd driven all the local women away from him. The very first time I met you I knew he felt something for you, Alexandra. I watched how he behaved around you. His eyes followed you across a room at his house. At the parties he never left your side. It was like he was afraid you'd disappear on him. And he hated it if another man even looked at you. He's in love with you.

"It was perfect for my plan. I made sure that as his feelings for you deepened, his hatred for Andrew would grow." Beau laughed. "You should have seen his face when he tore the cover off the portrait. He tried to tear it with his bare hands."

"How did you have that portrait made?"

"You met the painter at your wedding. He was the shorter gentleman who accompanied me."

Alex thought the man had stared at her too much, now she knew why.

"He was so struck by your beauty that he begged me to introduce you. He wanted to do your portrait. So I commissioned him. I attained a copy of your photograph from your wedding and one of Andrew. I gave them to him. When the portrait was done I held it until the proper moment," he said. "It was perfect. He went charging into the night to tear Andrew limb from limb, giving me the chance to prepare for our departure."

"Our?"

"Of course, my dear. Once your husband is dead, we will wed. I'll gain control of his lands, and my revenge will be complete." Beau laughed again. "Finally, I'll have everything I deserve."

Alex prayed he would get what he really deserved.

~

"Where the hell are we?" asked Trey, his voice soft so it wouldn't carry through the stand of trees that surrounded them.

"About fifty-five yards from your wife." Andrew pointed to the small ranch in front of them. It looked out of place in bayou country. "Beaumont owns it. He also left a trail so obvious he expected us to follow. He's setting us up."

259

"He knows we're here?"

Andrew nodded. "He still wants you dead and wants your wife. Beaumont is very versatile. He'll just adjust his plans to still have the same outcome. Beau thinks he's lured us here."

The door to the house banged open. Alexandra stepped awkwardly out onto the porch. "Trey?"

He clasped Andrew's arm. Just as he started to answer he found a cloth shoved in his mouth.

"That's what Beau wants. He'll be able to tell where we're located if you answer."

Cricket chirps filled the air.

"See, I told you—" Alex's voice cut off abruptly.

"I know you're out there, Trey, and I know Andrew and several of his men are out there too. Throw down your guns, and the women won't be hurt."

Trey turned his head toward Andrew. "Is he out of his mind?"

"His influence is very strong." Andrew shook his head. "He probably replaced the men we arrested by now."

"Then we're surrounded."

"Possibly."

Trey gritted his teeth. "Why doesn't this bother you?"

"I'm used to it. Now be quiet." He signaled several men to change location, then two more men to move closer.

A twig snapped behind them.

"We're bait, aren't we?" Trey asked, as he heard metal scrape as someone slid the bolt of a rifle home.

Andrew grinned just before they felt cold steel press against their cheeks.

"This really isn't funny," Trey said as he stood up at the same time as Andrew. After he turned toward his captor his eyes widened. There were four rifles trained on them. "Are you sure about this?"

"Trey. You have to trust me. Miss Alexandra's life depends on it," Andrew said just loud enough for Trey to hear.

He didn't respond as he followed Andrew into the clearing in front of the house where Beau stood. Alex and Miss Elizabeth stood against one of the posts. On closer inspection, he found they were tied to the post.

"Welcome, gentlemen," said Beau. "We've been anticipating your arrival." He gestured for them to step up on the porch with his gun. The wood vibrated with their steps. "This will be even better than my earlier plans. Now it will look like Andrew kidnapped both women, Trey chased him down, and you two killed each other, unfortunately a stray bullet will also do in Miss Elizabeth. And Miss Alexandra will be so distraught that she clings to the man who found her out here, which of course, will be me. We'll marry, I'll claim all your lands, Trey, and I'll live happily ever after."

Trey would have killed him then, if there hadn't been for the guns pointed at his head. "Why don't you fight me like a man, Beau?"

He didn't look at Alex. One glance at her face would crumble his resolve.

"Why should I?" Beau commented. He gestured for two men to step up and tie Trey's hands behind him first, then do the same to Andrew. "This is so much easier."

"Alexandra will know the truth. She won't marry you."

"She won't have a choice." Beau laughed. "I'll kill her if she refuses."

"You have an answer for everything, don't you?" said Andrew. "I'm amazed at how well you planned this out."

"I have worked hard to accomplish this." Beau preened at his compliment. "Of course, you two weren't difficult to manipulate."

Trey's hands clinched into fists. They did just walk right into his hands. He felt like an idiot. His gaze slid to the women for just a second. Alex's head was bowed. Some of her hair had come loose; several strands hid her face from view. He wondered what was going through her mind at that moment.

A few moments later her head snapped up. She wore a sly grin on her lips.

What was the woman up to?

A few seconds later he watched as Miss Elizabeth took several hesitant steps away from the post she had been tied to.

Andrew still had Beau's undivided attention so he knew he wouldn't notice right away. Trey started to struggle against his bonds to keep Beau's man from noticing her escape as well.

She moved as quickly as she could toward the woods.

Trey held his breath several times in fear of her getting caught, but she made it. Now he understood why his wife complained about the corset so much. Miss Elizabeth was hampered badly by it.

When his gaze fell on Beau again, he found his blue eyes narrowed as they stared at him. Beau turned toward where the women were tied. He shrieked at the absence of Elizabeth. He bellowed for one of his men, who came forward, but didn't come too close.

"Find her. Now."

The young man's head bobbed once before he hightailed it into the woods.

Beau grabbed Alex's chin. "Where did she go, my dear?"

Trey took one step toward them. The loud snap of a gun being cocked stopped him.

Beau never took his eyes off Alex while he pointed his gun at Trey's heart, then armed it. "I'll ask you again, Miss Alexandra, where did she go?"

Alex pulled her chin out of his grasp. "I don't know."

"You don't know?" Beau laughed as he backhanded her in the face with the butt of one of his guns. "I hate liars."

Trey watched in horror as his wife slid boneless to the floor.

CHAPTER 30

"I'll kill you for that," snarled Trey.

"You forget who is in control." Beau drew small circles in the air with the gun he had pointed at Trey's heart.

A light sound to the left made them turn in that direction. Beau smiled at the man who walked toward them. Trey noted his all black ensemble. A bible was gripped in his hands.

"It's about time you made it," said Beau.

"Had some things to take care of." He didn't seem to be afraid for Beau.

"I expect you to come when I summon you."

Trey watched the man size Beau up and, by the look on his face, the preacher found him lacking. Completely ignoring Beau's remark, he said, "You said there was a weddin' and a funeral you wanted me to take care of?"

Beau stood still for a few seconds, as if he fought some inner rage, before answering, "Yes. This young lady and I are getting married. These two gentlemen will be in need of your eulogy in a few minutes."

He looked at the pile of crinoline at Beau's feet. "It will cost you more for two of them."

"Fine, just get it done."

"Which first?"

"This one." he said pointing at Trey.

Metal scraped against leather as the preacher pulled out his Smith & Wesson and pointed it at Trey's head.

"The wedding first," said Beau.

"It don't look like the bride is ready to marry yet. Besides, isn't one of these fellows here her husband?"

"All in good time, my man."

"Fine." The preacher shrugged. "Wake her up. Let's get this thing moving."

Beau bent down beside Alex and released her hands. He tapped her face gently, trying to wake her up. When she didn't respond, he pulled her into his arms and shouldered her dead weight. "We're ready."

The preacher just stared at Beau, caressing his bible in his hand. "She ain't awake yet. The bride must say I do, or it's not a weddin'."

Trey watched as his wife came to life in Beau's hands as he turned her to face him. One minute she hung limply in his arms, the next minute her vibrant blue eyes opened, and her knee hit its mark.

Beau dropped his hold on her to grab his injured crotch.

"Beau, we're not getting married." Using the heel of her hand, she slammed his nose upward, shattering it. Blood spurted everywhere. The metallic odor hung in the air. Her foot came up and pounded into his chest, sending him flying backward through a glass window and crashing to the floor inside.

"Ever."

"You have two choices." She dusted off her clothes before looking up at the men who surrounded them with guns. "Leave or run the risk that I'll do the same thing to you next."

Alex watched as each of the men eased themselves away from her. Once they felt they had enough distance, they ran like their coattails were on fire, everyone, but the preacher.

He strode toward Trey and Andrew while he pulled out a Bowie knife.

Alex leaped from the porch.

"Whoa, ma'am. I'm just going to cut their ropes, nothing else."

The preacher moved slowly toward Andrew first. Keeping his blade in plain sight he split the ropes in two. "She's sure a live one."

"I know." Andrew grinned as he rubbed his wrists.

Trey's bonds fell from his hands seconds later. He raced to Alex's side. "You were beautiful."

Tears shimmered in her eyes. "He wanted... He was going to... Oh Trey."

Trey held her close as she blubbered all the fear and frustration she kept in check during those tense moments. He watched as Andrew checked on Beau.

Andrew stepped out on the porch in time to see the preacher enter the woods. "Beau's still alive, but barely. Miss Alexandra, I have never seen anything like that. You handled yourself magnificently."

"Thank you." She blushed, still holding on to Trey for dear life. "It was instinct. I couldn't stand by and let him take my life away."

Trey gently lifted her chin until he could look in her eyes. His lips lowered to hers. Love and joy coursed through his veins. She was safe. Neither noticed Andrew moving off to talk to his men, and to get all the men they arrested to the local jail.

~

*A*lex propped her head on one hand as she made another entry in her diary. After explaining to her grandmother about her frightening experience, she wrote a little of her love for Trey. The squeak of metal alerted her to the turning handle. She closed the book and slipped it under the bed. As she rolled over, her husband entered their room.

His eyes raked her, taking in the thin robe and gown she wore. She smiled. Just his gaze got her blood boiling.

"I didn't think they'd ever leave." He removed his vest and slung it over a chair.

"Beau has been arrested?" Alex stood up and helped him unbutton his shirt.

"I watched the marshal lead him away in irons. He'll finally pay for all his crimes." He drew her into his arms. "Seeing you at his mercy scared me so much, Alex. I never knew how much I loved you until I almost lost you."

"He terrified me," Alex admitted. A frown creased her forehead. "That gun he held on you made my palms sweat. I don't know what I would have done if he had shot you." Her voice broke.

"Nothing happened." Trey hugged her close as he kissed the top of her head. "We're here, no worse for the wear."

"But my mind keeps running it over and over in my head, with different scenarios." She looked up at him with tear-filled eyes. "Make love to me, Trey. Wipe out all the fearful memories."

She didn't have to ask him again. His fingers slid up her back to tangle in her hair at the base of her neck. His lips gently pressed against each eyelid, tasting the salt from her unshed tears. He kissed her temples and nibbled his way down across her cheeks to her full lips.

A sigh escaped her.

Trey's lips plundered hers. Their velvety texture intoxicated him, making him delve in for more. His tongue begged for entrance, which she gladly gave him. Their tongues entwined, dancing, stroking, exciting, and enticing them on. A few quick steps had them against the bed. He bent, lowering them down to its downy softness.

Breaking the kiss, he caressed her cheek. The rapid pulse in her throat caught his attention. He gently flicked his tongue against it, feeling her arch into him. A smile curved his lips as he placed feathery kisses all along that pulse point. His wife's rapid breathing told him how he affected her. Her hands roamed across his broad back, tracing an old scar here and there. He reared up to look at her when her hands slipped inside his trousers and cupped his derriere, pulling him harder against her.

"Alex."

She took advantage, placing kisses along his throat now. "Yes?"

"Keep that up and you'll regret it," he said as he moved himself against her.

Her eyes closed at the pleasurable sensation he caused with his movement. "I doubt that."

His heart started to race. Who would have known that one woman could arouse him so much with just words. He traced her collarbone with one finger. His finger then slid down, traveling between her breasts. He circled one through her gown, and watched the bud tighten. Desire sliced through him as he captured that tip in his mouth, but it was not enough. He wanted to taste her flesh, not linen. Grabbing the collar of her gown he pulled, tearing it in half and exposing the delights he craved to his gaze. "Much better."

Alex felt her blood heat quickly when Trey tore her gown off. As his lips recaptured her breast, she was already writhing on the bed. She couldn't stand much more yet didn't want this to end.

Trey moaned when she wrapped her legs around him. Her deft fingers worked on the waistband of his trousers, freeing him into her willing hand.

He rose up above her, giving her a chance to slide his trousers partially down his legs. Trey bent his head toward her other breast. As he laved, nibbled, and licked he kicked his pants off.

She slipped her hand between them, stroking him, trying to push him over the edge. His lips worked their way up to hers, pausing here and there to push Alex's arousal even higher. When his lips recaptured hers she moved against him, so that he would enter her.

Trey teased her by rubbing himself against her entrance, but not slipping in. When she tried to arch against him, he pulled away. He repeated this until Alex growled, locked her legs around him, and tightened them against him, trying to urge him on.

He nipped her collar. "It's my turn to drive you wild, my love."

"I need to feel you inside me," she panted, placing his hand against where she wanted him. "I'm hot and wet and ready for you. Now."

His large hand cupped her. Fingers rubbed and stroked against her delicate flesh. Trey watched as her eyes darkened due to his ministrations. One finger slipped inside, her muscled walls clenched against it. She moved, burying his finger deeper.

"Now," she whispered.

Trey's control snapped. He centered himself and plunged into her. Her legs wrapped around him like steel bands.

Their sighs mingled as they moved together. Alex matched his strokes. When he picked up the beat, she did too. He felt her muscles start to contract. Her breath became shallow.

"Oh God," she whispered. She moved faster beneath him, as if she raced for something that stayed just ahead. Her breath caught as she clutched him close.

He drove into her again and again, going deeper and deeper, until he couldn't tell where he ended, and she began. As Alex reached her goal, he felt her tighten against him again. He started to move faster. It felt too good. He knew he was close, so close. A slight shudder from his wife as she climaxed pushed him over with her.

~

*A*lex was the first to stir. "Oh wow."

Trey turned his face toward hers. He was still buried deep inside her and had no intentions of leaving anytime soon. The closest thing to his mouth was an ear, which he outlined with his tongue. "The night is still young, and so are we."

Alex purred.

Trey smiled.

~

*T*he next morning, after she had donned a day dress, Alex went down to the kitchen. Fleurette had a fresh pot of coffee on the stove. After pouring a cup, Alex moved to the small table in the kitchen. She inhaled the heavenly aroma. Noise from the front of the house drew her out of the kitchen.

"Good morning, Mr. Andrew," she said.

"Good morning, Miss Alexandra." He smiled. "I hope you are faring better today."

"Yes, thank you."

"Andrew, I'm surprised to see you here." Trey stepped out of his office. "Any problems?"

"No. Beau is now on his way to the judge, who will put him away for a long, long time. I just need a statement from you, and Miss Alexandra, to present to the judge."

"Don't we have to be there in person?" Alex asked.

"You want to travel to Washington DC, where he'll be tried?" Trey asked her.

"No," Andrew answered her. "Unless you're unwilling to sign a statement."

"I'll sign," she said quickly. That was a bit too far to travel by horse or train. Andrew had Alex write her statement first. Once she was sure he could read her handwriting, she signed it, and handed it to him. While Trey worked on his she left the study and wandered into the sitting room. Her curiosity about the painting pulled her in that direction.

There, hanging on the wall above the fireplace, like it did in 1997, was her portrait. This time, she knew the history of it. Staring at her likeness still sent a chill up her back. She found it hard to believe that just touching it sent her back in time.

What would happen if she touched it again? Should she dare? One step, then two, brought her closer to the painting. Her image stared back at her. In the background was a smeared image of Andrew. Angry gashes marred the back of the chair she sat in and part of Andrew's face.

"I'll have that repaired," said Trey from behind her.

She spun around. "I'm surprised you didn't completely destroy it. It looks like you wanted to."

"I wanted to destroy Andrew." He gave her a sheepish smile. "The portrait was just the first thing my hands found."

"Until you went after Andrew."

He nodded. "But he set me straight. Alex, I'm sorry I didn't believe you. If I had, we might have figured out it was Beau long before he tried to hurt you."

"Beau was too smart for us. Making Andrew the scapegoat actually led us to Beau quicker than we would have found him on our own." She wrapped her arms around him. "It is a wonderful likeness, isn't it?"

"Yes." He smiled. "Your eyes have the glow they did when we married."

"Glow?"

"I don't know how to explain it. When you look at me there is a special gleam, the artist captured that."

"Love."

"What?"

"He captured my love for you in that look." She planted a soft kiss on his lips. "Is that what pissed you off?"

"Pissed me off?"

"Made you angry."

"Oh. Just the thought of you being happy with another man tore at my heart."

"Not forgetting your pride," she added.

He grabbed her and twirled her around. "You belong to me."

She laughed. "Spoken like a true Neanderthal."

Jessie stepped into the room. "Excuse me, Mr. Trey, but Mr. Andrew needs to speak at you for a moment."

Trey planted a quick kiss on her lips before striding out of the room.

Alex turned back to the picture again. It fascinated her.

~

*T*rey had one foot on the porch, and the other on the top step when he heard Fleurette's scream. He couldn't get his body to move fast enough. Upon entering the sitting room, he took in his surroundings.

Every stick of furniture was in place. Knickknacks sat in their normal spots. The only thing out of place was Alex's portrait, and Fleurette's ashen face.

"Mr. Trey? How did she do that?" She bent to pick up the cloth she had dropped. Fleurette's hands shook as she stood back up. "One minute she was here and the next... She musta took out of here quick. Right, Mr. Trey?"

He turned on his heel. Dread filled him. She had to be in the house somewhere. She just had to.

CHAPTER 31

*A*lex found herself on the floor of the sitting room. There was only one problem. Five sets of eyes she didn't recognize stared at her.

"What are you doing on the floor? The next tour is coming in a second," hissed one of the women.

She stood quickly. Tour group? That only meant one thing. Her heart broke into a thousand pieces when she realized what happened. Somehow, she had returned to her own time. She made it through the next group, before excusing herself, saying she was supposed to be helping in the stables the rest of the afternoon. Once she found her way outdoors, she headed to the parking lot.

Her eyes widened at the sight of her jeep. It was still there. The heavy layer of dust made her wonder how much time had passed. How much did she owe on this renter? The door squeaked loudly when she opened it. The first thing she'd have to do is take it in to be maintained.

Alex wasn't sure if it would even start, but she had to try. It coughed, and sputtered but on the third try, started up. She drove to her grandmother's in a daze. She didn't remember walking into her grams's house or breaking into tears and crumbling at her feet. She spent four hours sobbing her story as she rested her head in her grandmother's lap, feeling her frail fingers gliding through her hair.

"What am I going to do, Grams?"

She patted Alexandra's head. "I don't know, chile, but before you make any decisions I think you should read this."

Alex stared at the diary she wrote one hundred and twenty years ago. "I know what's in that. I wrote it."

"You don't know everything that's in this. It's time that you did."

She took the journal.

"Go on. I'll bring you some tea and some of my famous pralines."

Alex smiled. Everything her grandmother cooked was famous. She nodded as she stood. Taking the book, she headed back to the bedroom she used when visiting.

~

A bottle smashed against the wall.

"Damn it, Alex, why did you have to leave me?" Trey yelled at her painting. "Why did you have to touch this damn picture?"

He hurled a vase at the wall. It smashed inches from where the portrait hung. The shattered glass tinkled to the floor.

His hands cinched at his sides, he advanced on the painting. Trey wrestled it off the wall, tearing a huge hole in the wall where it had hung. He ignored the tingle he felt as he held it in his hand before the weight made it slip through his fingers and crash to the floor. "You are the cause of all this."

"If you weren't here, she'd still be with me."

Trey grabbed a letter opener that sat on his desk. Wielding it like a weapon he thrust it toward the canvas. He hands stopped inches from its mark. The opener dropped from his hands as the portrait seemed to come to life. He rubbed his eyes. The image didn't go away. He heard Alex's voice.

"Don't. If you destroy this, you will destroy the vehicle that sends me back, and you'll never meet me." Her voice faded away.

Trey sat on the floor hard. "I think I need a drink."

~

*F*leurette flinched each time something smashed against the wall. She winced when she heard the painting smash against the floorboards. She turned to her father. "I think we need to get Mr. Andrew."

Jessie nodded. "Someone needs to talk some sense into that man."

An hour and two bottles later, Trey felt someone shaking his shoulders, but he chose to ignore it. He leaned heavily on the desk in the study where he now sat. He could only stare at Alex's portrait for so long before the anger and pain got to him. When the bottle he'd been nursing was snatched out of his hands, he growled as he stood. "Give it back."

"Why, so you can drink yourself into a stupor again?" asked Andrew. "I don't think so."

"I don't give a damn what you think."

He lurched for the bottle Andrew kept just out of reach. "How can you even begin to look for Miss Alexandra in this condition?"

Trey laughed. That laughter converted into a coughing fit. "We'll never find her."

"You haven't even tried."

"Andrew, believe me, she is beyond our reach." Trey reached for the bottle again.

"Convince me."

"You'll need to drink most of that bottle to begin to fathom what really happened to her." Trey ran his fingers through his hair. "I don't know where to begin."

"Try the beginning."

He took a big breath. "Okay, but first you have to make me a promise."

Four hours later, both were so drunk they couldn't see straight.

Jessie quietly came in to let them know Andrew's horse was ready.

Andrew pounded Trey on the back hard, as they staggered out the front door. "You know I won't remember a lick of this tomorrow."

"Probably not. You won't believe it if you do." He watched as Andrew made several false starts before actually getting his foot into the stirrup and plopping his butt into the saddle.

Trey wandered the house like a phantom. Without Alex his life meant nothing. He found himself lying across their bed about an hour later. His hand flopped over the side of the bed, landed on the floor, and hit something that protruded out from under the bed. He turned so he could look to see what he struck. A book poked out from under the bed. Reaching he snagged the book and pulled it up. He opened it to the first page.

Dear Grams...

He recognized it immediately as Alex's handwriting. He ran his fingers over the dried ink. Lord, how he missed her. Moving to one of the chairs next to the lamp, he settled down. This was as close as he might ever get to his wife again. When his wife read this again 120 years in the future, she'd find one more entry, one from him.

~

*A*lex sat the cup of coffee she just made on the nightstand next to the bed. Sleep eluded her, so she kept on reading. Turning the page of her last entry she was surprised to find a new entry. The handwriting belonged to Trey.

Dearest Alex,

I hope this journal finds you somehow. I never got a chance to tell you how much I loved you. How much you brightened my world. Knowing I'll never see you again gives me the strength to tell you everything I'll never be able to show you, now. You brought joy and color to my world and made me live again. My heart breaks every time I think about the time that separates us. I wish I could find a way to be with you.

You've been gone about a week now and Fleurette has already reverted back to her quiet ways. She wanders around sighing a lot and making far too much coffee in the morning.

Alex wiped the tear that escaped her eyes. She wished she could tell him how much she loved him and missed him. His entry went on for pages, but the tears in her eyes made it too difficult for her to read farther. Clutching the journal to her breast, Alex went out on the back porch of her grandmother's house. She wasn't surprised to find her grams out there waiting for her.

Both sat quietly. The scent of magnolias surrounded them.

"I have to go back, Grams."

"I know, chile. I wondered how long it would take for you to realize it too." She handed Alex a portrait of a loving family standing under the shelter of the old oak that stood in front of Trey's house.

Alex stared at her likeness in the photo. Hope swelled in her heart. "How am I going to get to the painting? I doubt they'll fall for your little trick again."

"Oh, I'm sure we'll figure out something that will work." Her grandmother winked at her.

~

*A*lex stood in the sitting room with the rest of the tourists, this time as a guide. She quit her job three weeks ago, closed out her account, and purchased a few items she could take back with her. Everything was now in order so that no one would miss her.

Dressed in the gown she wore in the portrait, she fit right in with the rest of the guides. The moment the curator laid eyes on her, he hired her. Her resemblance to the painting was too good for him to pass up, and her knowledge of the family surpassed their best historian.

The last tour group passed through a few minutes before. Alex sat on the floor and rested her head against the wall. She never felt so frustrated. Every time she thought she was alone, and moved toward the portrait, someone always came in, stopping her in her tracks. Every evening, for the last two weeks, she went back to her grandmother's house close to tears because she was still in 1997. The silence of the room filled her with serenity. Lifting her head, she noticed that she was finally alone for the first time all day.

She stood up and dusted herself off. It was now, or never. Her hand closed over the velvet ropes and unfastened it.

"Alex."

She jumped before turning around. "Yes, sir?"

"The photographer is here."

She nodded. The curator wanted to have her pose with the portrait. He planned on running her photo in some of the larger papers along with an article about the plantation to help drum up business.

The photographer set up his camera in the center of the room. "Now what I'd like to do is have Alex seated in front of the portrait the way the woman is seated."

A chair was dragged over and placed where he wanted it. Alex sat and waited for the flash.

"Next I want one with her next to it."

Like a robot, Alex stood up next to it, outside the ropes.

"Can we remove the ropes? It takes away from the painting."

The curator quickly removed the ropes.

"Now, Alex, stand right next to it." He looked into his viewfinder. "No. That's not right. Alex, could you point to it?"

She swallowed hard. Instead of gesturing to it like a Vanna White, she placed her hands on it, and stared up at her portrait. Silently, she prayed, *Please, take me back one more time. I want to go home.*

The tingling sensations started at her fingertips and spread up her arms. The flash of a camera went off before she felt her world go black.

～

Trey pushed his food around on his plate. Andrew had gotten him to stop drinking, and Fleurette convinced him that he needed to start eating again, but he just wasn't hungry. Life just wasn't the same without Alex.

A loud crash caught his attention. So did Fleurette's scream. Jumping up out of his chair, he ran to see what upset Fleurette this time. Reaching the door just as Fleurette exited it, she came close to knocking him down in her haste. He grabbed her shoulders. "Fleurette, what's wrong?"

"Mr. Trey, I have to find Mr. Trey." She blinked at him. Sucking in her breath she rambled on. "Oh Mr. Trey, you're here. Thank God, I found you. It's happened again. That crazy wife of yours has done it again."

"Wife?" Trey asked. "Fleurette what are you talking about?"

All Fleurette could do was point. There in the middle of the floor in the sitting room lay a pile of skirt and crinoline.

Hesitantly, Trey crept into the room. He wouldn't get his hopes up. He couldn't. His heart beat a little faster with every step he took.

A soft moan floated up from the pile of material. Then it started to move. "Man, I don't like traveling that way. I feel like I've been through the mill."

Trey watched in astonishment as the skirt started to right itself. Slowly, it started to move into a sitting position, giving him a chance to see the face clearly. "My God, Alex!"

Her head came up. Seeing Trey in the flesh brought a smile to her face. "Trey! I made it back, didn't I?"

"Yes, unless this is a cruel dream, you are back." He knelt beside her, running his hands all over her to be sure he wasn't dreaming.

She latched her hands behind his neck. "There is one way to find out." Alex pressed a kiss to his lips.

"I've dreamed of this too," he said as he ran his fingers though her hair.

"This is no dream, Trey, I'm home for good."

Fleurette discreetly closed the door so they wouldn't be disturbed.

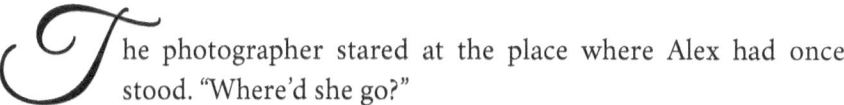

he photographer stared at the place where Alex had once stood. "Where'd she go?"

The curator was just as confused. "I don't know." He had the grounds scoured for two hours, but there was no sign of Alex Dalton. He picked up the phone and called the phone number on her application. "Hello, Ms. Thibodaux?"

"Yes," said Alex's grandmother.

"Um, I was wondering if you've seen Alex. We...she's missing."

"Missing, what do you mean? She flew in here about an hour ago. Mumbling something about the picture spooking her out. Alex packed her bags and headed north."

"You've seen her, then?"

"Yes. I was afraid that portrait would start to get to her. She never liked visiting the plantation, so I was surprised and a little worried when she took the job there. I'm sorry she left so suddenly, but it's for the best. Don't worry about her. She's gone where she'll be happy."

Betsy hung up the phone and smiled to herself. She gently rubbed gnarled fingers against the glass of the photo she held. "She'll be very happy."

EPILOGUE

Sunlight flickered through the leaves.

"Derrick, settle down," Alex admonished. She tried to wipe the dirt smudge from her son's cheek.

"But Betsy started it," he whined, pointing to a pretty brunette with a big white bow on her head.

"I don't care who started it. I will not have you picking on your little sister." She looked up to catch the daughter in question sticking her tongue out at her brother. "Betsy."

"Sorry, Mommy." She tugged discreetly on the bow. It made her head hurt.

Alex did a head count. There were only four. Looking around she asked, "Where is Andrew?"

"Here, Mommy," the voice came from over her head.

She glanced up and found her son wrapped around one of the larger branches. One just a little beyond her reach. "Get down here this instant."

"Yes, ma'am." He slid down the trunk.

Alex placed her hand on her chest and took a deep breath. Now she understood the curse every mother put on her children. *May your children be just like you.*

Trey came up behind her and gave her a squeeze. "The photographer is here. Is everyone ready?"

She nodded, at least she hoped so. The photo her grandmother had showed her burned brightly in her mind as she gathered her children.

They lined up by the tree Alex picked out. Carefully, she placed their three youngest first, with the two older children behind them. She and Trey stood behind their brood. A smile played on her lips because she knew where this photo would end up. The flash went off. Her daughter's bow was gone. One of the boys had his shirttail hanging out. The love she felt for Trey so strongly, flashed. Caught forever on film. True love captured in a portrait throughout time.

THE END

～

Don't miss out on your next favorite book!

Join the Satin Romance mailing list
www.satinromance.com/mail.html

ABOUT THE AUTHOR

Writing for Barbara Donlon Bradley started innocently enough, like most she kept diaries, journals, and wrote an occasional letter but she also had a vivid imagination and wrote scenes and short stories adding characters to her favorite shows and comic books. As time went on she found the passion for writing to be a strong drive for her. Humor is also very strong in her life. No matter how hard she tries to write something deep and dark, it will never happen. That humor bleeds into her writing. Since she can't beat it she has learned to use it to her advantage.

www.barbaradonlonbradley.com

~

Also Available

Love Is...
Love on the Run (coming 2018)
A Quest For Love (coming 2019)

www.ingramcontent.com/pod-product-compliance
Lightning Source LLC
Chambersburg PA
CBHW031103260626
47172CB00001B/190